Almost a Scoundrel

Ladies Who Dare
Book One

Tanya Wilde

Dragonblade Publishing, Inc. is an imprint of Kathryn Le Veque Novels, Inc.
P.O. Box 23
Moreno Valley, CA 92556
ceo@dragonbladepublishing.com

Produced in the United States of America

First Edition December 2023
Print Edition

ARE YOU SIGNED UP FOR DRAGONBLADE'S BLOG?

You'll get the latest news and information on exclusive giveaways, exclusive excerpts, coming releases, sales, free books, cover reveals and more.

Check out our complete list of authors, too!

No spam, no junk. That's a promise!

Sign Up Here

www.dragonbladepublishing.com

⇒⇒⇒✕⇐⇐⇐

Dearest Reader;

Thank you for your support of a small press. At Dragonblade Publishing, we strive to bring you the highest quality Historical Romance from some of the best authors in the business. Without your support, there is no 'us', so we sincerely hope you adore these stories and find some new favorite authors along the way.

Happy Reading!

CEO, Dragonblade Publishing

Chapter One

LADY PHAEDRA SHARP never thought a kiss could ever rob her of breath. She hadn't thought about kisses at all until Deerhurst, the mysterious earl-next-door, planted his lips firmly on hers.

At first, she thought her imagination had run wild again, which seemed like the only explanation for why she found herself in the earl's arms beneath the moonlit sky in the middle of the night. However, there were certain parts of the event that were too vivid for even the most robust of imaginations.

For one, there was the woody flavor of tobacco that clung to the lips kissing her. There was also no denying the velvet stroke of the earl's tongue that smoothly glided over her bottom lip. Or the hand that pressed against the lower half of her back. So sensuous, it drew a gasp from Phaedra.

His tongue swept into her mouth, claiming entrance. A thousand butterflies flitted down her spine.

Intoxicating.

And scandalous. The stuff of ruin. There were no words to describe the sensations flooding her body. And certainly, no way to mistake the tension that sparked within the space between them. But not the kind where the air turned thick and heavy with pressure. Rather the kind that one never wanted to step away from. It sizzled. Danced from one nerve ending to another and absconded with all her senses.

The man tasted like pure, molten sin.

The promise of broken vows.

Phaedra had always thought a kiss to be just the smack of two lips together. Not this . . . this . . . loss of composure!

The arm curled around her waist pulled her up against him. No thought of refusal entered her mind. No thought that this might be a trap and she'd thoroughly been ensnared. On the contrary, not to be outdone, she shoved her fingers through his silky hair.

The sound that rose from the back of his throat startled her.

No. Not his throat. *Her* throat.

Feminine.

Sultry.

A sound she did not recognize as her own.

God's breath.

He kissed her like a man who had found water after years wandering the Sahara Desert. But it was a short track through the wilderness, as Phaedra was jolted out of this entrancing world of two by distant laughter, a sobering reminder of her whereabouts.

What on earth had gotten into her?

Sanity injected into her consciousness, and Phaedra's mind, which had conveniently blocked out reality, swung open the gates once more.

She wrenched away from Deerhurst, not forgetting to cast a reproachful glance his way. Her heart still pounded, partly because of the kiss but mostly because of what may come next. She had no plans to fall into a matrimonial trap. Ever. Even one of her own accidental making.

"You kissed me . . ." she accused.

"I did," Deerhurst drawled with half a scowl, as though he, too, couldn't quite believe what he'd done. "You kissed me back."

"I was caught off guard."

"So was I."

"How were *you* caught off guard?"

He shrugged, folding his arms behind his back. A smooth mask fell over his face. "It's not every night I stumble across a beautiful woman in my garden."

"I am searching for Puck."

"Ah yes, the elusive cat that wandered onto my property."

Did he not believe her?

Phaedra narrowed her eyes, then blinked. She hadn't paid attention to him before, too distracted with her search, but she took notice now.

He wore a suit of evening clothes, as one would expect from a man about town, except he had stripped down to a white linen shirt, and his cravat had been disregarded as well. The opening of his shirt provided her a glimpse of his robust chest. He seemed wild, untamed, and yet he stood like a man accustomed to power.

His gaze, sharp as a blade, never left her. Not once.

Phaedra let out a slow breath.

Her attention shifted to his tousled hair.

She had done that.

She ought to be thankful she hadn't ripped open his shirt! Come to think about it, the gossip rags always described the earl as a tightly contained man. After tonight, Phaedra was not so sure about that.

"Puck is here somewhere," she said in the hope of distracting him. And herself. Where was that dratted cat when she needed it?

"Of course."

Phaedra stilled. Did the man have to sound as if he was merely indulging a rambling woman?

"What other reason could I possibly have for being here?" she demanded before she thought better of it. "I saw Puck leap into your garden and came to retrieve him."

"Animals wander. Ladies should not."

"Puck is an Angora; he is not supposed to wander either. Neither does he care for strangers." Phaedra thought his lips might have quirked up at the corners, but she couldn't tell with certainty. "I, at least, have a reason for being out and about. What are you doing here?"

He arched a brow. "Besides the fact that I have every right to take a stroll in my garden, what do you imagine men do upon discovering a woman on their property in a state of dishabille?"

Phaedra glanced down at her attire and inwardly cursed. She'd forgotten she'd been about to turn in for the night. She wouldn't be surprised if the man thought her to be a shameless seductress. After all, she hadn't pushed him away when he'd kissed her. She had brought this entire situation on herself! She refused, however, to cower, and met the earl's gaze head on.

"Since I am at fault for interrupting your evening, I shall forget everything that happened here tonight and take my leave." She paused. "If Puck does cross your path and sharpens his claws on your flesh, I am not to be held responsible."

He said not a word, but Phaedra could practically feel the amusement rolling off his body. She shot him a final look before hurrying to the side gate from which she'd entered. The chuckle that followed her both incensed and inflamed her.

Insufferable oaf.

But the man had been right. She should never have ventured onto his property. Not at night. And to think, for years she'd avoided the traps set by fortune-hunters only to be foiled by her own foolishness and whatever madness had beset her to kiss him back.

Phaedra had always thought of Deerhurst as nothing but an exemplary neighbor, unseen and unnoticed. She decided to reassess her opinion of him.

Roguish.

That seemed to describe the man of tonight perfectly. A problem, no matter how she looked at the matter. Whether good or bad, gentleman or scoundrel, Deerhurst had pulled the fabric of her world inside out with his untimely kiss. But she wouldn't be swayed, no matter what. She hoped for the earl's sake he didn't come to seek trouble at her door. A rude awakening awaited him if he did. She was not the sort of woman to be forced into anything against her will. She'd fight him like an animal—tooth and nail.

Speaking of animals . . .

Just where *was* that traitorous cat?

⇶⇷

DARING. FEARLESS. DANGEROUSLY tempting.

These were the words Marcus Lawson, The Earl of Deerhurst would use to describe Lady Phaedra as he watched her retreating, and they did not begin to do her justice. Neither did he mean to describe her in any sort of way.

He also hadn't meant to kiss her.

When he spotted her through his bedchamber window, skulking in his garden, his first thought had been to draw the drapes. However, after a moment's pause, curiosity had won out.

What was the woman doing in his courtyard?

The question had led him to his garden where an invisible force had pulled and tugged until his mouth had claimed hers. He could no more resist the impulse than a sailor could turn away from the bewitching call of a siren.

Bathed in moonlight, her hair cascaded to her waist in waves of rich, alluring chestnut. He had wanted nothing more than to run his fingers through the silky strands.

He had resisted that compulsion.

Until the moment her eyes touched his and all his wits evaporated. Wide and innocent, filled with unflagging resolve—probably to find

5

her cat—she'd twisted his gut up in knots. A thousand of Napoleon's cavalry could not have dragged his gaze away from her. Raw impulse overtook rational thought.

Thus, he had broken his one, chief, superior rule—no entanglements with any lady of any sort. Most troubling of all, he did not regret it.

A problem.

A big problem.

Because he wanted to break it again.

Not that startling, considering that over the years, he'd been a reluctant observer of Lady Phaedra and her family's private incidents. A phenomenon only he seemed subjected to. He'd borne witness to the time she pulled a pistol on a suitor. Also the time she'd tossed a tray of sandwiches at a man who Deerhurst presumed had insulted her. He'd even been there the day she brought home a kitten, otherwise known as Puck.

Well, he hadn't been *there*, there.

It seemed to be one of those mystifying quirks of the universe. Whenever Deerhurst passed the Sharp residence, his gaze would stray to the windows of their drawing room, and every time *that* happened, he would glimpse some scene or another. This would have been fine if he hadn't, on occasion, caught the Earl of Huntly frolicking with his wife.

Deerhurst shuddered.

Perhaps he should gift Huntly a pair of curtains that left no crack after being drawn shut.

But tonight . . .

Once again, that foreign force propelled him forward, and he caught up to Phaedra in a few long strides. He couldn't let her go yet. One more interaction, just one more, and he'd be done.

"Lady Phaedra," he called and hid a grin when her back stiffened. "You should be more careful where you follow Puck in the future.

Perhaps the feline is in want of male companionship."

She turned to him with a black look. "Your attempt at humor is as ill-suited as your behavior tonight."

"My kiss must have affected you greatly for you to bring it up yet again."

"Hardly, but I am a woman. We like to assign meaning to everything."

"Oh? And what meaning have you assigned to me?"

She crossed her arms over her chest. "What's your intention here, Deerhurst? You could have overlooked my presence, yet you chose the completely opposite path."

Deerhurst lifted his hands in the air. "No intention, I promise."

"I see. Then it seems I was right. Only a scoundrel would take advantage of a woman in the middle of the night."

Slightly astonished, Deerhurst laughed. "You wound me."

"Scoundrels rebound quickly."

"Touché, Lady Phaedra. Yet I'd hate for you to form such a low opinion of me."

"It has been formed."

"There is no alternative to me being a scoundrel?"

"I'm afraid not."

Deerhurst smiled at the determined lift of her jaw. There was something delightful about teasing Lady Phaedra.

"Your cat must truly be something for you to follow him about in the middle of the night. An Angora, you said. You'll have to forgive me, but I haven't heard of that breed."

She gave him a skeptical once over. "Puck is a very ancient breed of Turkish cats."

"I see."

"And they are very sensitive to their environment."

"Naturally."

"They also have a very curated diet and can't be fed just anything."

He caught her glance at the bushes in his garden. "What exactly do you think he'll find to eat on my property?"

She lifted her chin. "How should I know what skeletons you have buried here?"

He arched a brow.

"Puck has a sensitive belly," she said.

Deerhurst studied the woman before him, growing intrigued with each passing second. "Very precious indeed."

"He is also very feral if provoked." Her gaze met his straight on. "Just like his mistress."

Deerhurst wanted to laugh, instead, he held up his hands. He paused, shelving the urge to tease her further. "Noted. Well, scoundrel that I am, I shall admit to enjoying tonight."

She snorted. "Well, it's over. Let's not tempt fate anymore."

Deerhurst inclined his head, amused. "Agreed."

He shook his head as Lady Phaedra fled to the sanctuary of her home. There had always been something about her—repressed until tonight—that seemed to call to him in the most unnerving way. Perhaps because he had witnessed so many of her spunky moments through their drawing room window. How else to explain the madness that had prompted him to act on his desire tonight? He supposed he had been lucky. The kiss had been innocent enough.

Well, maybe not *that* innocent.

In any event, the woman seemed determined to sweep their momentary lapse in judgment under the rug. So did he.

Deerhurst had only one goal—to keep the secret of Abigail at all costs. His life had no place for a woman. Especially a woman that would *delve*. And Lady Phaedra was precisely such a woman. So he called upon years of discipline to stow the lingering intrigue she presented.

No attachments.

No entanglements.

All he had to do was keep his distance. That shouldn't be hard at all.

From a patch of nearby shrubberies, a snowy cat emerged, padding leisurely over to Deerhurst. The feline rubbed against his black boots, purring.

He chuckled. "Naughty Puck. You got your mistress all riled up. As did I."

After one more look in the direction Phaedra had disappeared, Deerhurst strode back to the lonely confines of his home, Puck trailing after him. He hadn't been entirely honest. The cat had been visiting him every night for the past year, not happy until Deerhurst allowed him to curl up on his lap. Sometimes, he even came to visit during the day.

He had grown quite fond of the feline.

So long as his affection didn't spill over to the delectable owner, all would be fine. No woman deserved to settle beneath the dark cloud of his past.

Chapter Two

BREAKFAST AT THE Sharp household was generally a peaceful affair. The Earl of Huntly, Phaedra's father, always read the daily paper while the women poured over the latest gossip columns. Not to gossip, mind you. Sharp women did not gossip. But they did keep up with the latest accounts of fashion and topics of interest such as foolish lords who gambled away their fortunes. This morning, however, Phaedra's mind dwelled on the matter of a certain Sharp woman who might have gambled her reputation away.

No one saw.

True. But that did not mean there couldn't still be consequences. Especially if the earl decided to go back on his word.

He said he wouldn't.

Which, in truth, was the crux of the situation. Phaedra had no choice but to place her trust in the man. And she did not trust men. Period. The mere thought gave her the shivers.

She cleared her throat, and opened the topic, "The Earl of Deerhurst."

As soon as his name left her mouth, Phaedra felt the tips of her ears heat. She truly questioned her sanity at this moment. Would her mother or aunt be able to tell she had shared a swoon-worthy kiss in the garden of the earl next door with said earl? A woman's intuition—especially her mother's—was a damnable thing.

"What about him, dear?" the countess asked, sipping her tea.

"What exactly do we know about him?"

"Besides the fact that he is our neighbor?" Portia, her aunt on her father's side, asked. "He is quite withdrawn, I believe."

"Reserved." Her mother agreed with a nod.

"Rather austere," Portia added.

"But handsome," her mother offered.

Phaedra felt the beginnings of an ache in her temples.

"Yes," Portia wrinkled her brow, "in an aloof sort of way."

"I get it," Phaedra said, motioning for them to stop. "He is handsome and every other word related to withdrawn. What *else* do we know about him?" Phaedra asked.

"Marcus Lawson," Portia murmured. "I believe his name is derived from the Roman God of War."

"Well, that sounds ominous," Phaedra muttered.

From behind his paper, the Earl of Huntly chuckled.

"Hardly, dear," her mother said. "Besides there isn't much to say. The earl has an impeccable reputation. Why do you ask? Has he shown interest?"

Her father lowered his paper and Phaedra found herself the recipient of three curious stares.

"Of course not," she managed to say evenly, though inside her heart galloped like a horse speeding down the racetracks. Interest, indeed. Just not the kind her mother meant. Even though a small part of her still expected the earl to beat down the door and demand an audience with her father.

"Puck wandered into his garden last night, is all." *And I wandered after him.* She had woken this morning with the traitorous little beast curled up in her bed, but she suspected he had been gone a good deal of the evening.

"That's hardly something to worry about," her aunt said. "Puck's a cat."

"Cats wander, dear," her mother agreed.

So did Deerhurst's lips.

Phaedra shoved the intruding thought, along with its accompanying image, into a box. "Puck's an Angora housecat, mother. They're supposed to remain indoors."

"You can't keep a cat locked up, my dear. It's in their nature to roam," her father pointed out.

Roam . . .

Phaedra nipped the image of Deerhurst and his roaming mouth in the bud. The man had thoroughly corrupted her mind.

"Puck has no instinct to defend himself, Papa. It's how they are bred."

"Perhaps Puck is drawn to something in Deerhurst's garden?" Portia offered helpfully.

Phaedra nodded. "Like a body buried beneath a flower bed."

"Goodness, Phaedra!" Her mother coughed behind her hand. "Must your imagination run so rampant?"

Phaedra shrugged. "Cats are attracted to dead things."

And, well, the thing of it was, she didn't quite know what to make of Deerhurst. She'd rather not make anything of him, but since her mind was stubbornly engaged with the memory of their kiss, she needed something to put her off him. Something like a proverbial skeleton entombed in the earl's garden, twisted in the roots of the flowers blooming above.

"How ridiculous," the countess said. "They are attracted to rodents, Phaedra, not bodies. You're reading those horrid novels again, aren't you? Your father should never have encouraged you to read those books of his."

"They are called history books, Mama. They recount history."

"They detail the accounts of London's criminals and their atrocious deeds. That's hardly the sort of history a young lady should be entertaining herself with. Do you not agree, Robert?" The countess looked to her husband for aid.

"They are just books, Eleanor."

Phaedra knew better than to grin at her father.

Portia winked at her.

Poor Mama. Both Papa and her aunt were quite mischievous. A trait Deerhurst seemed to share. Perhaps that is why she recognized it so easily in him. After all, while she still had no idea what the man was about, she hadn't sensed any malice or ill intentions from him.

"You are incorrigible, Robert," the countess admonished, but a smile pulled at her lips. To Phaedra, she said, "Rest assured there are no bodies in the earl's garden."

"What about bodies of cats?"

"Phaedra!"

"Is that so impossible? I heard Lord Royce did away with a cat that wandered into his house. It's only natural for me to enquire after the earl's character."

"Who told you that? You shouldn't be lending your ear to such nonsense. Lord Royce is an honorable man."

"He is also allergic to cats," her father murmured, lifting the newspaper to continue his reading, impervious to his wife's glare.

Portia chuckled. "You might want to brace yourself, Phaedra. Your mother is about to set that paper on fire."

One glance at the countess and Phaedra thought her aunt might be right. She attempted to change the subject. "Mama is right, of course. I doubt we have anything to worry about, skeletons or otherwise."

"Agreed," her father said from behind his paper. "Deerhurst strikes me more as a man who would dispose of a body permanently rather than have it connect back to him."

"That is quite enough, Robert."

"Your daughter is curious."

"She's your daughter too, and you are too indulgent with the child. Goodness, who speaks of dead bodies at the breakfast table?"

"Criminals and grave robbers?" Phaedra offered.

"Phaedra Rose Sharp!"

"Very well, my love, no more talk of dead bodies," her father placated. To Phaedra, he directed, "I once read that cats are drawn to the supernatural."

"Robert Charles Sharp! How do you expect your daughter to find a husband if you indulge her grim imagination?"

"I found you, did I not?"

Phaedra bit her lip when her father winked at her.

"We were engaged at birth."

"You fell for my charm anyway."

"To this day I cannot explain why."

"No need to worry about my future, Mama," Phaedra said. "I have no plans to marry."

"What if you change your mind one day?" the countess said. "That can happen, you know."

Phaedra spared a quick peek at her aunt, who had not been as fortunate in a match as her brother. She had married for love, yes, but it turned out that the man she'd fallen for had been nothing but a fortune-seeking scoundrel. Put aside how the man had ultimately died in a duel that his family had taken great pains to cover up, so much heartache had been caused by that one match. For Phaedra's entire family.

This was why Phaedra had vowed she would steer clear from the scheming entanglements of men and become a cat-raising spinster. And after the harrowing events that followed her aunt's marriage, no one in her family protested her choice. She was content with that.

"Let Phaedra be, Eleanor," Portia spoke up.

Phaedra directed her attention to her toast. It would take a miracle for her to change her mind, but she'd rather not rile her mother up any further. Neither did she want to rouse her family's suspicion by pressing for information about Deerhurst even though she was burning with curiosity.

Perhaps it was for the best.

Last night would never be repeated, and Phaedra had no plans to ever cross over the earl's property line again. Things would go back to how they were before.

Yet . . .

It was just a kiss.

A knee-wobbling kiss.

Somewhat troubling—her knees certainly hadn't wobbled when Sir David Murray had stolen a kiss a year prior—but not at all alarming. However, that *had* been more of a peck than the storm that Deerhurst's kiss had been. But the only thing *that* indicated to Phaedra was that different kisses prompted different responses.

Nothing to dwell on.

Forgetting about what happened in Deerhurst's garden and purging his touch from her mind *was* for the best. She inwardly snorted. No doubt the scoundrel had long since brushed the encounter from his mind. Well, no matter, as long as they kept to the confines of their own property.

Yet she couldn't shake the feeling that she hadn't seen the last of the earl.

⇶⥲⥲

The following evening

"LADY PHAEDRA SHARP."

The name sent a thousand pricks trickling up Deerhurst's spine. His breath seized. Not a good sign, he thought to himself.

Usually, his ears pricked but mildly at the mention of her name. After all, they were neighbors, and Deerhurst had witnessed so many events in their drawing room, he could practically be counted as family. This was different, however. Sharper.

She was on Avondale's list.

His gaze sprang to Phineas North, Marquess of Warrick, who had spoken her name. He, Warrick, and Field Savage, Earl of Saville, sat at a table in White's with Harry Spencer, Earl of Avondale, who found himself in somewhat of a quandary. He required a wealthy wife, and they were pouring over a list of heiresses Avondale's mother had compiled for him.

Deerhurst hadn't told his friends about the insanity that had led him to the beguiling lady. He wanted to keep that moment in a place in his mind that was free from ridicule and speculation and the nitpicking of the men around the table.

But Lady Phaedra and Avondale?

No.

Absolutely not.

No.

He couldn't explain this objection. Naturally, he did not harbor any deep affection for his next-door neighbor. Neither was he in any position to form an attachment with a woman. He'd already broken his one cardinal rule, but he figured a kiss could neither be seen nor be categorized as an entanglement. So long as he did not kiss her again, which he certainly did not plan to do.

Yet the instant protest that swelled in his gut at the thought of Phaedra wedding Avondale led to the disturbing revelation that he felt possessive of her, illogically so.

Admit it, she feels like yours.

Deerhurst absolutely refused to give credence to that intruding thought. And he would not object, in any way, if Avondale showed interest in Lady Phaedra.

He simply had no right.

Deerhurst held his breath.

Avondale shook his head, and Deerhurst exhaled slowly. Thank Christ his resolve would not be put to the test, and for the purpose of agreeing with his friend, Deerhurst shook his head as well. *No, she is not the one for you.*

But even as he shook his head, he knew that logic and reason didn't seem to carry any weight. His objection seemed to be driven by something much deeper. Primal. He didn't want Avondale to set his sights on Lady Phaedra. Even though he didn't plan to explore the connection either.

After all, he had to think about Abigail.

Confound it.

He should never have given in to temptation. Now he couldn't forget about the woman, and all he wanted to do was kiss her again. Perhaps if he hadn't succumbed to his instinct that night, he might not have opened his mouth to say to the group of men, "She once threatened a suitor with a pistol."

Fortunately for him, his friends did not so much as blink at this revelation. They had already moved on to the next woman on the list.

Deerhurst tossed back his brandy, welcoming the slight burn down his throat.

"What of Lady Ophelia Thornton? I recall my mother wrote her name at the top of the list." Avondale said to Warrick, who was poring over the list.

Deerhurst relaxed. "Not bad," he spoke up. "If you can get past her watchdog." And a much better prospect for Avondale. In truth, Deerhurst didn't know all that much about Lady Ophelia, or any of the women on the list other than that they were all in possession of sizable dowries. Which, he supposed, was the point.

Avondale's mother had compiled her list wisely.

He listened half-heartedly as Warrick and Saville launched into a discussion about the women and debated their flaws over their talents while Warrick scribbled notes next to the names. Lost in thought, Deerhurst nodded when they nodded and shook his head when they did.

His mind spun.

What flaws could Lady Phaedra possibly possess?

The answer was simple.

None.

He thought back to her rosy lips and the soft blush that had infused her cheeks after their kiss. Even the flicker of fire in her eyes could not detract from her softness. It felt like mere hours ago that they shared that moment in his garden.

Deerhurst was sure the moment was exaggerated in his mind. It didn't matter. His concern lay in the fact that he'd stood the better of the previous night staring out into his garden, hoping to catch a glimpse of a certain garden sprite.

"What about Lady Harriet?"

"Chatterbox," Deerhurst said without thought. He blinked. He hadn't been paying attention to their conversation. What had been decided about Lady Ophelia?

"True," Saville piped up. "But also demure. A good trait for a wife."

"What about Lady Phaedra's biggest flaw?" Warrick asked.

Deerhurst's head jerked to Warrick. He should intervene, he knew. But he could invent no flaw. And he hoped beyond all hope that any flaw offered would be enough to fully divert Avondale's attention elsewhere.

He was a bastard, he knew.

He couldn't even provide an explanation as to why his sanity left when it came to the woman. It seemed implausible that one kiss had affected him this much. There was no attachment between him and Lady Phaedra. Avondale had the right to court whomever he wished.

"Have you heard her laughter?" Saville asked Warrick. "I swear it could scare an alley cat."

Deerhurst wanted to punch Saville in the face.

Warrick pulled his brows together. "I heard it above the orchestra once. Ear-splitting, I'll give you that."

Deerhurst glared inwardly at Warrick. Lady Phaedra's laugh was merriment itself. She laughed from a place they could only hope to ever discover—her heart. It was a piece of magic.

"What about her greatest attribute?" Avondale asked.

"Wealth," both Saville and Warrick answered.

"Other than that," Avondale interjected.

Both men shrugged.

Deerhurst could have throttled his friends. However, selfish as he may be, their comments served his purpose, so he held his mouth.

Avondale took a deep breath. "While it's good to know you're taking my mother's search for a wife seriously, it doesn't matter anyway," Avondale said. "I plan to restore my wealth another way."

"Are you going to pillage England's villages?" Warrick asked.

"Don't be absurd," Avondale muttered. "Nothing as extreme as that."

"You have a plan, then?" Saville asked with interest.

"Not yet, but marrying for wealth is akin to admitting defeat. I'm not ready to admit surrender yet."

"Noble," Deerhurst murmured. "But building wealth takes years—centuries, even."

"Legally, yes," Saville said and chuckled when all of them raised their brows. "I would never suggest Avondale do anything under-handed."

"Would *you* marry one of the women on the list?" Avondale challenged Saville.

"Christ, no. I'll fulfill my duties in my fifties *after* I have tasted all the pleasures of life.

Deerhurst couldn't argue with Saville's logic.

It was a truth that few men would admit: no man wanted to marry for duty. It went against their very nature. Men were born to conquer. Which was why Deerhurst envied the simple man. Of course, men in the upper crust of society were told they could still conquer anything they wished. As long as it fit within the bounds of accepted society and they did not lose sight of their responsibilities. Simply put, they had a leash around their necks, and it wasn't very long.

But it was a fair deal longer than a woman's.

Deerhurst did not blame Avondale or Saville for their aversion. He, too, had held the same view before Abigail had entered his life. That day had changed everything for him. He loved his daughter more than he cared for duty.

Of course, the weight of that duty had never lifted. In fact, it became even weightier, because with Abigail came another secret. A secret not even his friends knew. A secret that could cost them both everything.

The only people who even knew about his daughter were his servants—all carefully selected and loyal to a fault—and the men that sat around this very table.

And her.

Cassandra Heath, the Duchess of Linley.

Abigail's mother.

A she-devil in disguise, but one that wouldn't dare breathe a word about her daughter for fear of what the duke would do if he ever learned the truth.

Yes, he had made many mistakes in his life. He couldn't afford to make more.

Deerhurst directed his focus back to his friends and noted the list was now filled up with Warrick's scribbles. What had begun as a bit of fun suddenly felt unfair and unprincipled, and Deerhurst could not help wondering how many of these women's leashes would tighten if word of this list ever got out.

It was going to be a long night.

Chapter Three

The next morning

PHAEDRA POKED HER head through the door of the pink drawing room and peeked down the hall to where a light buzzing sound came to the fore and rippled throughout the lower level of the house. There were two drawing rooms on the lower level, one where they received guests—the purple drawing room—and the other where the family lazed about reading, playing piano, and embroidering. The room embodied comfort. Papers were strewn over the table, books were piled up on the floor, and a quilt was carelessly flung over the back of one of the sofas.

A haven.

Unlike the other room.

A shiver ran down her spine.

That buzzing sound was the drone of sixteen men in conversation.

Fortune-hunters.

How did she know this? Well, of course, the Sharp women made it their business to be informed about every fortune-seeking fellow in London.

And the men in the receiving room refused to leave. Phaedra was in no mood for shallow compliments and syrupy falsehoods. She could chase out one or two at a time, but sixteen? She hadn't mastered the art yet.

Still, something about this congregation did not sit right with her. Never had there been so many suitors calling on her at the same time. The most she had endured had been eight, perhaps nine, callers.

Something must have happened. Something they hadn't been made aware of yet.

She glanced over to Millie, her maid, and gave her a panicked look. "What is going on? Why do I have half the gold-digging scoundrels in London at my door?"

"I cannot say, my lady. The gentlemen started arriving about an hour ago. Some have left."

"There were *more*?"

Millie nodded.

"Certainly Mama cannot expect me to greet all of them at once?"

But she could, which was why Phaedra was hiding in the pink drawing room.

And it would be impolite not to receive them, no matter their reason for calling. Downright rude. And a lady ought never to be rude. She snorted. What would be the point of entertaining a mob of gentlemen she had no intention of wedding? No, Phaedra didn't care how ill-mannered she seemed today. She would do just about anything to avoid her duties.

Her mother's laughter rang through the hall.

Phaedra squirmed at the notes of impatience coiling beneath the whimsical sound. She felt only a pinch of guilt at leaving her mother to the mercy of their callers. Their presence, quite frankly, alarmed her. She had recognized some of their voices as well. Suitors of old, ones she had thought had given up their quest for her dowry months ago.

What had reawakened their interest?

"You cannot hide from her ladyship forever," Millie whispered, as though anything louder would give away their presence.

No, but Phaedra could certainly try.

A soft tapping sound at the window startled them. Phaedra

glanced over her shoulder and promptly frowned at the man on the other side of the glass.

"Deerhurst?" Phaedra asked in astonishment.

What madness was this now?

An instant rush of awareness flooded her, spreading down to her belly and then her toes. Her lips tingled, and Phaedra had to resist the urge to scrub the sensation away with her fingers. Those sharp eyes would certainly notice the action.

And just what was he doing sneaking about her home?

He motioned her over.

"My lady?" Millie asked uncertainly. "Should I call for help?"

"Heavens no," Phaedra quickly said. "Do not worry, Millie, I'm acquainted with the gentleman. Stay on the lookout for Mama and let me go see what he wants."

Millie nodded, and Phaedra hurried over to the window. Her gaze locked with startlingly vivid green eyes, and for a moment, Phaedra forgot to breathe. If she could say one thing about the man . . . he was handsome as sin. He had that look about him that could make a woman question her morals—both powerful and wicked. Much too dangerous for comfort.

Sin was a bad thing. She had to remember that.

"What are you doing here?" she asked in a low voice.

"Open the window."

"Why?" When he narrowed his gaze at her snippy reply, Phaedra sighed. "Oh, very well." She cast a quick glance over her shoulder to confirm Millie still stood at her post by the door before pushing the window open. "This is highly irregular, Deerhurst, not to mention suspicious."

"And here I thought I was doing you a favor."

"A favor?" Lord, help her. Could this morning become any more bizarre? "What favor would that be?"

"I'm rescuing you."

Phaedra gave a startled laugh. Marcus Lawson, the Earl of Deerhurst, *saving* her? "Whatever gives you the impression that I'm in need of rescuing?"

"Then you don't have over a dozen men waiting to vie for your attention?"

She raised a brow. "Hardly a scene to be rescued from."

"Why are you hiding, then?" He craned his neck to peer into the room. "Not the best spot you chose. It's only a matter of time before you're discovered."

"How *do* you know about my callers?" Phaedra countered. The earl hardly struck her as one of those people who spied on their neighbors through the slits of their drapes.

"One has to be blind to miss all the gentlemen piling into your house."

"And you thought to save me?" Phaedra crossed her arms over her chest. "Why? We are not friends."

"Think of it as me making amends for my behavior."

Phaedra considered him. "I can manage quite well on my own, thank you very much."

"My apologies, then. I did not mean to imply that you were incapable. Since you do not require my rescue, I'll take my leave." He backed away from the window.

"Wait," Phaedra called in a loud whisper. She pinched the bridge of her nose. Accepting his offer would not be the worst thing in the world, would it? Perhaps she might even ease her curiosity about the man a bit.

"How were you planning on rescuing me?"

A slow grin spread across his face.

"I thought to whisk you off for a drive through Hyde Park."

Public. Pleasant. Safe.

She still couldn't quite make heads or tails of the earl's bizarre actions, but why not embrace it? He hadn't been wrong. She'd be discovered one way or another. It was just a matter of time. Plus, the earl seemed sincere. Although she knew better than to fully believe in his sincerity . . .

Sixteen versus one. The decision seemed clear. Phaedra could handle one man.

"I suppose I could tell Mama I accepted your offer before any of the callers arrived."

"Or you could tell her after you return and come with me now." He held out his arms.

"You want me to climb through the *window*?"

"It's that or pass the brood of gentlemen collecting in your receiving room."

That settled it. She reached for Deerhurst's arms.

"My lady," Millie protested, rushing over. "You cannot leave in such a manner! What am I to tell the countess?"

"Tell her I accompanied the Earl of Deerhurst for a ride through the park." The time had come to draw a line in the sand. She refused to act as the courteous hostess to gentlemen callers when she did not plan to marry. She understood her mother. Phaedra may have decided not to marry, but the countess didn't want her to become a complete pariah and offend anyone by not performing her social duties. Even if those social duties included entertaining a bunch of opportunists.

"My lady, the countess will enquire the time you left. How shall I explain?"

Phaedra shot Millie a reassuring look. "Just tell her the truth. All but for how I left. I can handle my mother's ire."

"My lady . . ."

"I shall see you later, Millie," Phaedra said before she leaned out and clasped her hands on Deerhurst's shoulders as he stepped up and reached for her waist. He felt solid and strong, and the scent of coffee and tobacco clung to him.

Not at all unpleasant.

The tiny hairs on her skin shot up to attention as he pulled her through the window and set her on her feet. For self-preservation's sake, she ignored every single one of those little ripples that spread across her arms.

"You prefer coffee over tea?" Phaedra asked.

"In the mornings, yes. I quite like the aroma." That soul-snaring gaze touched hers. "Why do you ask?"

"You smell like roasted coffee." *Lord, Phaedra.* A woman did not refer to a man's scent! Especially if said woman found the scent to be utterly enthralling.

"Is that a good thing or a bad thing?"

"A compliment, I think."

"One I shall accept," Deerhurst said.

He guided her to the small gate that led to his property. A thrill danced down her spine. The garden looked much different than it did during the night. More pristine. Like there were no secrets hidden within its bright landscape.

"I cannot believe I just climbed through a window to escape boisterous callers," Phaedra said more to herself than Deerhurst. A sudden thought occurred to her. "How did you know where to find me?"

"I didn't. I meant to catch the attention of a servant and instead I found you."

That sounded reasonable.

Yet a small bud of suspicion formed in Phaedra's heart. By the time that doubt had bloomed fully into wariness, she had already entered the earl's home.

Drat it.

Had she leaped from the frying pan into the fire?

※≫≪※

Deerhurst's entrance hall, five minutes later

EVERY LITTLE NUANCE of Lady Phaedra tugged at Deerhurst's aware-ness. From the way her chest rose and fell with each inhale of breath, to the sweet scent of honeysuckle clinging to her skin, to the way she tucked a single ringlet of hair behind her ear only for it to escape a few moments later.

He hadn't given his plan adequate thought, or else he'd have al-lowed her time to retrieve a bonnet or a shawl, which was why he decided to send for a closed carriage rather than his phaeton.

He felt another pinch of guilt.

That little pinch was overshadowed by a much larger stab of re-gret. *He* was the reason for the flock of rogue callers in her drawing room.

Well, part of the reason.

That damn list.

He felt like the bloody devil himself. The worst sort of scoundrel.

Debating certain attributes of women over brandy was one thing, writing the content down was quite another, but losing the list? That was deuced unacceptable. And yet Warrick had done exactly that.

He had lost the list.

Damn his foxed hide. Words could be forgotten or passed over. Ink, on the other hand, could neither be overlooked nor denied.

And Warrick couldn't have misplaced the list at his home either. No, he had to lose it at White's, only for the scrap of paper to fall into the hands of Cromby, who, curse his wretched soul, had pinned it to the betting book.

Wagers were running rampant.

"And you just happened to notice the lineup of my suitors?" Phae-dra asked with a hint of mistrust.

Deerhurst debated whether to tell her the truth or not. In the end, he couldn't see any harm, so he admitted, "I seem to have the damnedest luck whenever I pass your house."

"Oh?" Her tone suggested she still didn't quite believe him.

Deerhurst nodded. "My gaze seems to be drawn to the double windows of your receiving room," he confessed. "I always witness something inappropriate."

"Inappropriate? That cannot be."

He arched a brow. "You would be surprised at how much goes on in that drawing room."

She laughed, and the sound set Deerhurst's heart thumping at a strong pace. Not as all as his friends described. There was nothing ear-splitting about her laughter. They had it all wrong.

"Prove it. Tell me something you witnessed."

"You drew a pistol on Lord Lowbrow."

Her eyes widened, and he grinned down at her. Deerhurst could practically feel the wheels of her mind spinning.

"At first," he ventured on when no words from her were forthcoming. "I couldn't believe what I was witnessing but after my initial shock, it was rather entertaining to watch."

She blinked at him.

He smiled. "I never thought that one day I would be a participant in one of your incidents."

"Let us not forget that you instigated this incident." A small pause. "Did anyone else see that besides you?"

"Not that I'm aware of. Although, I do wonder—" he sent her a thoughtful look. "Do you always carry a pistol at the ready?"

She lifted her chin. "Only when I receive gentlemen I know to be suspect."

"Have you ever been wrong?"

"The marriage mart is like a jungle, Deerhurst. You must learn who the vipers are before you get struck by one." She gave him a look that spoke volumes. "I suppose it's different for men."

"Not so different. Entrapment goes both ways."

She gave a thoughtful nod. "I suppose that is true."

"No gentleman has come up to snuff? Caught your interest?" His eyes dropped to her lips. He couldn't help it. They seemed to be drawn to their delicate arch. Like bees are drawn to honey.

"Nor will any."

"And why is that?"

"You ask as if England were awash in eligible bachelors. And by the by, it's not the bachelor part I'm denouncing, it's the *eligible* part. I suppose our definitions of that word are a bit different."

"Wealthy. Unattached."

"That describes every other titled lord in London."

"Not every lord is wealthy."

"Yet they all appear to be embroidered in gold silk."

Deerhurst laughed. "True enough," he conceded. Appearances were everything.

"It doesn't matter anyway. I have no plans to wed any man."

This surprised the hell out of him. "No marriage?"

"No marriage," she confirmed.

"A brave choice."

He didn't question her further. Her future plans had nothing to do with him. Yet the weight of that blasted list pressed down on his chest even more. The last thing he wanted to do was ruin a woman's plan for her own life.

"What else have you witnessed through the windows of our drawing room?"

"Trust me, my lady, you do not wish to know the answer to that."

"Of course I do."

"No, you don't."

"My curiosity has been aroused, Deerhurst. Now I simply must know. Is it worse than drawing a pistol on a man?"

"It's certainly more sensual."

Her eyes went wide. "Romantic, you mean?"

"No." It was madness—utter madness—but he lowered his head to whisper in her ear. "Kissing." His gaze caught hers. "Carnal."

Her lips parted and closed again. "I'm not sure what you mean," she said. "Did someone kiss in our drawing room?"

"Amongst other things."

"Who? I cannot think of anyone who would . . . well, *kiss* in the drawing room."

"You have much to learn about people and the desires that drive them."

"Are you going to tell me or not?"

"I doubt they'd want me to reveal their identities. Just like you wouldn't want me to reveal to anyone what *you* did, correct?"

She pursed her lips.

"Will you at least tell me what *carnal* means? I don't believe I've ever come across the word."

Show her.

Deerhurst ignored the voice in his head.

"Are you in possession of a dictionary?" he asked instead.

When her eyes narrowed on him, Deerhurst almost laughed.

"Of course," she said, sounding offended. "I get the point. I shall look the word up myself."

"Books are the best tutors." He should leave it there. He didn't. "Better yet, a husband, although that doesn't count for you as you don't plan to take one."

"Are those my only options? Books or a husband?"

Deerhurst doubted Lady Phaedra understood the significance of her question. She had plenty of other options—none respectable. He sensed the woman before him would be enthralled rather than shocked, but he had to draw a line somewhere. Putting forth a roadmap that could lead a lady onto the path of debauchery was out of the question.

"Those are the only two that will keep you from ruin."

"How unfortunate."

Deerhurst furrowed his brows. Disappointment laced her voice, and it was all he could do not to kiss her then and there. He couldn't help his eyes from sliding again to her lips—it was becoming a damn obsession—surveying the tempting curve of her mouth.

He looked away.

He should never have kissed her. Now he knew her taste. Which made him want to kiss her again.

And never stop.

It was madness.

Burning idiocy.

He felt like he was perilously hurtling toward a collision, and he could no more stop the impact than he could turn back time and undo the chaos that one lapse in judgment had caused. And now, because of the blasted list, he couldn't steer clear of temptation. He had to make things right. He had to protect her from this mess until the dust settled.

Ridiculous amounts of blunt had been wagered on Lady Phaedra's name. It made Deerhurst uneasy. Some men would go to horrid lengths to get their grubby hands on that sort of coin. They would put their hands on *her*.

Because of him, she might get caught in a trap she seemed very determined to avoid. He may as well have put a death sentence on her dreams. This was why Deerhurst had approached her today. He would do anything in his power to protect her. His honor demanded it. He just had to do it *while* keeping a fair and safe distance from the temptation she presented. Which meant no touching. Not in any way, shape, or form.

Rhodes appeared. "The carriage is ready, my lord."

Deerhurst nodded and offered his arm to Lady Phaedra. "Ready?"

"Are you?"

The corner of his mouth twitched. "Always."

Not even a little bit.

Chapter Four

Phaedra squinted through the window of Deerhurst's carriage as she took in the scene playing out in her drawing room. She wanted to experience firsthand the view Deerhurst had told her about, so she had convinced him to give her a moment to observe her house as an outsider. She had never given any thought to what a curious passerby would witness when they took the time to peek through the large window. Did people even peek through windows? Well, she supposed there were a lot of people that would. But an earl? *Deerhurst?* Every time she met him her view of him tilted a bit more. Not exactly a bad thing, and not exactly a great thing either. The more her view changed, the more her curiosity bloomed.

Lud, Deerhurst had not been jesting.

Three men stood in conversation near the window while six others were seated in various spots sipping tea. Some were inspecting the artwork on the walls while the rest just hung patiently about. Every now and then the gentlemen cast an expectant glance at the door.

The red hue of her mother's dress appeared particularly vibrant, and Phaedra watched as the countess laughed at something the gentleman to her right said.

It felt to Phaedra as if she were a spectator looking in on a stranger's life. She thought of all the times *she* had been in that drawing room receiving callers. Besides the pistol incident, she once spilled hot tea over a suitor's breeches, threw a sandwich in a baron's face, and feigned casting up her accounts, which led to a viscount dashing from the room in a panic. And that was just off the top of her head.

How many of those little theatrics had Deerhurst glimpsed over time? As for the kissing and carnal part—she made a mental note to look the word up later—she simply could not imagine anything intimate occurring in a drawing room.

"See something of interest?" Deerhurst asked across from her.

She shook her head. "How queer to catch a glimpse of my life like this."

"Isn't that your maid?" Deerhurst asked, peering through his side of the window.

"Yes, that's Millie." She'd appeared in the doorway and was now speaking to the countess. "She must be informing my mother of my escape with you."

Phaedra stilled. It suddenly occurred to her that her mother might connect her outing with Deerhurst with her curiosity at the breakfast table the other morning. And, dear heavens, all that talk of dead bodies in his yard. Lord knew what her mother would make of this.

Another thought occurred to her. She glanced at Deerhurst. "You don't have views into other parts of our house, do you?" *Such as bedchambers.*

He cracked a smile, one that made her break out in gooseflesh.

"I could show you."

She blinked at him. *As in taking her for a tour of the chambers in his house?*

"The view," he clarified, the smile that stretched across his face widening, as if he had caught her outrageous thought. "From my windows."

Scoundrel.

Heat suddenly charged through Phaedra's veins, though she had no idea why. The man was a reprobate for certain. Mischievous to the core of his being. Come to think about it, there was nothing aloof about him. At least, not that she could find.

"That won't be necessary."

"Are you certain? I can take you on a tour of my home now."

She narrowed her gaze. "A simple yes or no will suffice."

He chuckled. "No, then, my lady, there are no views worth mentioning."

"Good."

He arched a brow. "You will simply take my word for it?"

Phaedra shot him a look. "Are you not a man of your word?"

"I am," he said, then shrugged. "I suppose I did not take you for a woman who would put herself at the mercy of it."

"And what sort of woman do you take me for?"

"The sort of woman who would march through my house and inspect the views for herself."

She probably would have done that if the man hadn't been so captivatingly dangerous.

"You forget, Deerhurst, that I do not know you, thus I do not trust you. For all I know that might be a ploy to entrap me."

"You trust me." His grin was back.

"And you arrived at this conclusion how exactly?"

He nodded to his residence. "You climbed through a window, followed me back to my house, and are now sitting alone with me in my carriage. Need I say more?"

He made an excellent point. If the earl had wanted to force the issue of marriage, he could have done so after their moment in the garden. Besides, for some unfathomable reason, she did feel a smidgeon of trust toward the man. Though, she had to wonder if being this close to him was a good idea. He seemed to take up all the space in the carriage, leaving the air between them charged with an intoxicating energy.

"I suppose I ought to be thankful you are not a ravening wolf."

He rapped on the roof, and the carriage jutted forward. "Speaking of animals, did your elusive feline return to your bosom that night?"

"I woke with him in my bed."

"Damn lucky cat."

Her breath caught, and Phaedra swore his eyes flashed with heat. They held her captive with their intensity. She couldn't look away, and to her surprise, she found she did not want to.

Lud, the man knew how to set a woman's pulse leaping.

"Tell me, Deerhurst, do you always end mischievous behavior on more mischievous behavior?"

He laughed. "Since you are participating in this mischief, does that make you mischievous by default?"

Phaedra snorted. "You have hoodwinked society."

"And how have I managed that?"

"I'm not sure, but my mother believes you to be quiet and withdrawn. It's not easy to pull the wool over her astute gaze."

"You asked your mother about me?"

Phaedra felt her face burn at the slip. "Do not get ideas, Deerhurst. I simply wanted to reassure myself that you are not the worst sort of hound."

"Noted," he said. "The countess is not entirely wrong. I do value privacy."

"So you kissed me to scare me off your property?" Phaedra teased.

"I kissed you because I couldn't resist."

Oh.

The question had passed her lips before she could give thought to the consequences. Whatever answer she expected, that hadn't been it.

"Was that not the answer you expected?" He plucked the thought straight from her mind. "You realize, my lady, if you marry, your fortune-sniffing problems go away. You will never have to worry about a man's intentions again."

A dousing of cold water could not have been more effective to extinguish the fire in her belly. Phaedra thought of her aunt.

"Who is to say marriage wouldn't be an even worse problem than a few overexcited suitors?"

He frowned. "I am not sure I follow."

"My aunt married a man she loved and believed returned her affections," Phaedra said. "He turned out to be a monster who only married her for her dowry."

"I see. You wish to avoid the same fate."

Phaedra nodded. "I do."

"Your parents seem rather enthralled with one another," he observed.

"They were promised to each other at birth and fortunate to have found love in each other."

"You do not foresee the same in your future? You could hold out for a love match."

Phaedra could detect nothing but curiosity in his voice, so she said, "I suppose you believe that is every woman's dream. Marriage. Love. Children."

"No," he said slowly. "I cannot begin to understand what occupies a woman's mind, but no woman, or man for that matter, longs to be unhappy."

"That is true," Phaedra said. "Yet it's a terrifying thought to entrust your life to another person's hands."

She did not care to inspect why she was confiding in Deerhurst. Phaedra certainly did not dream about a love match. She dreamed about booting every single fortune-skulking knave from her residence. She fantasized about waking up in the morning without having to entertain London's penniless. She longed for her drawing room to be filled with friends, not question marks. She wanted to enjoy the season without having to examine the intentions of the gentlemen who asked her to dance.

If only she could lift that pressure.

Just enough to breathe.

She considered Deerhurst. His intentions, while not fully clear, appeared honorable enough. Though Phaedra still was not quite sure what to make of the mysterious man yet. He had helped her, which meant he could not be all that bad.

Handsome. Lordly. Full of mischief.

The perfect man to enlist in a scandalous proposition—a wild proposition that suddenly formed in her mind. What if there was a way for her to get everything she wanted without having to spoil her time dealing with unwanted suitors?

In fact . . .

Phaedra cleared her throat and smiled at the man opposite her. "Why not throw your hat in the ring?

"And what game would that be?"

"Courtship."

He arched a brow. "Courtship? No need. I'm not interested in anyone at present."

"Must you be interested in them?"

"Why else would I court a woman? A man courts a woman who has caught his interest. Simple as that."

"Have I not caught yours?"

Both brows rose. "Where are you going with this, Lady Phaedra?"

"Well, Deerhurst, I want you to court me."

❧⟫⟪❧

OF ALL THE infernal things Lady Phaedra could say, no words could have shocked Deerhurst more than the ones that rolled off her temptress tongue.

She wanted *him* to court *her*?

Denial rose swiftly.

Absolutely not.

He felt sure the devil was cackling at him from down below, dealing out punishment for his past sins. A reminder of all he could never do, all he could never have.

She could never understand what she was asking of him. It was like dangling a carrot before a horse then, after getting the horse to do your bidding all for the sake of that carrot, taking the carrot away. Was that not a form of torture?

He had secrets. Secrets that had to be kept in a box and locked tight. Secrets that ladies like Phaedra would not tolerate. It wasn't something he could escape from. His daughter's future depended on this concealment. Lady Phaedra thought it scary to put her life in the hands of a husband. Deerhurst understood. The thought of putting his daughter's future partially in the hands of a wife was truly an alarming thought.

Kiss her senseless? He was her man. But court? His insides froze at the notion, and her declaration momentarily seized up his throat. If he tried to speak now, he would probably fill the space with nothing more than a croak or two.

An image of her between the satin sheets of his bed instantly invaded Deerhurst's mind. Phaedra . . . completely naked . . . He had meant it when he'd said her cat was lucky. *He* would like to be the one to wake up in her bed.

He choked the image down. That path was fraught with resentment.

"Do not look so alarmed, for heaven's sake," Phaedra said in a huff. "I did not mean court as in court-*court*, I meant as in reprieve-from-my-suitors-court."

Deerhurst stilled, his mind going blank. "A reprieve-from-my-suitors-court?" He sounded like a simpleton repeating her words, but dammit, she had caught him off guard. Again.

"You've already acted the knight today; all I ask is for you to act the knight a bit longer." She tilted her head in thought. "It should be as simple as two or three dances, calling a few times during calling hours, and perhaps keeping close for a while after that. All the gentlemen sniffing around my dowry will bow out, standing no chance against you, the knight."

Saints preserve him.

If only she knew. Those men weren't going bow out so easily. They had a pot load of incentives. And . . . "I am no knight."

"Let us beg to differ on that score."

"I kissed you," he reminded her and almost wished he hadn't. The memory always left him wanting more. But he had to dissuade the woman of this madcap idea.

"A momentary lapse in judgment, I'm sure."

"I want to kiss you again."

Her mouth formed a small *O*, and Deerhurst delivered his most crooked smile. He leaned forward. "How about now, Lady Phaedra? Do you still find me knightly?"

Her gaze narrowed. "Perhaps knight is not the right word."

"I certainly don't feel like a knight this very moment."

"I think you are trying to get a rise from me, Deerhurst. It won't work."

He sat back, and for a moment the only sound was the carriage rattling as it drove through the busy streets of London.

"A fake courtship is a terrible idea," Deerhurst finally said. His Lawson ancestors would roll in their graves if they heard this.

"I believe it's a fabulous one."

"For you, not me."

"I'm sure we can come to an agreement of some sort, no?"

"That depends. Are you sure you wish to enter a fake courtship? Because make no mistake, it will be fake."

And utterly reckless.

He should say no. He should return her to the safety of her home and wash his hands of her. That would be the best course of action. Deerhurst did none of those things. A refusal would no more pass his lips than his feet had been able to stop the night he found her in his garden.

"I am not looking for a husband, Deerhurst. I am looking for a respite."

"You believe a few dances will deter your string of suitors?"

"Will it not?"

No.

He thought of Avondale and the list. Avondale, for all his faults, found the idea of marrying for blunt abhorrent. It was the list, or rather the wagers, that presented the biggest problem. Besides the fact that money was a deuced strong motivator, once a wager was written in the betting book it couldn't be *un*written. The wager would stand until a decided outcome. So long as Lady Phaedra refused to marry, those wagers would be open. A fake courtship might aid her in the short term but not the long.

And yet, Deerhurst had appointed himself as her protector.

But courtship?

It won't be a real courtship.

"All I want is a short respite," she reminded. "In fact, we do not even have to label it." She tapped her finger against her chin in consideration. "It shall merely be a series of small actions that may or may not lead people to believe there is an attachment where there is none."

"That is the exact definition of a fake courtship," Deerhurst said, but his heartbeat settled into a semi-steady pace.

"Do not be such a stick-in-the-mud, Deerhurst. Say you will help me. I shall be forever in your debt."

Oh yes, it would be fine to have her in his bed.

Confound it.

Debt. Not bed.

This was a bad idea. He was going to help her anyway. And of course, the idea also held a measure of merit. It *would* present the opportunity to steal a kiss again.

No.

No kissing.

Absolutely no kissing.

And no beds. He would remove those words from his vocabulary. As a matter of fact, from this moment, a new rule would enter into force—no kissing Lady Phaedra Sharp. Period.

Kissing complicated matters. Complications led to curiosity. Curiosity led to questions. Questions demanded answers. He could not afford for her, or the *ton*, to snoop into his life. Too much was at stake . . .

In any case, a fake courtship could serve another unique purpose. It would provide the perfect opportunity for him to remain close while the wagers ran their course without her questioning his continued proximity.

With any luck, they would find an agreeable way to deal with those wagers, and this wretched guilt he'd been saddled with since Warrick lost the list last night would be put to bed.

"Surely I'm not asking for too much?" Challenge dripped from a syrupy tone.

He inwardly snorted. She could not phrase it as a plea either. *Infuriating, lovely woman.*

"Very well, I will help you."

Her eyes brightened. "You will?"

"I will." As long as he kept his private life separate from their fake courtship. Deerhurst could do that. Hopefully, he would not regret this decision.

The force of her smile knocked the breath from his lungs. Radiant. Infectious. And for a second, Deerhurst wondered what madness he had succumbed to for him to agree to her proposal. The woman addled his logic.

"Excellent!"

"Do not get too excited." Deerhurst waited until her eyes lifted to meet his before he said, "A fake courtship might have the opposite effect of what you hope."

She nodded. "You mean there is a chance your attention will attract *more* suitors to my door? That's fine. A courtship is a perfectly agreeable excuse to turn them away."

Speaking of which . . . "It will fall on to you to manage your family's expectations. I have no intention of becoming leg shackled because of this agreement."

"Do not be such a pessimist," she said with a wave of her hand. "I shall handle my family as long as you do your part. Besides, my mother will be granted a pardon from fortune-probing callers as well."

Deerhurst inclined his head.

"Shall we seal the deal?" She stuck out her hand.

His gaze flicked to her palm then back to her. "Should we not first establish some rules?"

A delicate brow rose. "Such as?"

"No midnight visits to my garden."

She shrugged. "I hadn't planned on any continued visits."

"What about you? Do you have any boundaries you wish to set for our fake courtship?"

She shook her head. "So long as we manage to fool those rogues into submission, all is good. Anything else?"

"Not to find ourselves in any situation that might cause *fake* to transform into *real*."

"Naturally," she said with a smile. "Do you believe me some seductress trying to trap *you*?" She laughed. "I suppose I couldn't blame you if you did. After all, I ventured into your territory first. Whatever terms you set, I will abide by them." She stuck out her hand again. "Shall we?"

Deerhurst nodded. He grasped her fingers between his and guided her hand to his mouth, placing a small kiss on the inside of her wrist. Her gasp brought him all measures of delight.

"Consider it sealed."

Chapter Five

That evening
The Morewoods' Ball

PHAEDRA TAPPED HER foot to the rhythm of the orchestra plucking away at the melody of the quadrille. She stood along the perimeter of gathering wallflowers, having found this to be a sweet spot where rogues dared not tread.

Beyond that border, wolves circled, and from time to time, one would venture dangerously close before a score of hopeful gazes, and Phaedra's bared teeth, sent him circling back to the pack.

More gentlemen were vying for her hand this evening than ever before, and almost all of them were after her dowry. She had long ago learned to separate the princes from the paupers.

Fortune hunters had a certain gleam in their eyes—a look of thrill and expectancy that entered their gaze when they saw nothing but capital and coin. Like a flash of light, as though *she* were a mountain of bountiful treasure and the glow of her jewels reflected in their pupils. Though, with some men, it was harder to spot than others. Those were the dangerous ones.

And London's destitute seemed to have turned into a pack of wolves overnight. With Phaedra as their prey.

Where was Deerhurst?

The earl had promised to meet her here tonight so that they could start the enactment of their play.

The inside of her wrist prickled at the thought of him, as it had been doing all day. Ever since he had sealed their deal with a kiss on that particular spot.

I want to kiss you again.

A jolting charge raced across her skin for the hundredth time at the memory of his admission. She wanted him to kiss her, too. But it was a futile desire. And dangerous. The earl had made it clear he had no plans to be—how had he put it?—*leg shackled* any time soon.

Phaedra would be wise to direct her focus elsewhere, such as the benefits of their agreement. She didn't want to scare the man away with any sort of enthusiasm. All she wanted at present was a measure of freedom and peace of mind. She hadn't quite thought beyond what she would do once she gained a bit of respite, but Phaedra supposed she'd figure that out later.

As for tonight, she had only one objective in mind—to dance with Deerhurst. She'd purposefully kept her dance card empty, claiming a sore ankle, all the while waiting for the earl to stake his make-believe claim.

Luckily, her mother had not questioned her drive with Deerhurst. Of course, the countess had been slightly put out, but she had also been happy that Phaedra had accepted an invitation from a gentleman rather than simply closeting herself away from all callers. After tonight, however, Phaedra would either admit the truth or find a plausible excuse for their continued involvement.

"Lady Phaedra." Lord Nash appeared before her. He cast a glance at the colorful array of wallflowers. "I never thought I'd witness the day where you forgo a night of dancing."

A longtime friend, Phaedra offered him a welcoming smile. "Nash, you are a vision in purple."

He laughed and motioned to the ladies beyond her. "And you're stealing the spotlight from those poor dears."

"On the contrary," Phaedra said. "I'm drawing the spotlight to this corner of the ballroom."

"Your humor is ever present, I see." He crossed his arms behind his back, lips twitching. "I know what you are doing."

"Am I that obvious?"

"I'm afraid so."

"My plan seems to be working then."

"I daresay it is, but your suitors are getting bolder." Nash motioned to a group of young bucks inching closer to her, their gazes flicking between her and the ladies at her back.

She sighed. "I suppose I shall have to take a seat soon."

"You are no wallflower."

True. "But I am hunted, Nash."

"My offer still stands."

Phaedra arched an inquisitive brow at him.

"The one I made last season," he clarified. "I shall help you find a husband. Don't tell me you've already forgotten?"

Phaedra shook her head. "I have no intention of marrying."

"You are serious?"

"Of course," Phaedra said. "That is unless *you* throw your hat into the ring. You, I shall consider."

Nash's face contorted before his gaze darted left and right. "Don't jest about such things. If Rochester hears you, I will have to spend days with his brooding."

Phaedra inwardly snorted. She would never understand those two. Such forbidden love. How could they stand it? She certainly didn't look down upon them, but the risk . . . trusting another person with your life and heart like that . . .

She glanced at the three men hovering on the edges of the invisible perimeter of their corner and shuddered.

"You know," she said after a moment. "Ever since I was a little girl, all I wanted was to dress in beautiful gowns and twirl the night away in glittering ballrooms. The reality is much less romantic."

"Reality and romance rarely ever go hand in hand," Nash said. "But when they do, it's quite magical."

Phaedra didn't refute Nash's claim, but neither could she comment on it. She had experience only with the first part, not the second.

"Do not look now," Nash suddenly said. "But Dare is staring at you."

Phaedra glanced from Lord Nash to the infamous libertine and shook her head in annoyance. "So let him look."

Nash raised a brow. "You are not worried that he's casting his sights upon you?"

"Why?" Phaedra questioned. "Dare looks at every woman who moves."

"You're not moving."

Phaedra smiled. "Everything with a skirt, then."

"Even skirt-wearing goats?"

She laughed. "Even *I* will look at a skirt-wearing goat."

Nash chuckled. "He's got wealth."

"So do I."

"Exactly. And his profile *is* exquisitely hewn."

Phaedra gave Nash a long, sideways glance. "You really think his profile is *exquisitely hewn?*"

He nodded. "But do not tell Rochester I said so. He gets dreadfully jealous."

"Perhaps he has reason to get jealous what with you ogling everything in a tailcoat."

Nash spluttered. He glanced around furiously, his shoulders slumping in relief when no one paid them any attention. Well, no one except the wolves pacing back and forth, searching for an opening to join.

"Will you be more careful with that tongue of yours? I do not ogle anything in a tailcoat." He lifted his chin. "I just voice what every woman secretly thinks."

Phaedra snorted. "That doesn't mean you must flaunt your opinion to the world."

"I'm not flaunting it to the world." Nash grinned at her. "Only to you."

"Well, I don't think Dare is all that handsome. The man is a fop." And Deerhurst was much more striking than Dare. The air of mystery that clung to the earl certainly had a way of making him more interesting. One look at Dare and a woman could tell what he was about.

"They say reformed rakes make the best husbands," Nash pointed out.

"The Pope couldn't reform that man."

"That's because the Pope isn't a woman. Truthfully, there are worse men to marry."

"From exquisitely hewn to marriageable? Did my mother send you?"

Nash laughed. "The countess doesn't agree with your decision to spend your days in the company of books and cats?"

"No, she supports me. That doesn't mean she hasn't also been planning her daughter's wedding since birth."

Nash nodded. "No mother wants her children to grow old alone."

A wry smile lifted the corners of her mouth. "But even mothers have dreams they must give up on."

"Amen, my lady."

Phaedra glanced again toward the fortune hunters. "I believe I shall take a turn on the terrace, Nash. It's getting quite stifling in here."

"I shall escort you."

"No, you block those three wolves while I slip away."

Phaedra retreated to a nearby terrace before Nash could stop her. Impatience stirred in her breast. She ought to have known better than to trust Deerhurst. He should have been here by now. How disappointing that he, too, when stripped bare of cloth and jewel, was all snuff and no substance.

She would fend for herself, then.

Phaedra tried to calculate how many minutes she'd have to herself before the wolves gave chase, but if ever an incalculable equation existed, this was it.

At the doors of the terrace, she did a quick scan of her surroundings to make sure no one had followed and spotted a familiar face in the crowd.

Her heart did a little flip.

He was here.

And then he was not.

A cravat suddenly blocked her view of Deerhurst. Phaedra frowned.

"My lady, will you honor me with this next dance?" Lord Cromby asked.

Phaedra cursed her luck.

"Unfortunately, my lord, my ankle is not up to the task."

"That is unfortunate, indeed." He advanced on her, and Phaedra balked at the ugly glint that sparked in his gaze. She retreated one step, two, three, and then gasped as cool air hit her skin. A quick sweep of her environment made her pulse leap.

He had backed her onto the terrace.

Drat it.

She should never have left Nash. She attempted to sidestep him, but he mirrored her move, refusing to let her pass.

"If you will excuse me, my lord." She tried and failed again.

"Stay a moment, my lady."

"That wouldn't be appropriate, my lord. Please let me pass."

His lips curled into a smile, and for a moment, panic set in. That was not a grin any woman wanted to be at the receiving end of. It made Phaedra's skin crawl.

"I called on you today," he said, ignoring her request.

Phaedra froze. Cromby was by no means destitute according to her information. Just a slimy louse. Did he want to court her?

Never!

"Please excuse me," Phaedra said more forcefully, once again trying to sidestep him.

She gasped when he circled his fingers around her arm, halting her escape. Phaedra wasn't sure what was happening. Lord Cromby wasn't one of her usual suitors. He had never shown interest in her before tonight. She didn't have a pistol with her. Neither did she have a tray of sandwiches at hand. Could she punch him in the nose? Would that hurt enough for him to let her go?

Phaedra glared at him. "Unhand me, sir."

He gave a sleazy grin. "I don't think I will, my lady. You and I have something to dis—"

His words were cut off as he was suddenly yanked away from her.

"The lady asked you to let her go, Cromby."

Phaedra nearly sagged in relief.

Her knight had arrived.

⇛⇚

FURY, UNLIKE THAT which Deerhurst had ever before experienced, exploded through him like a thousand thunderbolts. He glowered at Cromby, who drew back at the force of his anger.

Good.

The man still possessed a sliver of self-preservation. Cromby was the bastard who had found the list Warrick lost and secured it to the betting book of White's. Deerhurst would be damned if he allowed the man to harass Lady Phaedra because of it. In fact, it took about all his discipline not to drag the man off to the garden and beat him to a pulp.

Cromby cleared his throat. "Lady Phaedra and I were merely enjoying a conversation, Deerhurst."

Deerhurst raised a brow. "Doesn't look like she is enjoying it much."

Cromby's jaw clenched. "That is my fault, indeed. I have been told that my humor is sometimes difficult for women to follow."

"I'm not a woman," Deerhurst said. "And I'm not following."

Cromby stiffened, and Deerhurst too, locked every single muscle in place. Cromby wouldn't win this round. Or any other rounds if Deerhurst had any say in the matter. He was damn lucky Deerhurst did not grab him by the lapels and toss him over the terrace railings.

His fingers flexed.

He ignored the little voice that called him a hypocrite. Yes, he had taken part in that damn list too, but not in the wagers, nor had they meant for the list to ever become known.

And he was attempting to make it right by protecting Lady Phaedra from blackguards such as Cromby. Intention ought to count for something, no matter how bloody little.

His friends were also keeping an eye on the other ladies, though one of them had already been betrothed because of the wagers, if the whispers at White's could be believed. Nothing had been formally announced.

Cromby shoved past Deerhurst, shooting him a glare. "I won't forget this, Deerhurst."

"I'm pleased to hear it, Cromby," Deerhurst said, lowering his voice to a menacing tone, "I very much hope that you don't." There would be no lenience for his tricks again.

Deerhurst waited until the man disappeared into the bustling crowd before directing his attention to Lady Phaedra. She looked so beautiful and out of sorts his heart ached.

"Are you all right?" Deerhurst asked. "Cromby didn't hurt you, did he?"

She rubbed her wrist. "No, but the man has a foul mouth and

poisonous intentions."

Deerhurst locked his gaze onto that little action. He cursed Cromby to hell and made a mental note to teach the bastard a lesson in manners.

He could do nothing about the list, but he could damn well make sure she did not suffer for it. He ought to warn her about the wagers, give her an even fairer chance, but Phaedra Sharp did not trust easily. He suspected she would break off their fake courtship, and if that happened, he had no reason to appear before her. Protecting her would become harder. And this confrontation with Cromby had taught him one thing: he'd have to keep a closer eye on Lady Phaedra.

"I'm sorry," Deerhurst apologized. "Morewood held me up when I arrived. I should have found you sooner."

She waved his apology aside. "These things happen. It's not your fault."

"Would you like to find a place to rest? Perhaps a glass of wine to temper this incident?"

"I'm truly fine."

"Are you sure? Mayhap I should escort you home."

She raised a brow. "You make it sound as though I escaped the toothy jaw of a ferocious beast."

"Didn't you?" Deerhurst smiled. "An impressive feat, if I may say so myself."

"Well, I had *some* help."

Deerhurst inclined his head. "Then laugh, dance, and forget about that beast. Don't let him think for even a minute that his efforts affected your evening."

She nodded. "Don't fret. It shall take more than Cromby—or the pack of wolves circling about—to affect my mood."

"The what?"

"All the gentlemen fighting for a moment in my presence."

"Ah." Deerhurst offered her his arm. "We cannot do anything

about them, but we can dance. Shall we?"

She laughed and placed her hand on forearm. "I have been waiting for this moment all night."

Deerhurst swept her up in not one, but two dances, and the audience took notice. His initial uneasiness settled. While he did not tolerate people prying into his life, and while after tonight, all eyes would be on them, a sense of calm enveloped him.

He would not let any harm come to this woman.

But dear Christ.

What he wouldn't give to pluck the pins from her hair and have her locks cascade down her back like the night in his garden.

"What are you smiling about?"

Deerhurst blinked. He hadn't realized that he had been.

"Your wolves are glaring at me," Deerhurst said, because he couldn't very well confess what he'd been thinking about.

"And you find that funny?"

"I find it *entertaining*. I have something they want."

"How positively arrogant of you to assume."

He chuckled, and they were separated for a few beats.

"I believe that is my fault," Lady Phaedra said when they reunited.

"How is that?" Deerhurst asked.

"I've claimed a sore ankle all evening," she admitted. "Now I'm here, dancing my second dance with you." She grinned at him. "My ankle has recovered significantly."

"No wonder." Deerhurst leaned in close. "And that would make my perceived arrogance your fault as well."

"More arrogance. What am I to do with you?"

He winked at her. "As you please."

She snorted. "You will come to regret that statement."

Deerhurst didn't doubt it.

"If you don't mind my asking," she cast him a glance, "why have you not fallen into the parson's trap? Undoubtedly, there must be many who have tried to lure you in."

Deerhurst almost faltered in his step at the question. Memories flashed through his mind, memories he'd rather forget altogether. That part of his life ended years ago, and it had given him clarity and acceptance.

She must have detected something on his face, for she said with a smile, "No need to answer. I should not have pried. I'd rather not listen to all your roguish encounters and how your scoundrel's heart longs to be free of any entanglements."

The tension drained from his limbs, and he chuckled. "Absurd."

Lady Phaedra glanced at the gathering crowd on the outer edges of the dance floor. "I think our plan might work. Everyone is taking note. Perhaps the wolves will turn tail after tonight."

Deerhurst wasn't so sure.

He should have pummeled Cromby. That would have made his intentions crystal clear—stay away from Lady Phaedra or else.

The dance ended and Deerhurst led Lady Phaedra from the dance floor. Blatant stares and loud whispers followed them to the corner of the ballroom where refreshments were arranged. Deerhurst supposed they were waiting to see whether he'd whisk her off into a third dance, which would be akin to a marriage proposal.

"Deerhurst, old chap!" Saville stepped into their path. A foxlike grin coated his face. "Are you going to introduce me to your exceptionally beautiful dance partner?"

Deerhurst glared at Saville and made the introduction, whereby he realized *he* had not been formally introduced to Lady Phaedra. She seemed to realize it at the same time as he for her eyes rounded like saucers.

Bloody hell.

Dare he hope no one had realized?

But of course, Saville had, or he wouldn't be wearing that deuced grin on his face. Deerhurst scowled at him.

"Phaedra Sharp," Lady Phaedra introduced herself, offering her hand. Deerhurst shook his head. This woman didn't need anyone to introduce her.

Saville bowed and planted a kiss on her hand, his grin stretching and stretching. "You seem to have enthralled my friend, Lady Phaedra."

"Don't you have to keep an eye on your sister?" Deerhurst asked, his tone filled with warning.

"Warrick is keeping her company," Saville replied easily. "I'm much more intrigued by what is happening on this side of the ballroom."

"Nothing is happening here." Deerhurst guided Lady Phaedra, who looked amused, away from Saville. "We are on our way to the refreshments table."

"Smashing idea," Saville said. "I could use a drink as well."

"You weren't invited."

Saville waggled his brows. "Well, look who is in a blithesome mood tonight. What does the lady say?"

Deerhurst wanted to throttle his friend.

"Oh, I don't mind," Lady Phaedra piped up.

"See, Deerhurst? The lady said she doesn't mind."

Deerhurst cursed.

He knew Saville. His friend wasn't going to let this go. Heaving a long-suffering sigh, he said, "Very well. Let us *all* head over to the refreshment table."

Then he would throttle his friend.

Chapter Six

THE NEXT MORNING, Phaedra entered the breakfast room with a skip in her step. For the first time in her life, she hadn't risen in time for breakfast but remained in bed two hours later. Not to sleep, but to reminisce.

Phaedra loved dancing. And last night . . . well, she had never had so much fun dancing as last night. Partly because of Deerhurst and partly because one of those dances was the Waltz. But mostly because of the curiosity that rippled through the ballroom.

After dressing in a simple day gown of soft pink, she hurried down the steps to the breakfast room, listening carefully for the tell-tale hum that signaled the receiving room was stocked with dowry-sniffers.

Nothing.

Not one laugh.

Not one voice.

Not one rap at the door.

Last night had been a smashing success. So what if the evening had started off poorly, what with the pack of wolves and the main beast, Lord Cromby, cornering her?

Deerhurst had rescued her.

Phaedra refused to entertain the thought of what would have happened if he hadn't run Cromby off. But that was neither here nor there since the night had ended in dancing and laughter.

And if the silence was anything to go by, Deerhurst had done more than save her—he'd ensured her much desired reprieve. And Phaedra would delight in every moment of peace.

Only one question remained. How could she ever repay him?

With a kiss? A slight peck on the cheek, perhaps? And why not? She could be just as daring and mischievous as the earl. There was no denying that she longed for another one of his kisses. Surely a kiss or two could do no harm. She'd never met a man she wanted to spend her time with, not to mention share intimate embraces with. Quite frankly, her curiosity about Deerhurst still surprised her.

Phaedra slowed to a halt when she spotted her mother and aunt in the parlor, pulling on their gloves.

"Phaedra, there you are dear," the countess said. "Your aunt and I have sent for the carriage. We are off shopping."

"This time of the day?" *Without her?*

"Well, I figured the earl would be calling soon. I have instructed Hammington to show all other callers away."

That explained the empty drawing room.

"Do not look so surprised, my dear. You went on a carriage ride with him, and you danced two dances in a row. Really, Phaedra, I asked if the earl had shown interest and you denied it to my face."

Phaedra pursed her lips at the reprimand in her mother's tone. A pinch of guilt flashed in her heart. She had decided not to tell her mother or aunt about the fake courtship simply because it did no harm. Many courtships began and ended with the drop of a hat. It certainly wasn't like this was a scandalous affair.

"I did not want to get ahead of myself," Phaedra said after a short pause. "Besides, I'm not sure if the earl and I even suit."

"Oh, pish. The earl is an accomplished man, and you are an accomplished lady. You suit just fine."

"It's a bit more complicated than us both being accomplished people, Mama, as you well know."

"I agree with Phaedra," Portia said. "There is more to consider than simple compatibility when it comes to choosing a life partner."

"Exactly."

"Just be careful dear," her mother said. "Apparently there are wagers going about town surrounding dowries and marriage, or so your father informed me."

"Excuse me?" Phaedra all but spluttered. "Is that why our drawing room suddenly filled overnight?" And why Cromby had made his sour presence known?

"It appears so," the countess said. "I am not clear on all the details."

Portia gasped. "How ghastly."

Phaedra agreed.

But so much made sense now.

"Well, I for one am glad you don't have to play hostess to those gentlemen anymore," Portia said.

Phaedra offered her aunt a small smile.

The countess snorted. "Who has been acting hostess in recent days? Surely not that girl. But you are right. At least now her mother can go shopping for a change."

Portia grinned. "Do not try to hide it, Eleanor. We both know teasing Phaedra's callers constitutes your daily noon entertainment."

Phaedra laughed, recalling her mother in a red gown entertaining a roomful of young men. "I do believe you are right, aunt."

The countess harumphed. "Keep in mind, daughter, that not all men are the same. I wouldn't want you to cast a perfectly noble earl under the same parasol as the common fortune hunter."

Noble?

Phaedra nearly laughed. She supposed the earl could be considered noble insomuch as he'd been born into rank.

"Or whoever is responsible for those wagers," Portia added.

"Well, I do appreciate your advice, mother, aunt. As for the earl, we shall see. At least the man has his own fortune." And he protected women, but Phaedra kept that for herself.

"We will see you later, dear." Her mother waved her off. "Do give the earl our best."

Phaedra nodded.

"And do behave, Phaedra," the countess sang over her shoulder. "Don't think I don't know about your theatrics when it comes to your callers."

Phaedra laughed and headed for the empty drawing room and stepped inside, pausing to breathe in the silence.

Peace and quiet.

Finally.

She wandered to the center, her gaze raking over every inch. Her gaze stopped on the sofa, and after a moment of hesitation, she lowered down into the cushions, then jumped up and shut her eyes as she spun in a circle, arms stretched wide.

Liberation.

With every step, victory and delight swelled in her breast, her muslin dress billowing out at the hem.

Phaedra laughed.

It was the sort of unrestrained laugh that came from her belly rather than her lungs. She thought of all the times she'd had to entertain dubious gentlemen with slick smiles, inhale their lavishly applied perfume, and laugh at dreary recitations of what she only presumed to be jests.

She spun about until she became dizzy and tendrils of hair sprang from their pins. With a low chuckle, she slowed to a stop, breathless. If every day could start like this, life would be heaven.

A prickling made its way up the back of her neck.

Her gaze lifted, and Phaedra's breath caught as she locked gazes with the deep stare of a man. Deerhurst stood watching her through the large windows of the drawing room.

How positively bizarre!

He'd told her of this phenomenon of his—always passing the drawing room window at interesting times—yet to be caught so thoroughly in the act of a private moment truly shifted her perspective on the matter.

She could not quite interpret the expression on his face either. He looked at her as one might believe a predator surveyed his prey. Phaedra immediately thought of Puck, the moment he prepared to pounce on a little bird. But not quite. Because predators devoured their prey. Deerhurst couldn't very well eat her.

Could he?

No. Do not be ridiculous, Phaedra.

She must not have interpreted his gaze correctly. She must be mistaken. The strange look was probably due to the fact that he *was* privy to her deepest, most shocking behaviors.

For one, he'd witnessed other of her moments in this very drawing room. They had also shared a midnight kiss in his garden. And they'd formed a secret agreement.

But no man had ever looked at her like that before—as though she herself were the object of great fascination instead of the size of her dowry. As though he and he alone had a right to witness all her private moments. It was almost . . .

Possessive.

It was a heady feeling.

Phaedra loved that look.

She could get addicted to that look.

She headed to the window and lifted a brow. "I never thought I'd live to catch the earl-next-door peeping through my drawing room window," Phaedra teased.

He chuckled. "I never thought I'd be caught in the act of peeping through your drawing room window."

"Sounds positively wretched."

"Only if the lady refuses to forgive me."

"I shall forgive, but only this once." She glanced beyond him. "Will you join me for tea, or shall we start a new craze of communication?"

A slow smile cracked his face, and Phaedra found herself grinning back at him.

Lord.

That was another thing about Deerhurst.

The man could smile.

≫≫≪≪

HE WANTED TO caress her face.

He wanted to run each loose tendril of hair through his fingers. Just when he thought he had everything under control—his heart under control—the universe decided to show him this side of Phaedra Sharp.

It didn't help that he had awakened this morning hard and wanting, Phaedra's golden eyes swimming in his vision, naked, breathless, her hands all over his body. Christ, just thinking about the dream made him hard again.

He pushed the lingering images of her in his bed aside. Later he would let his mind run wild. He couldn't very well knock on her door with a full-on erection. The butler will take one look at his breeches and shut the door in his face.

How the hell had he become like this?

If it hadn't been for that bloody curse. Again, without conscious thought, his gaze had ventured to the Sharp drawing room windows as he passed, but this time he had stopped dead in his tracks.

Lady Phaedra had been in the room twirling in circles and laughing. A more striking sight he had yet to behold. At that moment, he couldn't have looked away even if he'd wanted to. In fact, he had stepped up to the window and practically pressed his face up to the glass.

She was simply exquisite.

Carefree. Happy. Victorious.

What that laughter did to him. Never had a woman tied him up in so many knots.

Not even *that* woman.

Then their gazes had locked, ripples had rolled down his spine. Deerhurst found himself entertaining a lavish thought. An unbidden, wild, and thoroughly intolerable question.

Would she accept or reject him if ever she discovered the secret that he had spent blood, sweat, and tears hiding from the world?

The question was so unexpected, so startling, that Deerhurst exorcised it entirely from his mind. This question was not to be borne. Too much was at stake. And now he had another secret. The secret of the list.

Christ.

There were the secrets you want to keep hidden, and the ones you do not dare let out. Deerhurst might have too many of the latter. Sometimes the weight of them threatened to crush him.

The butler seemed to expect him, and he opened the door before Deerhurst could raise his arm and knock. He followed the servant to the drawing room where Phaedra waited for him with a bright smile.

He took her in. Dressed in a simple day gown, the same color as her cheeks after the excursion of her twirls. Her eyes sparkled. She was a vision.

"Hello," she said, as if they hadn't spoken just moments ago.

"Hello."

She motioned to the empty room. "It worked."

"I'm surprised." He stepped over the threshold. "If I were one of your real suitors, I would not have given up so easily."

Her lips quirked. "I'm not sure they have given up, to be honest. My mother instructed that all callers, except for you, be turned away. I suppose we shall have to wait and see the outcome."

Deerhurst nodded. He glanced around the room. "Where is the

countess? Will she be joining us?"

"Oh, no. She and my aunt went shopping."

"They left you alone knowing I would call?"

She laughed. "I am not alone. I have a house filled with servants."

Deerhurst took four steps into the drawing room. He motioned to the spot at his feet, and said with some amusement, "This is where the infamous pistol incident took place?"

"Two steps to the left."

Deerhurst took two steps to the left. "Here?"

She nodded and grinned. "And it's not infamous. There are only three people in the world who know about that day's events."

"I feel surprisingly honored."

She pointed to the green velvet settee. "That is where I emptied a cup of scalding tea over Lord Rodale's lap."

Deerhurst raised a brow. He hadn't seen that. "On purpose?"

"He told me I'd be lucky to consider myself Lady Rodale and then proceeded to recount the finer details of his annual income when I know his pockets to be all but empty. The little he does have mostly goes to gambling halls."

Deerhurst's gaze swung to her. "How on earth do you know that?" *He* didn't even know that.

"Ask me anything about my suitors' annual income. Ferreting out their secrets has become a hobby of sorts."

Deerhurst instinctively wanted to take a step away from the woman. The idea of her ferreting out *his* secrets was a truly terrifying prospect.

She laughed. "What is with that face, Deerhurst? Do you have secrets you wish to hide from me?"

He heard the teasing note in her voice, but his heart still thundered in his ears. He fought for steadiness. Won.

"We all have secrets," Deerhurst said. "We are keeping one now."

"Normally, I loathe secrets, but even I must admit there is a thrill in knowing something others do not." Her gaze met his. *Sparkled.* "We share two secrets, Deerhurst. What do you make of that?"

He arched a brow. "That you are the most troubling woman in Mayfair?"

"Only Mayfair?"

"England, then."

She nodded, satisfied. "Though, I only wish to be troublesome for the men who seek to cause trouble, which is why it's important to always take account of their affairs."

It almost sounded like . . .

"Dear Lord, don't tell me you have a file on each man that throws his hat into the ring?"

"Of course not," she said, but grinned. "That would be too excessive, not to mention tiring."

He gave her a skeptical glance. "So you have not penned down in your journal scathing retorts on all the rogues that enter this drawing room?"

"This idea sounds intriguing. The perfect way to vent." She laughed. "What do all the fortune-hunters have in common besides their lack of fortune? Cats. Apparently, they all love cats."

Deerhurst chuckled. Of course, *that* would be her first complaint. "They shouldn't like cats?"

"It's an insult to cats."

He bit back a laugh. Half curious and half teasing, he asked, "If you don't have a file on your suitors, how do you keep record of their annual incomes?"

She tapped a finger against her head. "I have an exemplary memory."

"You consult Debrett's."

"Debrett's is hardly an accurate account, I'm afraid. If it had been, my aunt would have had fair warning before her wedding."

Her aunt again.

Deerhurst tried to bring to mind what he could of Lady Portia's husband. She'd married the late Marquess of Rowley, and shortly after the marriage, rumors surfaced. Rumors of arguments and Huntly beating Rowley to a bloody pulp. But Deerhurst rarely ever burrowed his ears in gossip. However, if there was even a scrap of truth to the tales he'd heard, their marriage may well have been one of misery right up to the marquess's death three years ago.

No wonder Lady Phaedra did not trust men. Especially the type of men who wooed her.

Fate truly had a way of knocking a man on his ass. Not all men were Cromby and Rowley's ilk. There were honorable men in the world, and for the most part, he counted himself one of them. He would have loved to show Lady Phaedra that there were men she could trust.

But that wasn't his place.

His involvement in the wagers had forever set him apart.

His mouth twisted. "Rowley deserved his end." A pause. "Should I even ask how you procure the knowledge about their income?"

Her lips twitched. "You probably shouldn't."

The woman had some gumption.

"You have an unusual hobby."

She shrugged. "Do you not have unusual hobbies?"

"I peep through ladies' drawing rooms."

She laughed. "Unusual, indeed." She waved to the door. "Shall I send for tea?"

"I thought we could go for a drive through Hyde Park in my phaeton. It ought to go a long way to stave off unwanted suitors."

Her eyes lit up. "Can I drive? I love driving high perch phaetons." She rocked on her heels. "Let's not waste any more seconds."

Deerhurst swallowed. He suddenly had an ominous premonition. Not for her, but for himself. She was looking at him in a way that had the hairs on the back of his neck rise to attention, and not in a bad way. He couldn't decipher the exact spark, but dammit if she didn't look like she might kiss him at any moment.

Deerhurst froze.

Did her gaze just drop to his mouth?

Surely not.

He must be imagining things. He'd started the day with a desperate need for the woman before him. Now he was seeing all sorts of illusions that weren't there.

He adjusted his cravat and offered his arm.

"Shall we go?"

Chapter Seven

THE DRIVE THROUGH Hyde Park proved not to be as thrilling as Phaedra had hoped. In fact, Phaedra would go so far as to venture that if a drive could be equated to a nightmare, this would be the worst nightmare of them all.

Her mother had told her she'd instructed all her callers to be sent away, which meant there were possible callers to send away. Deep down, Phaedra had known an empty drawing room did not equal complete success, but she hadn't expected *this*.

Her solitude seemed to be reserved for the Sharp residence and *only* there. The moment they were spotted in Hyde Park, the wolves descended in packs.

Deerhurst's presence was apparently deemed inconsequential.

In fact, he may as well not have been there at all, the way the wolves behaved. And then Phaedra remembered the wagers her mother had mentioned. It had to be the reason they were so persistent. She should have warned Deerhurst, but she'd completely forgotten about it, too distracted by her delight at the empty drawing room and Deerhurst's arrival.

Beside her Deerhurst cursed.

They were completely surrounded, which forced Phaedra to bring the phaeton to a halt. The wolves had boxed them in. She couldn't just run them over, could she? The visual imagery the idea provoked gave her immense pleasure.

"Lady Phaedra!"

"—you look lovely today."

"Marry me, Lady Phaedra—"

She blocked them all out.

"Deerhurst," Phaedra's gloved fingers grabbed his wrist, "what are we going to do?"

He glanced at her, his expression grim. "You didn't bring a pistol, by any chance?"

"I beg your pardon?" she exclaimed. "Is that humor? At a time like this?"

"I am perfectly serious."

"Well, then, no, I did not bring my pistol," Phaedra said. Annoyance sank into her tone. "I thought I'd be *perfectly* safe with you."

Hot eyes narrowed. "Is that sarcasm? At a time like this?"

Before Phaedra could punch Deerhurst, another wave of shouts drowned out all reason.

"Lady Phaedra!"

"What a lovely gown."

"Your hair shimmers like the stars!"

Phaedra shut her eyes.

"Dammit," Deerhurst exploded.

"Whoa!" a voice exclaimed, and Phaedra opened her eyes to find the newest arrival pushing his horse through the man blocking their path.

The Earl of Saville had arrived.

He guided his horse up against the phaeton. "What have we here? A damsel in distress? Shall I save the lady?"

"You will do no such thing," Deerhurst bit through gritted teeth.

Saville arched a brow. "You don't want the lady saved?"

Phaedra shook her head, amazed that she could still feel amusement while boxed in by suitors gone mad.

"I will do the bloody saving," Deerhurst said.

Saville's grin was almost audible. "Even a hero needs a helping hand."

Phaedra intervened before Deerhurst could impart another growl. "I take it you have a plan of action?"

"A smart woman you have here, Deerhurst."

"Get to the damn point."

Saville leaned in low and said to Deerhurst, "On the count of one, I will leap onto your carriage, and you will jump onto my horse. On the count of two, I will snatch up your lady and swing her up into your arms, and on the count of three, you dash off into the sunset."

Oh. My. Lord.

The man was utterly insane.

As, apparently, was Deerhurst, for he nodded thoughtfully and then said, "Excellent plan."

Phaedra blinked. Was she the only one who thought it a terrible plan? Jumping, leaping, and being snatched up? There wasn't even a sunset to dash off into! Who even spoke like that?

"I don't think this is a good—"

"One!" Saville barked and swung his leg over the horse as Deerhurst reached for the reigns.

Phaedra gasped, expecting both men to tumble and land in a heap on the ground. It would serve them both right if they got trampled by horses and wolves today.

However, surprisingly, the men were in utter harmony. The phaeton wobbled as Saville landed on the spot Deerhurst previously occupied, Deerhurst now atop the big, copper horse.

"Two!"

Phaedra had no time to absorb what was happening before she was snatched around the waist—she gave an extremely unladylike yelp—and was tossed at Deerhurst, who, bless his soul, caught her in a firm, confident grip. He settled her at his front, his arms enfolding her in a safe cocoon.

"Three!"

They surged forward as Deerhurst dug his heels into the horse. Strong, powerful legs surrounded Phaedra, and she inwardly admonished herself for noticing Deerhurst's thighs during such a disturbing event.

She glanced over his shoulder.

"They're chasing us!" Phaedra cried as all but one or two of the men set out after them. What madness prompted these men to chase them? What could they possibly hope to gain? Surely they would not rip her from Deerhurst's embrace? Such behavior would be barbaric, but she wouldn't quite put it past them.

They were all acting barbaric.

She heard Deerhurst curse, then his lips pressed up against her ear. "Are you all right?" he asked.

This was certainly not the way Phaedra had anticipated their first public drive through Hyde Park to go. She leaned back against his broad chest. Neither did she care to complain, because suddenly, the nightmare seemed to disappear and, in its place, settled another sort of thrill.

Phaedra could get used to being rescued by earls who had strong arms and smelled like tobacco and coffee.

They raced across the streets of London, Deerhurst guiding them through alleyways and paths Phaedra did not recognize until no more buildings appeared familiar to her.

She had thought Deerhurst would take her home, but he hadn't, and she could no longer hear the pursuit of horses galloping behind them.

"Where, exactly, are we going?"

The earl had been tight-lipped during their escape, and Phaedra hadn't questioned him for fear that she might pull his concentration from their mad dash through town.

Now, curiosity bloomed. Phaedra was not sure whether that delighted her or made her unsettled. But she did feel something to the effect of fluttering in her chest.

She cast Deerhurst a sidelong glance.

Awareness pricked at the tips of her fingers. He appeared ever the posh gentleman. Yet there was a wildness to him. It was not a quality one noticed straightaway. It came slowly, beckoning to anyone who paid any notice.

They came to a stop before a decrepit old building.

Phaedra knitted her brows. "Why have we stopped?"

"We can find shelter here for the moment."

Shelter? Here?

She glanced at the building again. They'd ventured into a seedy part of London, not a neighborhood any lady wished to find herself in.

"Could we not find shelter at home?"

His gaze turned to her, the corner of his mouth lifting. "Are you worried for your safety, Lady Phaedra?"

"Of course not," Phaedra hedged. "I'm more worried for yours, Deerhurst. Look at you; you're dressed like the lord you are. I, at least, donned a simple day dress." Pink, but simple. She wished she'd brought a cloak.

He chuckled. "A potato sack couldn't hide your beauty, my lady."

"I should be flattered." Phaedra eyed the scoundrel. "Yet, I'm not."

"Are you so used to flattery that a compliment has no meaning anymore?"

Phaedra snorted.

But he wasn't wrong. Phaedra distrusted flowery words more than she distrusted the men who uttered them. Flattery could seduce; those wretched rapscallions could not.

"I see that I'm right," Deerhurst said, this thumb tracing her cheeks. "Am I not allowed to compliment the lady I am courting?"

"*Fake* courting."

"A fake compliment, then."

Phaedra narrowed her eyes. "You were right, Deerhurst. You are no knight."

A roguish smile stretched across his lips. "Then you thought of me as a gentleman before? Didn't you label me a scoundrel?"

Lud, the man was incorrigible.

Phaedra huffed. "I have not quite decided what to think of you," she lied, and to divert his attention from his question because she liked him more than she ought, she said, "Are we going to stand out here all day or are we going to seek shelter?"

"Do not sound so skeptical," Deerhurst said with a smile. "We are safe here."

Phaedra snorted. "Tell me, Deerhurst, do you take all the ladies to seedy parts of town or am I the first?"

Green eyes fastened on her.

Magnetic.

The word slid into her mind like the first glimpse of a shooting star. Vivid. Breathtaking. And wholly unexpected.

He cocked his head to the side as a devilish spark entered his gaze. "Only you."

Only her.

Now, there were two words that held immense power—*only you.* Phaedra would have to be made of rock not to feel a slight flutter that *she* was the only one. The only one he brought to . . . to . . .

The seediest part of London.

Phaedra frowned, then cleared her throat.

Right.

That was nothing to get her stays into a twist.

"What do you plan to do to me, Deerhurst? I warn you, I will hunt you down and gut you if your intentions are anything but sterling."

He laughed outright. "Upon my honor, Lady Phaedra, you have nothing to fear."

And once again he offered his arm.

Once again Phaedra accepted it.

⇒⋙⫷⇐

DEERHURST MUST HAVE lost every last one of his marbles to bring Lady Phaedra to the Lawson Home for Abandoned Children. His first thought had been to outrun their pursuers, and his second had been to find a place where they could pause and catch their breath.

He had thought about returning her to the Sharp house, but he wasn't so sure they wouldn't be ambushed on their way back home or that her suitors wouldn't have overpowered the butler and invaded the house.

This was utter bloody madness.

Never in his life had he experienced such uncivilized absurdity. It seemed impossible that one little list could stir up so much trouble. Had the men in London all lost their damn fortunes? Their dignity had certainly been placed in question after today. But Deerhurst knew the truth. This was no longer about money. This was about conquest. The thrill of the chase. The satisfaction of victory over others. Winning.

Even *he* brimmed with a misplaced sense of triumph at being the one at Phaedra Sharp's side.

"I must warn you, Deerhurst, I don't like surprises."

"Noted." Deerhurst smiled at the woman beside him "No surprises here, my lady. Just a shelter." In all senses of the word.

"I sincerely doubt that," she said. "Everything you do surprises me."

"Pleasant surprises, I hope."

"Pleasant or unpleasant, neither appeals to me. In fact, I'm not sure which is worse, the pleasant ones that give rise to expectations or the ones that pop up like a sore tooth. Like Cromby. They both bring me discomfort."

Deerhurst arched a brow. "Heaven almighty, where's the rosy chit from this morning?"

"You doused her spirits with all this suspense."

He laughed. "You are an impatient woman, Lady Phaedra."

"It's never been my virtue," Phaedra agreed.

"Come on, then." He leaned in close. "Don't wander from my side."

"Why? Is something going to jump out and bite me?"

Deerhurst grinned. "No, Phaedra, nothing is going to bite you." *Well, perhaps me. But just me.*

He pulled her close to him. She smelled nice. Sweet. Vanilla and fresh blossoms. He inhaled her scent deeply before guiding her to the building and rapping on the door.

There weren't many people in the street, but the ones who were about looked rough and weathered by time. Two men stared at Phaedra openly, and Deerhurst secured an arm around her waist and drew her into the crook of his arm.

He smiled at her small gasp.

Two seconds later the door swung open to reveal a stocky older woman, whose pinched look softened as it fell on Deerhurst, then broke into a wide grin.

"Well now, what a comforting sight to behold. Haven't seen you in ages, laddie. Almost thought you weren't coming here no more."

Deerhurst felt his ears burn. He suddenly regretted his decision to come here. He had forgotten how he always felt like a naughty child when in the presence of this woman.

Deerhurst straightened his shoulders. "My apologies, Mrs. Plum, I've been busy these past weeks."

"No matter, no matter. You're here now." She motioned them in. "And who might this young lady be? Have you married since you last visited? So beautiful! Ginny will be heartbroken, she will."

He ignored Phaedra's wide stare. This was definitely a mistake.

"Ginny?" she hissed in a low voice, shooting daggers at him. "Where exactly have you brought me to, Deerhurst? Certainly not—"

"Mrs. Plum," Deerhurst cut her off. "Allow me to introduce you to

Miss Sharp. She is a family friend." Better to keep her exact identity a bit ambiguous, though Mrs. Plum was no fool.

Phaedra gaped at him.

"Nice to meet you, Miss Sharp," Mrs. Plum gushed. "You're lucky to have a friend such as our Deerhurst here."

Deerhurst shook his head. "I am the lucky one, madam. Miss Sharp keeps me on my toes."

"A pleasure to meet you, Mrs. Plum," Phaedra said politely, though Deerhurst could feel the tension rolling off her. He probably should have warned her beforehand, but he was beginning to have fun now discovering and sparking the embers of her temper.

"You two come inside, I shall see to your horse and have Tom stand guard."

"Thank you, Mrs. Plum."

Deerhurst guided Phaedra inside and led her to a small parlor to their left. The moment they entered, three young girls ran up to them and threw their arms around Deerhurst's leg. He laughed and picked up the little blond one, pinching her cheek.

Deerhurst watched in amusement as surprise and shock lit Phaedra's vivid gaze.

Satisfaction filled him. He also noted some nerves. Not unexpected. Deerhurst was privy to a few of her drawing room secrets, and now she was privy to one of his. Though the orphanage could not be considered a secret exactly, his involvement was not something he advertised to society.

"This is Maddie," he told Phaedra about the girl in his arms. He pointed at the others. "And that is Macy and Evie. They've clung to me since they were infants."

Her mouth opened and closed again.

"Does she not know how to speak?" Evie asked.

Deerhurst patted the little girl on the shoulder. "I suspect she is merely a touch overwhelmed. We were chased by a group of scoundrels."

"Hello there," Phaedra greeted the girls, having found her voice. "We had quite the mad dash."

"Did bad men chase you?" Maddie asked.

"Well, perhaps not all bad," Phaedra said. "But certainly not well behaved."

"Doesn't that make them bad?" Evie asked.

Phaedra tilted her head thoughtfully. "Yes, you're right. Men that are not well behaved are bad, bad men and should be avoided at all costs."

"Mrs. Plum says good manners are everything," Macy said.

"Mrs. Plum is very wise," Deerhurst agreed. He cast his gaze at Phaedra. "You should also never venture out alone at night. You never know what scoundrels wait in the shadows."

Phaedra arched a brow.

Evie nodded. "Mrs. Plum says good manners will bring you happiness and bad manners will bring you trouble."

Deerhurst's gaze still held Phaedra's. "Just so."

"Mrs. Plum is certainly right on that score," Phaedra agreed as well, her eyes never leaving Deerhurst's. Tiny thrills shot up his spine. "A woman must learn to defend herself well lest she be devoured by wolves."

The girls giggled.

Then, Maddie said, "Then we must learn to defend ourselves. We don't want to be caught by bad men."

All the girls nodded.

"Interesting shelter," Phaedra remarked. "I daresay no rogues will venture in here."

"Come girls," Mrs. Plum said when she returned a moment later, taking Maddie from Deerhurst and ushering the other girls from the room. "You can help me prepare some tea for our guests while they take a moment to catch their breath.

Deerhurst almost called them back, suddenly hesitant and uncertain of how to explain the girls or the home. Phaedra stared at him, waiting for him to collect his words, as though she sensed his struggle to gather his thoughts and weave them into a satisfactory sentence or two that would explain their presence here.

And she would be right.

"I didn't think you to be such a philanthropist," Phaedra spoke first, ever impatient.

"I'm not," Deerhurst said. "One could say I happened upon this place by chance."

"How *did* you find this place?"

Deerhurst paused.

He had found this orphanage seven years ago on a freezing, rainy night, after having received word he had a child, and she had been abandoned here. A daughter conceived between him and the Duchess of Crane.

Deerhurst inwardly sighed.

That affair had nearly cost him everything.

But he had also gained so much.

Both a blessing and a curse. And a secret that could never be revealed to anyone. Deerhurst didn't even want to imagine what might happen if the Duke of Crane ever discovered his daughter's origin. No, he couldn't afford to let the man find out—not ever. The duke was a powerful man—and a vengeful one. Vicious to all who betrayed him. He and his wife had that in common, Deerhurst supposed. If the maid who had brought Abigail to this orphanage hadn't sent word to him, Deerhurst would still, to this day, not know he had a daughter.

He also dared not examine why he'd brought Phaedra here. Then again, he didn't really need to, as the reason was at the forefront of his mind already. He wanted to show her not all men were like Cromby. But he also had a more selfish reason for bringing her here—he wanted her to see a different side of *him*. Even if just to ease some of the guilt in his heart. Just so that he could for a moment believe he wasn't a bad man. A scoundrel. A beast. He had redeeming qualities as well.

He wanted to catch sight, no matter how briefly, of that version of himself reflected in her eyes. A good man. An honorable man. A knight.

Even though he would never be.

Just one glimpse would be enough.

"Welcome to Lawson Orphanage."

Chapter Eight

PHAEDRA'S HEART POUNDED as she stared into Deerhurst's eyes. His gaze refused to let her go, dared her to look deeper, past the surface of their color and into the very being of his soul.

She had never entered a children's home before today—a place that took in children who weren't wanted.

Phaedra had always been wanted. No matter how many proposals she declined. No matter how she vexed her mother with her reading material. Phaedra had never had a shortage of love.

She had been born into immense wealth. Had grown up with the promise of glittering ballrooms and gowns so pretty she had spent hours praying to reach an age where she could wear them. And then after she had come out, she had been the belle of the ball on more than one occasion.

But that was in her first season, before she had sharpened up to the dreary truth about the marriage mart—that women were put on an invisible scale and weighed for their talents and dowries.

Still, luxury and opulence were part of her life. She danced on the same floors as dukes, rode in extravagant carriages, and never had to worry about where her next meal would come from.

It was also the life of the man standing before her. Yet, she hadn't missed the significance of the orphanage's name.

Lawson Orphanage.

As in Marcus *Lawson*.

This was Deerhurst's orphanage.

And Phaedra, who loathed surprises, found herself once again surprised. And, though she couldn't claim she loved this particular surprise, she couldn't claim she hated it either. Every moment spent with Deerhurst wreaked havoc on her impressions of him. Just when she thought she had him pinned down, he did something completely out of her scope of imagination and forced her to change her opinion of him once again.

Was the earl a mischievous scoundrel, a noble knight, or a gentlemanly saint? Or was he perhaps all of the above?

Phaedra couldn't quite keep up.

She studied Deerhurst, who stood still as a garden statue, his gaze not once wavering from her.

Only you.

Those two words suddenly took on a whole different meaning. Deerhurst had only ever brought her here. She'd been the first person with whom he'd ever shared this side of him.

Her pulse leaped.

"This is your orphanage?" Phaedra asked.

"If you're asking whether I am its founder, then no. I'm merely their benefactor. They changed the name after my first donation."

She glanced around the small room. The furnishings were old, and the color of the walls had faded, but it was still neat. She had watched in fascination at the interaction between Deerhurst and this Mrs. Plum. She found it almost inconceivable that he could turn sheepish when speaking to the older woman and be so at ease interacting with small children.

"How long have you been their benefactor?"

"Seven years, give or take a few months." He stepped up to her, his lips turning into that roguish grin she'd come to expect from him. Mischievous to the bone. "What say you, my lady? Has my reputation completely crumbled in your eyes?"

She harrumphed. "I think it's . . ." Wonderful seemed like such an inadequate word, so she said, "Inspiring." A small pause. "Why doesn't anyone know of your philanthropic venture? I would certainly have read about it somewhere if you had allowed it to be generally known."

He arched a brow. "I am a private man."

"Ah yes, I had almost forgotten," Phaedra said. "Though I have always thought actions represent character better than words."

"Are you saying I'm not a private man?"

"I am saying I have yet to meet this man you speak of."

He chuckled, and something passed through his gaze, a flash of emotion Phaedra couldn't quite catch. But it made her belly clench with butterflies.

"It is worth remembering that sentiment in the future, my lady."

Phaedra was about to ask why when Mrs. Plum breezed into the room with a tray of tea and biscuits, the three little girls trailing after her with giggles.

Her stomach gurgled.

She shot a fleeting glance at Deerhurst, sighing in relief when he hadn't noticed such an embarrassing sound!

Mrs. Plum set the tray down and poured them each a cup of tea, motioning for Phaedra to sit. Phaedra snatched up a biscuit and lowered into a chair as she watched Deerhurst with interest.

Mrs. Plum turned to Deerhurst. "A word, my lord?"

Deerhurst nodded and said to Phaedra, "Do you mind keeping an eye on the girls for a moment?"

"No, of course not."

"They are a handful," he warned.

"They are just girls," she countered with a smile and reached for the tea.

The moment Deerhurst and Mrs. Plum left the room, Phaedra found herself surrounded by the three girls, none of whom could be older than seven years of age. She swallowed her tea.

"Are you a true lady?" Macy asked.

Phaedra paused, then lowered her voice. "What makes you believe I am?"

"Your dress," Macy said with confidence.

Evie nodded. "I've never seen such a pretty dress."

"And you're beautiful. Only true ladies are as beautiful as you," Macy said.

"Well, that's not true," Phaedra said, pinching Macy's cheeks. "I can tell—you three will be great beauties one day."

They all giggled.

"So *are* you a true lady?" Maddie asked.

Phaedra nodded. "I am." She lowered her voice to a whisper. "But keep it a secret, all right?"

The girls nodded.

"I would like to be a lady when I grow up," Evie said.

"You cannot become a lady," Macy said. "You have to be born one." Her little face turned to Phaedra. "Tell her."

Phaedra smiled. "Normally, I would say you are right. Times have not changed all that much, but we women grow stronger with each passing year. You do not have to be born a lady to become one. If you wish to be a lady one day, then go and claim your lord."

"Truly?" Evie asked in awe.

Phaedra smiled even wider. "You can be whatever you'd like to be, Evie. You too Macy. And you as well, Maddie."

"But Mrs. Plum said we should aspire to become seamstresses or maids in a grand house," Maddie said, still skeptical. "She says the world is not kind to people like us and we should always know our place."

Phaedra sighed. "Mrs. Plum is not completely wrong, nor is she entirely right. You should know the rules of the world. How else are you to break them?" She smiled. "Do not let anyone tell you how you must live. You and you alone are in charge of your life."

"Have you ever broken the rules?" Macy asked.

"Oh, all the time," Phaedra said. "I am breaking one right now by being here."

"But you're a lady," Evie breathed. "Ladies don't break the rules."

"On the contrary, dear. I'll let you in on a little secret. We ladies know how to break the rules best." Phaedra paused thoughtfully. "That being said, I do not mean you should disobey Mrs. Plum. However, whether you're a lady, a seamstress, or a maid, we are all still little girls inside our hearts, and little girls should never stop dreaming, don't you understand?"

"We do," the girls said in unison.

"That's good." Phaedra ate another biscuit. "You can be whatever you want to be so long as you go about it cleverly."

"What would you have liked to be if you weren't born a lady?" Macy asked.

"Mmm," Phaedra said, tapping a finger on her lip. "I'd probably be a spy."

The girls erupted into a fit of laughter.

"But that's a man's job!" Maddie exclaimed.

"Yes, and I wouldn't be able to be one unless I did so cleverly, like wearing men's clothing or not caring what other people thought of me."

"That is brave," Macy said. Her eyes brightened then. "*Are* you secretly a spy?"

"I still want to be a lady," Evie piped up. "A lady detective!"

"If I were a spy, I would never reveal my identity to anyone. Not even to pretty girls like you. But I'll tell you another secret that you should never let the men in your life know." Phaedra smiled and leaned closer to whisper. "Women have always ruled the world."

"They have?" Maddie asked with wide eyes.

Phaedra nodded. "Just read about Queen Elizabeth and Catherine the Great. They are women who ruled empires."

"I shall have Mrs. Plum read it all to us at once!" Macy declared.

"What if we don't have the book?" Maddie asked.

"Then I shall have to give you one," Phaedra asked. "Just ask Mrs. Plum to write to Deerhurst."

"Absolutely," a deep, gravelly voice said. "And also an excellent point about Elizabeth and Catherine."

Deerhurst leaned against the door, arms crossed over his chest, powerful and confident, an indescribable look on his face.

Her breath seized.

Phaedra thought herself to be a strong woman. She had just referenced two of the most powerful females in history. And yet, at that very moment, she could have laid an entire empire at his feet.

Her empire.

He suddenly looked different to her, which was utterly preposterous since he was still the same man that she had dashed through the city with an hour ago. Though, somehow, he resembled a knight, or a saint, or something beyond even that a little bit more each time her gaze found him.

Dear Lord, she could *not* be falling for this man. She had dreams of spinsterhood and cats. *Cad*, he had no wish to be *leg shackled*.

No.

Absolutely not.

She could not be falling for Deerhurst.

⤜⟫⟪⤛

CHRIST, HE WANTED her.

Deerhurst thought he might just go mad from want. He stared at Phaedra, still reeling from the sight of her whispering conspiratorially to the girls, her laughter and teasing doing things to his body that no woman before her had ever accomplished. He had made many mistakes in his life. Far too many to count. Some of them horrid enough to bury deep in the bowels of his mind.

But bringing her here was not one of them. No, this had been right.

For it liberated him.

"Deerhurst?"

He blinked, having missed her question. "I beg your pardon?"

She rose to her feet. "Are we leaving?"

"Not yet. I've sent a man after Saville for a brief on the situation."

He shouldn't have eavesdropped. He should have announced his presence the moment he realized they hadn't heard him return. But he hadn't. There had been something about watching Lady Phaedra interact with the girls that spoke to the very heart of him. He had found himself alight with all sorts of questions.

Would she speak to Abigail in the same gentle way? Would she be just as accepting? Would it be different if she discovered Abigail was his illegitimate daughter? Did she truly believe these girls—and by extension his little girl—could rise above the circumstances of their birth?

In truth, what Deerhurst actually wondered was if Phaedra believed these girls could be happy following their dreams, going against the grain of society.

Deerhurst was no fool. Bastard males were much more acceptable on the fringes of society than by-blow females. Most respectable men wanted respectable matches. The ones that didn't . . . he wouldn't even consider them.

Which was why Deerhurst had sent his daughter to his country estate as his ward, not his daughter—to protect her. Oh, Deerhurst knew Lady Phaedra would not condemn an innocent child. That much was clear after today. But this didn't mean she would tolerate a bastard child in her life.

Deerhurst cursed.

What the devil was he thinking?

Abigail was one of the reasons he'd remained a bachelor, but not the only one. There was still her mother. The duke. The fact that Abigail resembled the duchess more and more each day.

And there was Phaedra herself.

"I am going to be a lady detective someday," Evie piped up as she rushed to him.

Deerhurst caught her up in his arms. "What a terrifying prospect, pet. I feel sorry for all the criminals in London."

"What would you like to be, Macy?" Deerhurst asked.

"I want to write adventure novels," Macy said.

Dear Christ, what had Phaedra done?

"A grand idea," Deerhurst went along.

"What of you, Maddie?" Phaedra asked.

"I still haven't decided yet," Maddie said.

Phaedra patted her head. "Take your time."

"Girls," Mrs. Plum poked her head through the door. "Come now, class is starting."

The girls reluctantly said their goodbyes and hurried from the room after Mrs. Plum, but not before they extracted a promise from Lady Phaedra that she would visit again, who agreed without any hesitation.

"A lady detective, eh?" Deerhurst said when the girls left. He cocked one brow at Lady Phaedra.

"What? You don't think a woman can become a detective? I have remarkable aim with a pistol, you know."

"I do know. I've seen that firsthand," Deerhurst said. "Being a detective requires a bit more than brandishing a pistol, however. Resources, for one."

She smirked. "I have those as well."

"Ah, yes. How else would you know about every last penniless man in London?"

"I've also read thousands of books on the topic of criminals. I'm pretty sure I'll be able to spot one when he passes me."

"You read detective books?"

"Not exactly. I read true accounts of London's past criminals such as *The Hangman's Noose*. Have you read it?"

"I cannot say that I have." He knit his brows, a terrifying thought occurring to him. "Do *you* want to be a lady detective?" *Are you a lady detective in secret?*

"Honestly?"

Deerhurst gave a nod.

"Until today, I never thought about being anything other than what I am—a lady."

He blinked. "Christ, you *are* going to become a detective now, aren't you?"

She laughed. "Do not fret, Deerhurst. I have no desire to send my mother to an early grave."

"I'm sure she will appreciate it," Deerhurst said. "What of Huntly?"

"My father? Oh, it's his books I read. I'm sure he will join me in my practice, which would be the final nail in my mother's coffin."

"I hate to admit it, but I can actually envision such a scene." He held her gaze. "Thank you for being kind to the girls."

"They are very adorable."

Deerhurst sighed. "You have given them enough hope to conquer England."

"Good," she said. "By the time they become of age, the entire landscape of society may have changed."

What a beautiful thought. "It may not, however."

"Then perhaps they shall be the ones who change it." She winked at him. "Don't be such a man, Deerhurst."

She held him spellbound. "Then you believe that little Evie can become a lady?"

"If she so desires."

"That still doesn't mean she will be accepted by society."

He wasn't speaking about Evie anymore, he knew.

"Acceptance is a relative term, Deerhurst. What matters is what Evie accepts or does not accept, not the world."

"What about her husband?"

Phaedra arched a brow. "If he marries her, then he accepts her."

If only it were that black and white. He, more than anyone, knew better than that. But she had given hope with her words. Hope to him. Hope for those girls. And a little bit of hope was better than no hope at all.

"Besides," Phaedra went on. "What Evie does with her life is her choice, a choice that shouldn't be weighed and found wanting by us."

"I just don't delight in the thought of them being rejected one day."

"Of course they will be rejected. Rejection comes in many forms. Have you ever been rejected? I certainly have. And I've rejected many. You are asking the wrong question. What you should be asking is whether they can be content, even happy, if they don't break from the mold the world has cast them into."

Deerhurst thought of Abigail. He would protect her as long as he was able. But Phaedra had made some valid points today. His daughter's choices in life and the path she would choose to walk were hers to decide, and he ought to support and respect those choices. Hiding her away for all her life, unless that was what she wanted, was not an option.

Deerhurst cleared his throat. "Where did you learn to be so wise? Don't tell me from all the criminals in your books."

She laughed. "Don't ever mention that to my mother," she said. "You might be horrified, but these are just my opinions, Deerhurst. Make of them what you will.

He wanted to kiss that saucy mouth.

"I quite like your opinions."

Her cheeks pinkened. "Well, I might not know much, but I do know it is not for us to say what is and what is not. All I know is that hope keeps the soul alive. If these children are to survive this world and the obstacles they will face, they will need plenty of it."

He couldn't help himself. He reached out to caress her cheek. "You give me hope."

Her lips formed a perfect O, before she blinked and said, "Well, good. It seems you don't need my tutelage on all the famous women in history and how they overcame obstacles."

"Infamous women, you mean."

"Incorrigible."

Deerhurst thought back to the night they butchered the women on the list Avondale's mother had put together for her son and was barely able to contain a wince. What if his daughter ever made such a list? No matter how he looked at it, they were all bastards.

"I am." Deerhurst didn't argue.

She looked out the window in thought. "My mother informed me of wagers going about town about heiresses and their dowries."

Everything in him froze. Deerhurst could have sworn his heart had been gripped by an icy steel hand that squeezed and squeezed until he nearly choked for air.

"Do you know about them?" she asked, her gaze meeting his.

"Wagers," he evaded. "I have not heard about any wagers in particular, but that would explain your string of suitors."

Deerhurst could practically feel the shovel breaking ground on his soon-to-be grave. He was going straight to the bowels of hell.

No detours.

She nodded. "Well, if you do hear anything, please tell me. I must get to the bottom of this."

"Did your mother mention anything else about the wagers?"

She shook her head. "Only that I should be careful. Luckily, I've got you." She tilted her head. "And that crazy friend of yours."

Deerhurst would have laughed if he could get a sound past the back of his throat. He'd never been a good liar. But he'd always been an excellent evader.

If only she knew.

If only . . .

Now is your chance to tell her.

He let the idea slip from his mind as she wandered over to the drapes and peered through the window onto the street. Deerhurst felt certain he would quickly greet the end of her pistol if she learned the truth. And he wanted—needed—to stay close.

He just wasn't sure whether this need was because of the wagers or something else.

Her.

Chapter Nine

THE LIBRARY WAS one of Phaedra's favorite places in her home. It was also the most peaceful. She could get lost in the scent of books and the solitude of the room. Sometimes she would merely sit on one of the settees and stare at the books until she swore she could hear the whispers of all the stories contained within each binding. Those times, when her imagination was at peak performance and the library burst into a thousand voices, time would both stop and fly at the same time.

Today, however, time seemed to crawl at a pace that both annoyed and called attention to the fact that Phaedra could not get Deerhurst from her mind.

He was stuck there.

For better or for worse.

She glanced down at the dictionary, another flush stealing over her cheeks as her eyes passed over the one that would forever be branded in her mind from that day onward.

Carnal.

Fleshly.

Lustful . . . Lecherous . . . Libidinous . . .

Her gaze skipped to the next word: *carnality.* Compliance with carnal desires . . .

Dear Lord! What was this?

Phaedra thought of the very first kiss she and Deerhurst had shared in his garden. Did that count as fleshly and libidinous? Surely not. Definitely not lustful and lecherous!

But was it in compliance with carnal desire?

She did not even want to contemplate *that*. She did not need a wild imagination for pictures of a shirtless Deerhurst to flit through her brain at those provocative words. He would be all muscle. That she didn't doubt.

Lecherous? That sounded like an old man pinching young women's waists.

Phaedra shuddered.

Was Deerhurst a pincher?

Surely not.

Her gaze skimmed over the word again.

Carnal.

Phaedra shut the book sharply.

And just in time too.

Her aunt breezed into the library.

"There you are," Portia said with a smile. "We missed you at tea."

"Aunt." Phaedra clutched the book. "Did you enjoy your trip to the shops?"

Her aunt settled into the sofa on the opposite side. "Of course. How was your ride through Hyde Park with the earl? I heard there was some commotion?"

Phaedra sat up a bit straighter. "Does Mama know about that?"

"Not that I am aware, but do not worry. I won't mention anything, though I cannot promise she won't hear or read about it elsewhere."

"Deerhurst saved the day, again. Well, to be fair, Deerhurst and his friend, the Earl of Saville."

Portia lifted a brow. "Again?"

Phaedra hesitated, but in the end confessed, "Do not tell Mama, but Cromby cornered me at the Morewood Ball. Deerhurst interfered before anything could happen."

Portia lost a bit of color. "What?"

Phaedra put the book aside and saved her hand. "It wasn't all that bad. Deerhurst put him in his place."

"He seems quite the hero," Portia said, clutching at her breast.

Phaedra thought about Evie, Macy, and Maddie. "He is."

"He knows about the wagers?"

"Nothing in detail."

"Well, he seems like an honorable man. A protector."

Phaedra thought so as well. But something had happened today at the orphanage. She'd been introduced to another side of Deerhurst.

Yet, before they left, a subtle change had overcome him. Phaedra couldn't quite explain it. It was more instinct than anything else. The mischievous, roguish, sensuality-provoking Deerhurst, for a moment, had been replaced by a man filled with tension and something she couldn't even begin to place.

She had touched a nerve.

But Phaedra hadn't pressed mainly because she had wanted the carefree Deerhurst back.

"Aunt," Phaedra began. She'd been turning a question over in her mind all afternoon, and she wanted her aunt's opinion. "You've vowed not to wed again, but what sort of man would change your mind?"

Her aunt blinked, then picked at the hem of her gown, glanced away, back again, and then ultimately sighed. "Marry again?" Portia laughed lowly. "Does this man I might marry even exist?" She shook her head. "No. He does not."

Phaedra didn't argue.

"That doesn't mean you should not wed, love," her aunt continued. "My experience is not your experience. Who is to say what the future holds for you?"

That was the problem.

Phaedra valued certainty. And uncertainty . . . surprises . . .? They weren't for her.

Though she could still admit that Deerhurst had surprised her every day since they met, and she didn't mind his little bombshells.

"I have made up my mind," Phaedra said. "I am content with my decision."

"The earl . . ."

"Is helping me keep the wolves at bay," Phaedra confessed. "Please do not tell my mother."

A long pause. "I see. I won't tell Eleanor. So long as you know what you are doing."

"Do not worry, aunt. I am well aware. Besides, Deerhurst has no interest in marriage."

"He hasn't?" Portia asked in surprise.

"No. He has admitted as much." Phaedra found herself saying, tapping on the dictionary in thought. "Why would a man not be interested in marriage?"

Portia shrugged her shoulders. "That is not uncommon. Some men are more free-spirited and prefer to enjoy the advantages of bachelor life a bit longer than others. Sometimes even their entire lives."

That caught Phaedra's attention. "What are the advantages of a bachelor life?"

"No responsibilities," Portia said. "At least not those that pertain to maintaining a wife."

"Is that all?"

A light blush stole over her aunt's features. "Freedom to cavort," Portia clarified.

Oh.

"That doesn't seem to fit Deerhurst."

"Would he reveal such a thing to you—a lady?"

Probably not.

"That being said, if you have truly decided to spend your life as a spinster, there is no reason for you also not to enjoy the advantages of a single life."

Phaedra nearly choked on air. Did her aunt mean what she thought she meant? That word *carnal* flitted through her brain again. "Surely you are not suggesting seduction?" Was her aunt even allowed to suggest such a thing to Phaedra? Her mother would have a fit.

"Lord, no! Eleanor would have my head. I simply mean some flirting. Some kissing . . ."

Were those not the very acts of seduction? Phaedra wasn't completely unknowledgeable. She read *A Lot.* And Phaedra had already done all of that.

With Deerhurst.

Was her aunt suggesting she kiss Deerhurst? Her whole body heated with the idea of seducing the earl.

Then Portia suddenly asked, shaking the foundation of Phaedra's world, "If the earl changed his mind about marriage and asked for your hand, would you change your mind . . . for him?"

Phaedra froze—her limbs, her heart, even the hairs on her head. The moment seemed suspended in time. She stared at her aunt, the question bursting into a display of fireworks in her mind.

She couldn't answer.

Portia seemed to sense this, for she said, "You are scared of being hurt. However, all I can say is—the greater the risk, the greater the reward. Sometimes you must simply shut your eyes and take the leap."

"You still believe that after . . . after . . ."

"After Rowley?" Portia asked. "Yes, I do. My life hasn't been perfect, and I made a few wrong decisions along the way, but that doesn't mean no good came from our marriage. I learned valuable lessons in that relationship. What happened to me made me the woman I am today. And I quite enjoy her. Trust your instincts, Phaedra. You have excellent ones."

"You didn't trust yours back then?"

Portia shook her head. "I let myself fall in love with Rowley despite my instincts urging me to look a bit deeper at the man. Had I listened to that little voice, my life would be different today. But I still don't regret anything. There are no guarantees in this world. All you can do is make the best of the choices you made."

"You have no regrets?" Phaedra found that hard to believe.

Portia laughed. "I was a different woman back then, and to claim I regret my choices would mean I regret the woman I have become. That I could never do."

Phaedra hadn't known this about her aunt. She had only witnessed the aftermath. This, however, was quite inspiring. Listen to her instincts? She could do that. And her instincts told her that Deerhurst was different than all other men. It also told her he was a little bit of a scoundrel.

As for her aunt . . .

"You are a remarkable woman," Phaedra praised.

Her aunt winked at her. "I'm quite the adventurer now."

Phaedra blinked. "You are?"

The corners of her aunt's mouth tilted upward. "Oh yes, I'll tell you all about my adventures someday soon."

"Why not now?"

"I should not have said anything. Your mother will never forgive me if I told you, that is why, love."

"Mama knows? Aunt please, it is rude to leave your niece in such uncomfortable suspense."

Porta laughed. "You are worse than your father when you want information. Learn some patience."

"Does Papa know?" Phaedra asked, shocked.

Her aunt's cheeks flared pink. "Of course not! And you better not tell him anything either. He'll shoot through the roof if he ever discovers my little adventures."

"I don't know anything so I cannot tell him," Phaedra complained. But she certainly had her suspicions. Her aunt now possessed the freedom to cavort, so it was only reasonable to assume she was flirting, perhaps even kissing, in these little adventures of hers.

Phaedra was dying of curiosity.

"Like I said, love, all in good time."

Phaedra blinked as her aunt rose and flitted from the room like a colorful butterfly.

She slumped back onto the settee.

As much as she wanted to discover what her aunt was up to, Phaedra didn't have time to launch a full-scale investigation into her. She had other, more pressing matters to delve into, adventures of her own she wished to contemplate.

But the most important matter of all? Counting seconds.

The seconds left before she saw Deerhurst again.

⋙⋘

DEERHURST SHOVED HIS account books away from him in disgust. It was a dreary topic he usually reserved for a dreary day, but he had thought to distract his clamoring thoughts of a certain lady-next-door with numbers.

His gaze fell on the cat curled up on his desk. "It's all your mistress's fault I can't bloody concentrate."

The cat didn't move.

Deerhurst snorted. Now he was holding conversations with a damn cat. This was the beginning of him losing his mind.

No, that had started when he kissed Phaedra, who he very much wanted to kiss again. Christ knew, his restraint had been tested to its very limit.

A small head poked through his door.

Deerhurst smiled.

96

An unexpected surprise had delivered herself to his doorstep today. His daughter.

"Abigail." He motioned her over. Deerhurst scooped her up in his arms when she ran over. "Have you been threatening Miss Green again?"

"It was only this one time," she defended. "I really wanted to see you, Papa."

Deerhurst pinched her cheeks. "You are missing your classes. I'm sending you back in the morning."

"Can't I stay here?"

"Not until you are eighteen."

"Why?"

"Because there are big, bad wolves in the city, and they like to eat little girls like you for breakfast."

"They don't!"

"How would you know?"

She pouted. "I just know."

Deerhurst chuckled. "I will reconsider when you are taller than a sprite."

"I am tall! I am very tall!" Her attention fell on Puck. So easily distracted. "I saw Puck sneak into the house next door."

Deerhurst paused. *Well, that was his home.*

"Puck belongs to the lady living next door, pet."

Abigail titled her head, curiosity filling her little face. "Why is he here then? Does that mean he belongs to us too?"

"His owner is a distracting wench. No doubt he is looking for a reprieve."

"What's a wench?"

"A wench is a—" he stopped. This was not something a man explained to his seven-year-old daughter, right? He adjusted just in time, "a term of endearment."

"Then why do you call me pet and not wench?"

Christ above.

"Pet is an endearment for little girls while wench is an endearment for adult women."

Abigail nodded. "I understand. So you will call me wench when I'm an adult?"

"No . . ." Deerhurst said slowly. "I shall always call you pet because you will always be a little girl in my eyes."

"But I want to be called wench when I grow up!"

"That's still a while away, pet. Let us talk about it then." *Let's hope she forgets about it by then.*

"All right!"

Deerhurst let out a breath of relief. Conversing with children was like struggling blindly down a garden path overgrown with prickly hedges.

The talk that Phaedra had had with the girls at the orphanage sprang to mind. She truly believed the girls, and by extension his daughter, could rise beyond the circumstances of their birth and find happiness.

That gave him more hope than she could ever possibly imagine. But it had to be their choice—something he'd not considered for his own daughter. He wanted to protect her all her life. All he wanted for her was to marry well and live a peaceful life. However, his wants and his daughter's wants might not be the same.

It was a deuced uncomfortable thought, and not one he was fully ready to embrace just yet.

Mainly for his own peace of mind.

Deerhurst wasn't sure he could handle anyone rejecting Abigail with much grace. In fact, he was quite sure he'd lose his bloody mind. In any event, there was more to consider than just this.

Abigail tugged his hair, a tender, playful gesture, and he let out a mock grunt. "What is the lady next door's name?" she asked.

"Lady Phaedra Sharp."

"That's a pretty name."

"It is."

"Is she pretty like her name?"

"She is."

"Is she going to live here as well?"

Everlasting hell.

He shifted his daughter into a better position on his lap. "No, pet. Why would you think that?"

"Her cat is already living here."

"Puck is only visiting." And stirring up trouble again.

"But if she lives here then I would be able to live here as well, right?"

A child's logic . . . "How did you come to this conclusion?"

"I would ask her, and she would say yes?"

"You are full of confidence." He rubbed her hair. "Where does all this confidence come from?"

Abigail giggled.

"And what has inspired this newfound urge to move here?" Deerhurst asked. "You love the country."

"But Jeremy said he is moving to London to live with his uncle."

Ah. The cook's son. "So you don't really miss me, you just want to move after your friend, eh?" He poked the tip of her nose.

"If he leaves, who will play with me?"

Well, there you have it.

"Doesn't Miss Green play with you?"

"Sometimes, but she is busy too."

"How is she busy? Her entire job is caring for you."

"Lesson plans."

I stand corrected.

"What do you want me to do, then?"

Abigail pursed her lips as she thought for a moment. "Let me move here or order Jeremy to stay home."

Two impossible things.

"How about you make a new friend?" Deerhurst suggested.

"But Jeremy is my friend."

Deerhurst felt an ache in his temples coming on. He'd have to elicit the help of Miss Green to find his daughter another friend.

"I'll see what I can do, pet."

"Thank you!" she cried and hugged him around the neck. "Will you have tea with me and Miss Strumpet?"

Strumpet?

Deerhurst frowned. "Who is that?"

"Miss Strumpet is the newest addition to my tea party."

"I mean who named her?" Deerhurst asked slowly.

"I did, silly. It's a pretty name. Miss Green said so herself."

Miss Green was worse than him. "How about we call her Miss Trumpet?"

"Why?" Abigail asked skeptically. "Isn't it a pretty name?

"Yes, but I like Trumpet more," Deerhurst said. He thought on his feet when his daughter scrunched her brows. "I knew a bad—very bad—lady once with that name."

Abigail's eyes widened. "Ok, then we will call her Miss Trumpet. It sounds just as pretty."

Deerhurst nodded. "My thoughts exactly."

"Then you will join us?"

"Sure pet, I'd love to meet this Miss Trumpet of yours."

"She's a true lady."

"Just like you."

She pulled a face. "I'm a princess, not a lady."

If his daughter wanted to be a princess, Deerhurst would damn well find her a prince. "A princess, then."

"They wear crowns." She adjusted the small one on her head. "So do I."

"I cannot argue with that logic, princess."

"They also wear pretty gowns."

"That's right."

"They rule kingdoms!"

"Yes, yes. When they become queens," Deerhurst agreed.

"Not the ones I mean. They don't become queens to rule. They just rule."

"Fair enough." Who was he to disagree? "What else does the princess in these kingdoms do?"

"They feed the poor."

"Very noble."

"They also rescue little children from doglike monsters."

Deerhurst paused, but then nodded. "This is a very honorable kingdom."

"And they eat cake every day!"

"That sounds a bit unhealthy."

"It's healthy cake!"

"Is it made from vegetables?"

Her lips puckered. "No."

"Then it's—" Deerhurst paused when she crossed her arms over her chest, "—a good thing cakes aren't made from vegetables."

"Vegetables taste like dirt."

"In my kingdom, however, you must eat them."

"I don't think you should eat them in any kingdom."

"One day, when you rule your own kingdom, you can outlaw vegetables, until then, you must eat them."

"Very well, but only until I rule."

"Fair enough."

"Let's go drink tea, now."

Deerhurst rose with Abigail in his arms and set her on her feet. He could not help the grin that cracked his face as he followed his daughter from the room. He enjoyed their make-believe parties. He did not know of any other father who would willingly sit down and have tea with a pair of dolls, but Deerhurst had to make up for the times he missed with her.

He would do anything for his daughter. Even buy her a string of friends. All he wanted for her was love and acceptance. If a servant, a friend, or anyone else could not give her that, then they would not suffer to breathe in his presence.

No exceptions.

Not even ladies with pretty blue eyes.

Chapter Ten

B Y MUTUAL AGREEMENT among Phaedra's mother, father, and aunt, the Sharp family decided to forgo all events for the evening. They had claimed fatigue, but Phaedra suspected it had something to do with the wagers her mother had mentioned.

Just what were they about?

She wondered whether her aunt mentioned the incident with Cromby to her mother. Papa clearly did not know, or he would have had a fit of temper. And since they were staying in for the evening, there was no need for Deerhurst to seek her out.

Tonight, the earl was off duty.

The thought should not have left her so disappointed. But it did. Immensely so.

Mary slipped into the chamber and said in a hushed tone. "My lady, you have a visitor."

Phaedra put aside her book and sat up in bed. It was past ten in the evening. Her entire family had already retired for the night.

"Who is it?"

Mary lowered her voice even more. "The *earl*, my lady."

Phaedra froze. "Deerhurst is here?"

"He is waiting in a carriage outside."

Phaedra shot from the bed. "Hand me my cloak, Mary."

"My lady! You aren't dressed!"

"That is why I'm putting on a cloak."

Mary handed her a cloak. "Do you want me to accompany you?"

"No need, Mary. I'll be fine."

Phaedra slipped out of her room and hurried outside using the back entrance, and then stole through the narrow gate that separated the properties.

The door of the awaiting carriage swung open as she approached, and Deerhurst jumped out. Lord, the man looked handsome. Dressed impeccably in all black, hair styled in the latest fashion, he looked powerful and dangerous. Her heartbeat sped up.

He quickly ushered her inside.

Phaedra settled into the carriage. "I did not expect to see you this evening."

He removed a mask from the inside of his jacket. "I thought you'd like to go on an outing."

"A masked ball?" Phaedra asked. "I'm not dressed for an evening out."

His gaze dropped to her cloak. "What you're wearing is fine."

Phaedra grinned. "It's what I'm wearing beneath that won't do."

His eyes met hers. "Christ, Phaedra. You can't say that to a man."

She chuckled. "So where is this ball you wish to whisk me off to?"

"I'm not sure you are dressed for the occasion," Deerhurst half said, half muttered.

She laughed. "Oh, come on. As you've said, it's a masked ball." Excitement unfurled in her breast. "But if anyone recognizes me, I might as well not return home. My mother will have my head."

"Rest assured, no one will recognize you at this ball, and if they do, no one will dare breathe a word."

Intrigued, Phaedra reached for the mask. She had heard married ladies whisper about these sorts of clandestine balls in hushed tones at soirées before. She'd always been curious but never thought she'd attend one of them.

"Why Deerhurst, I'm not sure whether I should be thrilled or worried that you thought to escort me to one of these balls."

"After Hyde Park, I thought you might be in need of some adventure."

Phaedra inhaled the clean scent of Deerhurst, that familiar prickle traveling across her skin again. "You have perfect timing indeed. I'm indeed in need of a rousing distraction." And perhaps a chance to figure out what these wagers were about. Plus, hadn't Aunt Portia encouraged her to have some fun? At least that was how Phaedra chose to see it. Deerhurst's invitation to this ball was just the thing.

She dangled the mask from her fingertip. "Will you help me secure it?" She turned to give him her partial back.

"Of course," his deep voice came.

Phaedra shivered as his hand covered hers, taking the mask from her. She wore no gloves, neither did he, and the heat of his touch burned through her skin.

A shiver trickled down her spine and back up as he secured the mask, his touch hovering a moment longer than it ought to have. Every movement seemed deliberate, slow, and gentle, and cast a spell over her. Her pulse beat frantically in her breast. It had recognized the magic of the moment before Phaedra had.

When he pulled the strings tight, she turned back to face him, startled by the emptiness that followed the withdrawal of his touch.

"Thank you," she murmured, wondering why her voice suddenly felt so shaky. Then she realized . . . his touch had been sensual. Perhaps even *carnal*.

She felt her face flush. She should never have looked up that word. Now it would be forever stuck in the forefront of her mind.

"I have rules for tonight," he said, a slight rasp in his voice. Phaedra's body reacted to that alluring note by breaking out in another round of gooseflesh.

"Oh?" Phaedra murmured. More intrigue.

"You will not leave my side," Deerhurst said. "No matter what."

Phaedra nodded. She certainly didn't mind that. She'd plaster herself right up against him if that was what he wanted.

Phaedra smiled, deciding to test his boundaries. "What if I am asked to dance by another gentleman?"

"No dancing with anyone but me."

Phaedra pursed her lips to keep from breaking out in a stunning grin. "And the other rules?"

"Do not drink or eat anything anyone offers you. In fact, do not accept anything from anyone except me. And also, no smiling at other men. Follow those four simple rules and everything will be fine."

Amusement filled her. "I'm not allowed to smile at other men?"

"Your smile is very recognizable."

Phaedra flashed him that smile. "Really?"

He cursed.

"What about you?" she asked. "This seems like a lot of responsibility you're taking on, catering to my every need."

"It will be my greatest pleasure."

My oh my oh my.

She could not help asking, "Is this a mischievous ball with mischievous people?"

He grinned. "The very most mischievous of the mischievous."

"How thrilling." She gave him a curious look. "Normally, a gentleman would not take a lady to such a ball. Why are you? Surely, it's not just to distract me?"

"I admit, this was the only event tonight that offered a measure of concealment."

"Very stealthy, I agree. And you received an invitation to such an event?"

"I receive many invitations to many sorts of events. If you do not wish to go, we won't go." Deerhurst's lips twitched as if he already knew her answer.

Phaedra wanted to kiss him.

Should she let that be her confirmation? It would be a degree more fun than saying a simple *yes*. The moment the mask had fastened at the back of her head she felt transformed. As though "Phaedra" had been shelved for the night, replaced by a brazen, daring, provocative woman.

Deerhurst broke her train of thought by leaning forward, reaching for her mask.

She held her breath. "What are you doing?"

He tugged at the edges with gentle fingers. "That's better."

She cleared her throat, hoping her voice didn't sound too affected when she said, "Thank you."

The air crackled between them.

What would he do if she kissed him? Could she kiss him? She should kiss him. Definitely kiss. But would that be too brazen?

So what if it is?

Even her aunt had alluded to flirting and kissing—the freedom to cavort.

"Where is your mask?" Her whisper weaved through the heightened tension like a sensual touch. She watched the skin around his jaw flush.

His gaze drifted over her face, and he removed a matching black mask from a pocket. "No one will recognize us, so let's have some fun."

"You are even more memorable than I am."

He grinned at her. "But no one expects the two of us to attend such a ball."

Phaedra's gaze dropped to his lips.

He didn't seem to notice or perhaps he did but chose to ignore it. Either way, a dangling mask entered her sight. She lifted her gaze to meet his. His green eyes were full of devilry.

"Would you mind helping me secure it?"

This was too much. This was the best.

Phaedra nodded and scooted forward. Her fingers artfully drew the laces from his, the delicious brush of their hands sending sparks of electricity down her spine. She thought she heard his intake of breath.

Perhaps it was hers.

She inhaled sharply, drawing the familiar aroma of tobacco and coffee into her lungs. She swore his scent took root there, ensuring that no other man would ever smell as good as him.

Her fingers worked lazily to loop the ties together, lingering a moment—just as he had done.

"Is that secure enough?" Phaedra asked.

"No," he said roughly. "Do it over."

She laughed and undid the knot, carefully renewing her efforts, this time lingering a bit longer than the first time. "How is that?"

"Better."

She settled back in her seat, her face flushed with warmth from being so close to the earl. She made a decision then. She would kiss Deerhurst tonight.

No matter what.

>>>«««

DEERHURST ENTERED THE masked ball with Phaedra on his arm, his chest tightening in a sort of awareness he hadn't considered possible. He had thought turnabout was fair play, which was why he'd asked her to fasten his mask, but Saints, he still felt her fingers tugging and looping and brushing against his neck. It was just a bloody mask. But in Phaedra's hands, the very act of securing the piece of cloth had become seduction. The hardness that still strained against his breeches had been proof of that.

Thank Christ she hadn't noticed.

He spared her a brief glance. How could one woman look so

bloody beautiful? She smelled like an ocean breeze after a hot summer day. Much too good for his jaded heart.

He was a selfish bastard.

He had no business escorting Phaedra to a ball such as this. She was an innocent. And he hadn't had any obligation to protect her tonight since she had been safely tucked in her home. Yet here he was, with her on his arm, at a ball that would probably shock the hell out of her sensibilities.

But when he'd heard that Huntly had cancelled all engagements, Deerhurst had known he had found out about the list. After all, as a fellow member of White's, it had only been a matter of time.

Momentary panic had set in. Why?

Good bloody question.

The thing about it was he hadn't been able to stay away. He'd planned to, honestly, he had. He had plenty of other things to do. Meet up with Saville and Warrick. Pore over ledgers and matters of business. Find a woman to satisfy this growing need inside of him.

None of those options tempted him.

He'd been too restless to stay home. The only person he wanted to see stood beside him. The only thing he wanted to do was enjoy her company.

So, he had brought her here.

Deerhurst didn't know how long it would take for the dust to settle on the wagers, but he was beginning to suspect it would last until every single one of those women on the list was married. He didn't know how this would end for Lady Phaedra, but he knew he wanted to give her one night where she could be free to socialize without having to worry about wagers, fortune-hunters, or men like Cromby.

"This is so thrilling." The excitement in her voice was tangible.

Deerhurst smirked.

Her face lit up when she spotted the dancers. Not willing to pass up on an opportunity to spend time up close with this beauty, he asked, "Do you want to dance?"

Her sparkling gaze turned to him. "That would be wonderful."

He leaned over to whisper in her ear, "I serve at your pleasure."

She snorted. "That is such a roguish thing to say."

"Am I misbehaving again?"

"We have already established you are a man full of mischief. Though you hide it well when you're out and about." A thrill of anticipation and desire spun down his spine.

"I don't hide it from you."

"I'm not sure if I should be thankful or alarmed."

"I prefer you be grateful and in awe."

She laughed. "Be glad I'm not about to order you to get me wine all night."

"You'll be toting around along with me."

She arched a brow. "Is that so?"

He lowered his head so that his lips brushed the skin of her cheek. "Remember rule number one."

"Never leave your side," she whispered.

"No matter what."

Deerhurst swept her up into the dance before she could offer a witty retort. He couldn't promise not to kiss her saucy mouth if she did. His restraint had a limit where this woman was concerned. He'd rather she not talk, since he suspected he would not be able to deny her anything. She possessed an unfathomable power over him.

Best that she never discovered that.

"Oh!"

Deerhurst went on alert as they twirled about the dance floor. "What? What is it?" He lowered his voice. "Are you all right?"

"The couple to our left is kissing," she exclaimed under her breath. "*Kissing*, Deerhurst."

Deerhurst followed her gaze and chuckled.

Indeed. They were practically shagging for all the groans and fondling going on.

"Are you shocked, my lady? Didn't we already establish that this is a ball where mischief occurs?"

"I just hadn't expected such displays out in the open."

"Well, this is not your average ball." Deerhurst pulled her closer than was acceptable at a normal ball. "Which is why everyone is wearing masks."

"So all of these parties are masked?"

Deerhurst shook his head. "There are some parties where you don't have to wear a mask, but those result in—" *full on orgies* "—more sensual pastimes."

She lifted her chin. "*Carnal,* you mean?"

Blood surged through him at the purr of that word, a wave of heat exploding him into spiraling need. Christ, he wanted this woman in his bed. There, he finally admitted it to himself. He wanted this woman so badly it hurt.

"Carnal," he repeated, finding it impossible to pull his gaze from her. "You looked up its meaning?"

"Of course. You thought I wouldn't?"

He hadn't thought much about it at all. Mainly because he had thought she'd forgotten about it, but also because *he* had forgotten about it.

He cleared his throat. "Naturally, you would. And yes, carnal is the name of the game at balls such as these. There is something about masks that allows you to liberate yourself from the straps of society." His gaze dropped to her lips. "Don't you agree?"

She tilted her head. "Not fully in the Cyprian world and not fully in ours."

"Somewhere in between," he agreed, his grip on her waist tightening. Something he could do in this world but never in theirs.

"A space where we can be whoever we want for the night."

"*Yes.*"

Christ, yes. And what he wanted to be tonight was *hers*.

She smiled at him. Not her usual smile. This one was provocative. Coy. Filled with a promise that made Deerhurst's lungs contract in a painful yet expectant manner.

Her words gave life to that promise when she said, "Then I could kiss you and no one would bat an eye?"

Deerhurst's mouth went dry, any reply smothered by the burn of desire that bolted straight to his groin. He'd never come so close to dragging a woman off to some darkened corner and shoving himself inside of her.

If he said yes—that no one would bat an eye—was he giving permission? Aiding in ruinous behavior? If he said no . . . could he even say no?

In the end, he went with the theme of the night and said, "No one would bat an eye."

"No one would care?"

"Not one person."

He should have expected what happened next.

He should have anticipated how she would lift onto her toes, grab hold of his upper arms, and plant her lips on his, and kiss him.

But he hadn't.

Astonishment made its way to his gut, which in itself was rather astonishing since he had practically told her she could do so.

The moment her mouth connected with his, the same pull that had urged him to kiss her in his garden returned with a force stronger than the impact of a ton of bricks. This was what he wanted. This was what he had craved every moment of every day since he met her. She was magic. Pure magic. His hands lowered to cup the soft flesh of her derrière and squeezed.

Her lips parted with a gasp, and he did not hesitate to take control and thrust his tongue into her mouth. There was nothing gentle about his kiss. She had opened this floodgate. Christ knew whether he'd be able to close them tonight.

He wanted to devour her.

All of her.

The instinct was unprecedented. And yet he could no more fight it than he could fight off an army. Indeed, it might be safer to fight off an army than share one kiss with her.

He pulled her close, his fingers digging into her soft, pliant flesh. She tasted sweet and inviting, like a substance a man could never get enough of—like a drug. Deerhurst suddenly understood why opium users ruined their lives chasing that smoke.

She was his opium.

Their kiss was interrupted by a group of rumbustious men entering the room at that moment. Deerhurst pulled away and cursed under his breath.

"I'm afraid we're going to have to cut our attendance short, love," he said as he tracked the group's progress across the room.

"Why?" She followed his gaze. "Because of those men? Who are they?"

"Troublemakers."

"Not the playful kind, I take it?"

Deerhurst's eyes never left the newcomers. "Let's just say their arrival never bodes well for gatherings such as these."

And on the heels of that sentence, everything went to hell.

Chapter Eleven

PHAEDRA SHOULD HAVE known, with the luck she'd been having of late, the masked ball would somewhere take a turn—and this time not for the better. Deerhurst's rules and been simple enough. Stay at his side. Do not dance with anyone but him. Accept nothing from anyone. *Smile* at nobody but him.

In the end, she broke every last rule.

The night might have been salvaged if the exuberant new arrivals had headed for one of the other rooms, but no, they turned their sights to the dance floor. Up until the moment they had entered, Phaedra had believed them to be a small but loud party, but as they stumbled and cheered through the throngs of dancers, it became clear that Deerhurst hadn't exaggerated. A mob of rabble-rousers had arrived.

It all happened so fast.

One moment Phaedra was in Deerhurst's safe embrace, the next they were forcefully separated, and she was in the arms of another, being twirled—if one could call it that—by a large man that smelled of sweat, spirits, and cheap cigars.

Phaedra tried to break loose of his hold, her gaze attempting to find Deerhurst, but this big ruffian blocked her view. She could only assume that Deerhurst had lost sight of her as well.

"Well, aren't you a little beauty," the man slurred. "Care to have some fun with me?" His smile turned foxlike. He had dark eyes and a hideous bird mask covering the upper part of his face. Phaedra wanted to punch the man.

"Unhand me, sir!"

His smile never faltered. "You don't want to have some fun with me?"

"I'd rather die!"

"You are one of *those*, are you? I seem to have hit a pot of luck tonight."

"I beg your pardon? One of what?"

"Women who like to make a man work for his prize."

A shudder ran through Phaedra's entire body. She had to get away from this man. "Sir, I have no idea what you're speaking about. Now let me go before I club you over the head."

He laughed heartily. "You are indeed a prize."

"I already have a companion, sir."

"Where is this man?" the rogue asked slyly.

"You stole me away from our dance!"

Still, it was a good question. Where on earth was Deerhurst? Was he in trouble? She craned her neck to try to find him, but to no avail.

"If I was able to steal you away, then he isn't much of a man, now is he?"

Phaedra refused to argue with a foxed man. She tested her kidnapper's grip on her, alarmed to find he only held her with one arm, an arm that tightened when she squirmed. The other hand held a goblet-like cup.

Great.

She had to be accosted by a beast who was strong as an ox. She should really start to carry her pistol with her. She attempted another method—and gave him her most charming smile.

"Sir," she practically purred. "I believe we can come to some sort of understanding if you let me go."

He blinked. And then his smile broadened as he brought the cup to her lips.

"Have a sip of wine, and I shall consider it."

Her eyes widened, recalling Deerhurst's words. "I will not!"

"Come now, little beauty. It's the best money can buy."

The wine? She doubted it. "I'd rather eat dirt."

He laughed. "I'll let you go if you have a taste. Imported it from Italy myself. Truly, it is the best." He gave her a sloppy wink.

Phaedra flicked her gaze to the goblet and back to him. This was all he wanted? Someone to praise his wine?

She narrowed her eyes on him. "If I have a sip, you will let me go?"

"On my gentleman's honor."

Ha! He was no gentleman, but Phaedra had no other choice. She had to find Deerhurst and see if he was all right. He must be worried to death by now.

This might be her only chance to escape this man. If he believed her cooperative, and she took a sip, his hold on her might relax, and she could slip away.

Phaedra scowled and snatched the glass from his hand. With an unladylike mutter—a curse, really—she took a sip and damned the man to the bowels of the earth. But as she would have pulled the glass away from her mouth, the ruffian's hand applied pressure to the bottom and held the goblet firm. The contents rushed down her throat.

Phaedra sputtered and fought to swallow the liquid before it spilled all over her.

The scoundrel!

The rogue!

"You big beast!"

He laughed.

"There," she shoved the glass back into his hand. "I took a sip, *more* than a sip, now let me go."

He nodded. "First, tell me how it tasted."

"It tasted like wine," she snapped.

"I mean, what flavors did you detect?"

"I–" she was about to lay into him but paused. It seemed to only taste of wine, but the gleam in his eyes sent a chill down her spine. Was this not the usual sort of wine? It tasted the same as one might find at a normal ball. Perhaps a touch stronger. But just a touch.

"It *is* wine, is it not?"

"Of course."

Why did those two words sound so ominous?

"Then why are you asking me about flavors?"

He leaned in close. "It's my own brew."

His own brew? Why did that sound even more sinister?

Instinct screamed at her to escape this man.

Something about him, the wine, the entire incident seemed off. An odd sensation overcame her, so unexpected and foreign that Phaedra almost lost her train of thought.

"What's wrong?"

"I . . . I'm not sure . . ." It was as though the entire world narrowed until she was the only one left.

This was not right.

He was not right.

Deerhurst. She needed to find Deerhurst.

Run!

Kick him and run!

She started to do exactly that, and club him over the head for good measure, but her limbs refused to obey her instructions. She blinked, and everything around her slowed to a crawl. All at once, the fast rush and boisterous laughter of the ballroom cut to a whisper. And in the wake of her panic a glow of euphoria settled.

Phaedra stared into the knowing eyes of the beast that held her captive in some corner of the dance floor. He was a bad, bad man. She had never met such a bad man.

A giggle erupted from her throat.

"That's better," the man said, and Phaedra vaguely noticed they weren't on the dance floor anymore. They were floating on a cloud away from the dancers. They reached a flight of stairs.

"Where are we going?"

"A more private setting."

Another man's face flashed in her mind. "I don't think that's—"

His face suddenly came closer to hers. Almost like he wanted to kiss her.

This is not right.

If she didn't do something, this knave was going to kiss her. While a part of her found that funny, another part—a more instinctual part—recognized that she could not let that happen, no matter what.

A stranger wanted to kiss her.

Phaedra tried hard to collect her scattered thoughts. There was something she should be remembering. A reason why she should be fighting tooth and nail, but her body seemed to have surrendered all rational sense. Her mind seemed like a faraway star, one whose sparkle diminished as it pulled away farther, leaving her no control of her body.

And what her body wanted . . .

Deerhurst.

Ah, Deerhurst.

The missing thread that guided her back to semi-reality. She was here with Deerhurst. Danced with him. Kissed him. This man was *not* Deerhurst. He had stolen her away from her earl! Their kiss had been so enthralling, Phaedra hadn't wanted it to end. Now, this rogue's friends might even be causing Deerhurst trouble. If she allowed this barbarian to touch her, everything would be ruined. Deerhurst would scold her. He would be disappointed in her.

She didn't want that. *Ever.*

Slowly, some of the fog lifted from her mind.

Phaedra pushed the man away from her as he came closer. She

struggled from his grip, and almost wished she hadn't. Her leap turned out to be more of a stumble, and the world spun around her. She staggered forward, she thought, but couldn't be sure, and then suddenly, before she could hit the ground, she was hoisted up into an unwelcome hold.

The man had tossed her over his shoulder.

"No more of that," he growled.

She was about to cry out for help when the weight of his body disappeared from beneath her and she was placed aside. Punches and grunts followed soon after. It was over before she could scramble to her feet, and then a familiar scent enveloped her, and she was lifted into a strong embrace.

Deerhurst.

His voice rumbled in her ear, "I am going to beat you within an inch of your life."

Phaedra blinked.

"Four rules. Four! That was all you had to follow. Always stay at my side. Don't dance with anyone. Don't accept drink from anyone. Don't smile."

Phaedra slumped her head against his shoulder. She wanted to explain, she truly did, but her brain hadn't yet been able to connect words together into a coherent sentence. Whatever that man had put in that drink, it had thoroughly rendered her a dimwit.

"Then I find you following a man to the private chambers," Deerhurst bit out. "Do you know what would have happened if I hadn't intervened in time?"

I didn't follow him.

"Thankfully, your mask is still in place."

She frowned.

She also wanted to laugh. And cry. In the end, she chose to focus on the warmth of Deerhurst's body. He alone gave her comfort. She wanted to ask if they were leaving, but her answer came a moment later when he shoved her into a carriage.

Phaedra scrambled to sit upright, but wouldn't you know it, the only position she could manage was a slump. Why was he scolding her? Where had *he* been this entire time?

"Deerhurst . . . Explain yourself."

⫸⫷

DEERHURST NEARLY SPUTTERED at the unexpected command coming from the woman before him.

Explain *himself?*

By Jove, she better explain *herself.*

He still cursed the bloody bastard that had knocked him to the ground. And then when he'd shot to his feet, he'd tripped over his own damn boots. Seven seconds. Seven deuced seconds and she'd slipped through his fingers.

A terrifying prospect.

Not only had she disappeared from his side, it had felt like a lifetime as he frantically searched the dance floor for her. Never in a thousand years had he imagined he'd find her dancing—*dancing!*—with one of the bloody rancorous devils that had separated them. Fury had overtaken him almost instantly.

Rule number one and two—ashes.

Rule number three—dust.

He'd all but fought his way through the dancers on the floor, which had turned into something of a circus, those men testing every last ounce of his patience, only to then catch a glimpse of Phaedra drinking from a cup before he lost them again.

Rule number four—vapor.

But anger over those rules fell far short of the feeling that followed. Deerhurst's chest still burned at the sight of her being carried off by another man—one second away from disappearing from his sight completely. Perhaps even forever. He had wanted to slap his own face in the hope that he'd been hallucinating, but no, the heat in his chest had spread through his body, touching every nerve he possessed—down to the very pit of his soul.

But he couldn't—didn't—blame her. He should have been quicker to remove her from the party. He should have held on tighter and not allowed them to be separated.

So, yes, he *did* need to explain himself. He had brought her here. He had been caught off guard. He had let those bastards separate them.

But none of that stifled the fire in his heart. "What the bloody hell happened? Why didn't you run away?"

"I tried . . ."

"Christ," he dragged a hand through his hair. "Do you know what could have happened to you tonight?" The rage that tore through him at the image that question evoked ought to have shaken the heavens. Though in the back of his mind, he realized her actions didn't fit. Why *would* she allow a stranger to carry her off? The woman he knew would have fought tooth and nail to break free and escape.

Deerhurst inhaled three long breaths in order to reign in his temper. By the third, she leaned forward and gave him such a pitiful look, Deerhurst had to blink twice.

"Are you all right? You seem a bit out of sorts. Did I do something wrong? I tried to follow your rules." She tugged at her cloak. "It's so hot."

Bloody hell.

"What are you doing?" Deerhurst demanded when she reached down and removed her slippers and lifted her skirts. "Are you undressing? You cannot undress."

"Aren't you hot? I'm so hot."

He cursed. "*Phaedra.*" What the hell was wrong with her? And . . . "Why are you sitting that way?"

She was pulling her skirts up, showing off a pair of beautiful legs, but her slouching position had her falling over repeatedly.

He stilled.

If he didn't know any better . . .

"Phaedra," Deerhurst asked urgently, shifting to the edge of his seat. He grabbed her hands, stopping her from raising her skirts to her knees. "What was in the cup I saw you drink from?"

"The cup?" Her brows knit together before her eyes lit up. "Oh, that ugly goblet? Wine. Apparently the best wine in the country. Imported from Italy."

"So you drank it?" Deerhurst let out another oath, this one fouler than the last. "Did you forget my rules so easily then?"

"He said he would let me go if I took a sip."

"And you believed him?"

She shook her head. "I thought it would be the best time to slip away from him."

Deerhurst wanted to punch that man again. He had heard about a certain group that went around drugging unsuspecting women. Usually with wine laced with a combination of other drugs. It was said to affect the consumer almost instantly. Up until now, Deerhurst had never seen it with his own eyes.

"Phaedra, love," he pressed the back of his hand to her forehead. "Describe to me exactly what you're feeling right now."

"Hot."

"Yes, hot, but what else?"

"Sluggish." She pulled her hands from his and tugged at her cloak. "Almost like falling into a puff of clouds."

Deerhurst let out a foul oath.

She paused, blinking at him. "Do you know why I'm feeling this way?"

"The wine you drank was laced with drugs."

She frowned. "What drugs?"

"Damned if I know." He rapped on the roof. He had to get her home and summon a doctor. She lurched onto his lap as the carriage jerked forward. Deerhurst grabbed her by the shoulders and put her next to him so that she could slump against him.

"We were rudely interrupted, were we not?" she murmured.

Deerhurst clenched his fists.

They still hurt from the beating he'd given her assailant. Had he known the man had drugged her, he would be dead right now. The blackguard was damn lucky Deerhurst did not recognize him beneath his mask. He had half a mind to go back and hunt the bastard down.

"What do you mean?" he asked, his mind still on the drugs.

"Our dance. Our kiss. And just when I was enjoying it the most."

Phaedra broke into Deerhurst's murderous thoughts by leaning forward and clasping his thigh with her hands, invading his space with puckered lips, her lashes sweeping down.

He blinked. "What are you doing?"

"Coaxing a kiss from you," she murmured, puckering her lips again.

Deerhurst suddenly wanted to laugh. "Listen to me, love. You've been drugged. Do you understand? The wine you drank was laced with a dangerous substance."

She smiled at him and placed a finger over her mouth—to silence him? She looked so silly, so innocent, in that moment that he wanted to pull her into his arms and kiss her senseless. But he wouldn't take advantage of a woman befuddled from drugs.

Though it seemed she had other plans.

Deerhurst caught her in his arms when she crawled onto his lap, pulling herself up to his chest. Dammit. Just give the woman what she wanted. The last thing *he* wanted was for her to hurt herself. Better he keep her close where at least she'd be safe from tumbling around the carriage.

Christ, she was not going to make it easy for him.

"All you had to do was follow four simple rules," he muttered, more to himself than to her.

"Don't you want to kiss me?" she asked him, then pouted.

"I want to kiss you very much, but I can't."

"Why not? You kissed me earlier while we were dancing."

"Because you're high on wine and God knows what else, love."

"That's not good."

No, it was not. "Although I should kiss you for what you put me through this night. How did you think you could escape by drinking the wine?"

"If I took a sip, he would think he won." She rubbed her cheek against his. "Then I would have blindsided him with a kick and run off."

Deerhurst frowned. "But you didn't take just a sip, did you? You had more." Or she wouldn't be so out of her head.

"He tipped the glass over."

"Bastard," Deerhurst exploded, sighing when she pulled back and her eyes widened at his outburst. He hoped he had cracked the man's jaw.

"I never thought you to be a man with such a temper, Deerhurst. I find it quite—"

He shut her up with a kiss.

She didn't object. Her hands circled his neck, her breasts pressing close up against him. His hands spanned her back, keeping her tightly locked against him as he teased her lips open with his tongue. She obliged.

He claimed her mouth, slow but demanding, leaving no doubt that no other man would ever kiss her like he did. It was primitive. It was possessive. It was damn madness. He didn't care.

How the hell was he ever going to walk away from this woman?

Not a question he dared to contemplate.

But if he did not stop at this very moment, he wouldn't stop at all. In Phaedra's state she wouldn't deny his advances. A dangerous situation to find themselves in. Because Deerhurst's beast roared for release.

Reluctantly, he broke away from her lips.

His gaze darted to her scattered slippers and gaping cloak, revealing a snow-white chemise beneath.

He sighed.

Perhaps he was more of a saint than a scoundrel. Be that as it may, he had to sober her up. And there was only one way he could think of to do it.

His special brew.

Chapter Twelve

"L UD, WHAT IS in this stuff?" Phaedra pulled a face.

"Coffee beans."

"It tastes nothing like its aroma." *Like you.*

Phaedra felt happy, as though she belonged to the moment she was in—with the man she was sitting across from—and she never wanted to step out from it. She still felt as though the world might tilt at any moment, but that she could manage.

She didn't know why Deerhurst was urging her to drink this ghastly black liquid. She felt fine. They had remained in the carriage, and a doctor had come to check on her as well. Three hours ago. And yet, Deerhurst had kept vigil over her every single second.

He'd told her the wine she'd drunk had been laced with druglike substances. Phaedra had a vague impression of drinking wine. Everything after that felt hazy. As though she had entered into a dream and the memories retreated farther and farther until nothing was left but the moment she found herself in.

Even their kiss had floated toward that haziness, leaving her with naught but a hot, black drink in her hand.

"Where did you get this anyway?"

Deerhurst had jumped from the carriage, ordered the driver to keep her inside no matter what, and dashed off to his residence. He had returned with this travesty.

"Wilson brewed it."

"Your servant? Where is he?"

"At home." He shot her a worried glance. "We are currently pulled up three houses before yours. Drink up and I'll escort you to your chamber."

In her current state, Phaedra found that immensely funny. Also a bit thrilling. *"You'll* be escorting me?"

A grim look passed across his features. "You're in no condition to make it to your chamber without waking the entire household."

"We cannot let *that* happen." Her mother would have her head. She was also still a bit dizzy. Anyone could take one look at her and know she'd indulged in liquor.

"No, we cannot," the earl agreed.

"Will this help?" Phaedra motioned to the drink.

"Wilson swears by it."

Phaedra blew on the contents. She could not drink it in one smooth motion at this temperature. She'd already scorched her tongue once.

She stared at Deerhurst, who had tried his best to provide an exciting night away from all the drama only for them to find themselves in another hot pan. He watched her like a hawk, his lips pursed and tired lines forming around his eyes.

Her heart melted.

"How many moons have you lived, Deerhurst?"

He shook his head. If Phaedra did not know any better, she'd thought he was exasperated with her. She grinned at him. All she wanted to do was wipe the worry from his brow and make him smile again.

"More than you can count at the moment."

Could she even deny that claim? "Then, how old are you this year?"

"Four-and-thirty."

"Do you plan to be one of those men who wait until they've all but turned grey before taking a wife?"

He arched a brow. "And what sort of man would that be?"

"My aunt says men who do not marry enjoy the freedom to cavort. I have gathered there are three sorts of man in the world. The eager man that marries young, the reluctant man that marries later when they're old and grey, and the carefree man that never marries."

"By that definition, there are three sorts of woman in the world as well."

Phaedra paused before she laughed. "Right you are. But where lack of marriage hoods us in bronze and copper, it colors you in gold."

He chuckled. "Does that even make sense? You have an interesting imagination, love."

"The point is merely that men don't lose their appeal when they don't marry, Deerhurst. Women do."

"I can't help but argue that point," Deerhurst remarked.

"And why is that?"

"You won't ever lose your appeal."

Her pulse quickened. "So, in which category do *you* fall? Two or three?"

"Why not one?" He grinned at her. "I am still young, and I believe I'm still eager, am I not?"

Phaedra bit back a laugh. "Eager you may be, but four-and-thirty is close to five-and-thirty which is closer to forty which—"

"Good Christ, woman, I'm a long way from forty!"

"But not young enough to fall into the first category."

"Fine," those sharp eyes delved into hers, "then I propose you add another category."

"Call me intrigued, Deerhurst."

He smirked. "The man that gets married when he meets the *right* woman."

Phaedra arched a brow. "Then you don't mind being leg shackled as long as it's with the right woman?"

"Perhaps."

"Well, you must let me know when you find her. I should love to meet this paragon of a woman who catches your heart," Phaedra teased.

His gaze never left hers as he said, "You shall be the first to know, then."

"How accommodating of you, Deerhurst." She paused, testing the temperature of her coffee on another sip. Much more tolerable than before. "Thank you for tonight."

"Don't thank me." He dragged a hand through his hair. "It was an utter disaster."

"Every part?" Phaedra asked. Surely not every single part. Yes, the night could have gone better, yet despite what happened, it still ended quite nicely, she thought.

A short pause, then, "Not every part, no."

Phaedra grinned. Perhaps it was the effects of the wine, but Deerhurst had taken on a new degree of handsomeness. He had moved beyond the title of protector or knight.

He was a hero.

The kind that makes a woman want to toss her bonnet into the wind and leap into the unknown. A feeling of giddiness spread through Phaedra. How had she lived next door to the earl all these years without paying attention to his existence? In any event, she was making up for that now. He seemed to have quite completely taken over her mind.

She took another sip of coffee, finding the temperature had lowered to where she could finish the cup. She pulled a face. Truly ghastly stuff. She preferred the subtle, sweet taste of tea.

"All done."

Deerhurst nodded and took the cup from her hand, placing it on the floor of the carriage. He then reached for her slippers and slid them carefully onto her feet. His gaze raked over her cloak. He nodded once more in satisfaction and reached for the door. "Let's go."

Phaedra waited for him to inspect the area before shifting to follow him out. He did not offer his hand as expected. Instead, he leaned into the carriage and scooped her up into his arms.

"What are you doing?" she said with a gasp.

"I'm not taking the chance of you stumbling about the street like a foxed wench."

She snorted, half amused, half offended. "Admit it, Deerhurst. You just want to hold me."

He snorted back. "Your wild musings never fail to entertain me, love."

"Likewise, Deerhurst."

He hurried her across the street, his hold steady—safe—slowing as they reached the big, arching windows of their purple drawing room.

Phaedra shot a sideways glance at Deerhurst. "This shall be the first time you pass on the street without witnessing anything in our drawing room." To prove her point, she craned her neck to peer through the windows. The drapes had been drawn shut. Not the slightest crack—

Phaedra's eyes widened, and she placed a hand over her mouth as she gasped.

"What?" Deerhurst instantly went on alert. "What is it? Are you unwell?"

"Deerhurst . . ." Phaedra, still in a state of shock, couldn't quite explain what she caught a glimpse of because there *was* a crack in the drapes. Very slight, but there.

"What is it? Did something scare you?"

She patted his arm and pointed to the set of windows. "My aunt's there."

Deerhurst suddenly hunched down with her in his arms, his grip on her tightening. "In the drawing room? Are you sure?"

Phaedra nodded. "Unless I am hallucinating," she paused, "which could well be the case." Because her aunt was with a man, and they appeared very much entangled with each other.

He cursed, then tugged her back into his arms. "Let's go."

"No." Phaedra squirmed out of his hold. "She's not alone. I want to see who she is with."

"Trust me, love, some things are better left unknown."

Some things, yes. "Not this."

She scrambled onto her haunches and slowly rose to peek through the crack. Phaedra's jaw went slack as the sight before her stabbed through her hazed mind.

Her aunt reclined on one of the sofas—the same one she'd sat on this very morning. The sleeves of her dress had been pulled over her shoulders, allowing her breasts to spill out. That was not all—there was a man between her legs. A very naked man, and he flexed his hips against her aunt.

She watched in shock as the man suddenly flipped her aunt over and took position from behind.

Somewhere, in the depths of her mind, a word whispered through the fog.

Carnal.

"How—"

She was yanked back to the ground, her words cut off as Deerhurst covered her mouth with his hand. He must have thought she would cry out in alarm. But all Phaedra wanted to say was: *How could her aunt be engaged in such an act?*

Her gaze found Deerhurst, and he seemed as flustered as she was. Color rose high in his cheekbones, and pearls of sweat coated his brow.

"We need to go. Now."

"My aunt, she . . . he . . . they . . ." She couldn't finish the thought. In that moment, another image rose in her mind: her and Deerhurst.

Carnal.

﹥﹥﹥﹦﹤﹤﹤

UNBELIEVABLE.

The one time, the absolutely only time Deerhurst had thought there would be no surprises in that cursed drawing room, the most provocative scene yet would unfold. He ought to have known this would happen, given his luck tonight.

And dammit, why did *he* look? He should have kept his arse on the ground. He should have dragged Phaedra away the moment he suspected something caught her attention. He should have known.

And he. Should. Not. Have. Looked.

Christ above.

Lady Portia had a lover. He would never have guessed. Or suspected. And by the looks of it, they held nothing back.

Bloody hell.

His body was on fire. It burned with need. The scene inside had been too vivid. The moment he set eyes on the couple, his imagination flared with scenes of him and Phaedra.

Phaedra provocatively displayed on that couch. Phaedra's head falling back as she cried out in pleasure. Phaedra's thighs parting as he thrust in deep.

Sweet Mother Mary.

His erection strained uncomfortably. It wanted out. It wanted her. Phaedra Sharp. She'd ruffled a lot more than his feathers. She ruffled every damn bit of good sense he possessed.

It took all his strength to tug her away from the windows and not push her up against the wall and claim her right there and then.

"We need to go before someone sees us," Deerhurst commanded, his voice brooking no argument. Really, they had to go before he took her on the pavement in the street.

He pulled her toward the narrow gate that led down the side of her house. He didn't have time to smooth over any of her sensibilities that had probably shocked her into immobility. The masked ball was one thing, this quite another.

And it was all his damn fault.

Because he couldn't stay away from her.

"I was not hallucinating, was I?" her low voice came.

"If I say yes, would you believe me?"

"No." She shook her head, and whispered, "My aunt said she had a secret. I just never thought it would be so scandalous. No wonder she didn't want to spill the details when I asked."

That was one hell of a secret.

"I never imagined . . ."

Neither had he.

It appeared the Sharp women were creatures of great passion. He glanced at Phaedra. Would she be just as passionate? He thought so, thinking back on their embraces.

She gripped his arm. "Did you recognize the man?"

Had he?

He'd glimpsed the scene as a whole, not catching any minor details. The man could have been anybody.

"Deerhurst?"

He cleared his throat. "No."

"I wonder who he is. He must be someone my father would not approve of if my aunt is keeping him a secret."

Deerhurst could think of a host of reasons why her aunt would keep her lover a secret. None of them had anything to do with Huntly.

"He is younger, I think."

Deerhurst frowned. "How do you get that?"

"His back seemed taut and powerful. A man in his prime."

"You looked at his back?"

"Didn't you? It was hard to miss all the naked flesh."

Deerhurst scowled. "You weren't to see that scene at all."

"Well, now that I have, it cannot be unseen. Lord, how am I ever going to look my aunt in the eyes again? All I'm going to see is that man's hips—"

"Please stop," Deerhurst choked. His restraint hung by a thread. If she kept talking about thrusting hips, there would be more thrusting to be had tonight, thrusting that would thrust that image right out of her mind.

"Oh, right, I completely forgot. You must be just as disturbed at the scene as I."

"Yes," he breathed because he could manage nothing else. He was so bloody disturbed he wanted to set fire to that drawing room. Paint the windows black. Carry off Phaedra to his bed this very second.

"I should have listened to you. I never should have peeped. Some things truly are better unseen."

A little too late.

They rounded the corner and Deerhurst cast a cautious glance over the shadows. "Did you leave the door unlocked?" he asked.

Phaedra nodded.

"Well, let's hope no one locked it since you left."

No one had, thank Christ.

The door opened with only the smallest of creaks and they both slipped inside without being detected.

"You don't have to escort me from here," she said in a whisper. "You can go home. I'm quite capable of making it to my chamber from here."

Amusement filled him. "Then why are you gripping my arm like you might drown if you let go?"

She gasped and let go. Deerhurst anticipated the move and caught her around the shoulders as she swayed. She still hadn't fully recovered from the wine.

"Do not argue with me, love."

She sighed. "Very well."

He grasped her elbow. "Lead the way."

They quietly made their way through to the main staircase, careful to avoid the purple drawing room, tiptoeing up the flight of stairs. There was a brief moment where they heard soft grunting noises, but Deerhurst quickly led Phaedra away. A man can only stand so much.

Deerhurst released a relieved breath when they reached her bedchamber. Though at this point it didn't matter if Lady Portia caught them together, as *she* had been caught in a much more compromising position.

Two positions, in fact!

And they were branded into Deerhurst's skull with an iron poker. Just like all the other scenes he'd witnessed in that drawing room. He redirected his focus and led Phaedra into her bedchamber.

"As you can see, I am safe and sound. You should leave before anyone finds you."

He should. He really bloody should.

Deerhurst shut the door behind him.

Her lovely blue eyes widened. The chamber was dark, but the curtains hadn't been drawn so the light of the moon spilled through the window, and soft embers still crackled in the hearth. Her maid must have made sure Phaedra would return to a glowing chamber and not a cold one.

"Deerhurst? What are you doing? Why aren't you leaving?"

"I cannot go until I'm satisfied you are over the high."

"I'm fine," she said. "I am over the worst thanks to you."

"No, you are not," he denied. She might wander off in her condition. And though it was completely irrational, he didn't want her to wander off where she might find a naked man whose back was taut and powerful. Who was to say that man wouldn't be wandering the halls too? God knows what might happen. Given Phaedra's curiosity, he didn't even want to contemplate the thought.

It was better to stay.

The woman had already been kidnapped by a stranger tonight. He wasn't about to take a chance. Christ, he himself was still recovering from the terror of the first one.

Her gaze narrowed on him. "Then when, according to you, will I be fine?"

"In the morning."

Her eyes widened. "You plan to stay the entire night?"

"I'll leave before dawn."

"This is highly un—" her voice tapered off at the raise of his brow.

"Fine." She stumbled over to the bed and fell onto it with a sigh. "I am too exhausted to argue with you."

"Good." He approached the bed. "Scoot over."

She did as she was told, and Deerhurst settled in beside her. He turned to his side to stare at her.

"Puck usually sleeps on that spot," she remarked.

"Puck's not here." He was over at his house.

She gave a soft snort. "That cat is never where he is supposed to be."

"Just like his mistress."

She rolled over to her side, mimicking his pose. "We are breaking all the rules, aren't we?"

"We are." He reached out to touch her cheek. "You are an adorable rule breaker."

"Oh?"

"One I have trouble staying away from."

"I shouldn't be so pleased at that remark." She smiled. "But I am."

"You shouldn't."

She suddenly laughed.

"What is so amusing? Are you laughing at me?" Deerhurst asked. His gaze narrowed. "I suppose that is better than gawking at me speechless upon hearing my confession."

"Your confession is not as shocking as sharing my bed. And I believe I kissed you tonight. You ought to be the one speechless."

"I was. But I'm more speechless at my own actions than yours."

Her brows puckered. "Because you hit that man? Are you mad at me?"

"Furious."

"I am terrible, right?"

"The absolute worst."

Her lips lifted at the corners. "Do you ever spare a lady her pride?"

"I suppose not. I must do my utmost best to repair it."

"How ever shall you do that?"

He leaned over to brush his lips against hers before he slowly pulled back. "How was that?"

"My pride still feels a bit bruised."

He kissed her again. "How about now?"

"Better."

He chuckled and settled back into the mattress. "Sleep, love, I will watch over you tonight."

She might as well sleep. For he certainly wouldn't tonight.

Chapter Thirteen

PHAEDRA GRIPPED THE small missive sent from Deerhurst tightly in her grasp. He hoped she would feel well soon.

She sighed.

She had opened her eyes that morning with a keen sense of dread. At first, she hadn't known what stirred such a horrid feeling, only that it was no pleasure rising with it. Then the flashes of impressions sparked a flood of memories she was wholly unprepared for, all but bursting through the banks of her mind.

The masked ball.

The kiss.

The rancorous crowd of rousers.

The wine.

Deerhurst in her bed.

More kisses.

Embarrassed and alarmed by all that had transpired the previous evening, Phaedra had hastily penned Deerhurst a note, thanking him for his protection and that he had brought her safely home, and letting him know that she would also take a day or two to rest.

In truth, Phaedra had entered full avoidance mode.

Lud, and her aunt.

That had been her biggest shock.

Not only was she avoiding Deerhurst, but she was also avoiding all the drawing rooms in the house, one in particular. She'd never be able to receive another caller in that room. Ever.

They took tea there!

All she would be able to see now was her aunt, breasts on display, and a naked man doing unspeakable things. And Deerhurst had been right by her side, witnessing everything.

The library seemed the only haven for her now.

Honestly, she didn't quite know what to make of their relationship. Fake courtship aside, they should not be kissing, sleeping in the same bed, and slipping out to gaudy balls. What did it mean for them? Nothing either of them wanted. They both had different futures. Different paths to walk. They were only brought together by a cat and a moment of madness. Some might call that fate, but Phaedra didn't believe in such nonsensical things.

There really was only one thing left to do.

End it.

"There you are, dear." Her mother breezed into the library with a stocking dangling on her fingers. "Is this yours?"

Phaedra frowned. "I don't believe so. Why?"

"I found it tucked behind a pillow in the drawing room."

Phaedra's eyes widened.

Oh no.

No.

No. No.

No doubt the stocking belonged to Portia. She must have misplaced it after last night's assignation!

Curiosity blossomed once more.

She almost wished Deerhurst hadn't pulled her away from the scene. Not to spy, but to catch a glimpse of the gentleman's face. Did they know the man? Was he part of their circle? Where did he and Portia meet?

Ah, curiosity was such a terrible thing!

"Well, it's certainly not mine," her mother said with a frown. "I suppose it must be Portia's."

Speak of the devil.

"Eleanor," Portia entered the room with something in her hand. "Is this yours?"

Drat. Phaedra was not ready to face her aunt, so she peered down at the book she was clutching in her hands. Already she felt her face heat. She doubted she would be able to face her aunt anytime soon without blushing several shades of pink. On the other hand, she was so dreadfully curious.

Although, a part of her was glad her aunt had found some form of happiness. She deserved any joy she could find after her dreadful marriage to Rowley—even *carnal* joy.

The word made her cheeks heat even more.

"I found this on the stairwell last night. Hello, Phaedra," Portia said when she spotted her burrowing into the couch.

Phaedra mumbled hello and then spotted the slipper her aunt held up. She felt the blood rush to her face.

That was her slipper!

It must have slipped off her foot on their way to her bedchamber. It was also one of the reasons she couldn't face Deerhurst. She'd practically undressed before him. Her palms broke out in a sweat. She had never experienced these feelings of uneasiness, mortification, and distress at the same time. Highly discomfiting. She should have stayed in her chamber today.

We're breaking all the rules, aren't we?

Phaedra groaned. For a woman intent on avoiding compromising situations, she sure had trouble with this man. Was there a way to extract humiliating memories from the brain? Surely science had advanced to such a stage. Gah! How was she ever going to look Deerhurst in the eyes again?

"That's not my slipper," the countess said with a small frown.

"That's my slipper," Phaedra admitted, knowing she couldn't hide this. "Puck must have gotten into my drawer again."

Sorry, Puck. You must carry the blame this once.

The countess held up the stocking to Portia. "This must be yours then, as it is neither mine nor Phaedra's."

Portia's eyes rounded, and Phaedra inwardly snorted. Caught twice.

"Where did you find this?" Portia asked, snatching the stocking from the countess's fingers.

"In the drawing room," the countess said. "An odd place to find a stocking, Portia."

Lord. This was too much.

Both women turned to her in question.

Phaedra blinked. Had she spoken out loud?

Phaedra cleared her throat. "I mean, whatever is going on with our apparel. Bits seem to be strewn all over the place. They must have acquired a life of their own."

Her mother opened her mouth to reply, but as the fates apparently thought this a wonderful scene and wished to expand upon it, her father entered at that precise moment.

"Eleanor, Phaedra." He held up a stay, which looked grossly out of place in his hands.

"Robert!" Her mother snatched the garment from his fingers. "How rude to display my undergarments so!"

"It's *yours*? I thought the cat had gotten into Phaedra's laundry again."

Phaedra wanted to laugh.

"Of course it's mine!" Her eyes narrowed. "Where did you find it?"

"I found it beneath the dining room table." Her father's face suddenly flushed. "Devil knows how I spotted it. Just caught my attention as I rose."

Phaedra nearly dropped her jaw.

Her father and her mother? In the dining room? This truly was too much for her mind to grasp. Was there anywhere in this house people hadn't become carnal? She should never have looked up that word. Never have looked through the window.

Her entire reality had shattered.

Phaedra would have loved nothing more than a glass of water just now. Or air, she needed air. For women of propriety who took part in carnal pleasures and inappropriate behavior, they really ought to be more careful with their undergarments.

"Whatever would your garment be doing in the dining room?" Portia asked innocently, much too innocently.

"I cannot say," her mother answered. "I last saw it in my chamber. Perhaps Puck got into my drawers as well."

How ridiculous! Phaedra had made that up. Puck had no interest in undergarments or slippers. He preferred to steal cook's fish or hunt for rodents.

Portia nodded thoughtfully. "Puck is really something, don't you agree? He also got hold of my stocking."

Phaedra couldn't listen to this. There had to be a way out for them all. It was only a matter of time before they asked her about her slipper since they well enough knew their garments hadn't been carried away by Puck! And given what they had been doing, who knew what they would believe Phaedra had been doing to lose a slipper! Unless they believed her fib, but she'd rather not have that scrutiny on her.

As though the heavens had heard her turmoil and looked down on her with mercy, Puck sauntered into the library and headed straight for her legs, rubbing his face against her, purring.

Thank you, Puck!

The feline had caused her enough trouble; he might as well get her out of it for once.

"What a little troublemaking cat," the countess was saying. "He got into your chamber too?"

"Puck!" Phaedra exclaimed, picking up the cat.

All eyes turned to her.

"It's fine if you chew on my slippers," Phaedra said, giving all the Sharps an out. "But you mustn't play with mother and aunt's clothing items, or I shall restrict your snacks for a month."

At their bewildered stares, Phaedra went on. "It's a recent habit he developed. I have to hide my slippers, or he drags them off somewhere, usually outside. I'm not sure why he does it, but it's a troublesome recent practice."

Her father nodded. "Cats are wont to do that. It's in their nature to scavenge."

"That's right," Phaedra said. "I read about it in one of the books. They tend to steal the clothing of the people they like the most." She sent an apologetic look to her father. "Sorry, Papa. It seems Puck favors us more."

The earl snorted. "That's because he is male. It's only natural. He senses my dominance."

"Robert!" the countess exclaimed. "Don't spout nonsense about dominance. Not in front of your daughter."

Her father drew his thick brows together. "What's wrong with it?"

Phaedra glanced at her mother. She would like to know too. She had a suspicion her mother's mind was still on the garment and how it got underneath the dining room table, which meant her mother's mind remained solidly rooted in the gutter.

"Like father like daughter," the countess said in a huff, turning to march from the library.

Phaedra let out a relieved breath.

A footman appeared in the drawing room. "The Earl of Deerhurst for Lady Phaedra."

Deerhurst was here?

Her pulse leaped.

DEERHURST WAITED FOR Phaedra in the purple drawing room—the one and only—with her crumbled missive in hand. He hadn't wanted to leave her bed this morning. He'd badly wanted to snuggle in closer and stay. She had looked so peaceful, so beautiful in her sleep.

He had stared at her soft, delicate features for what felt like hours before dawn had beckoned and with it the need to leave before they were caught together by her maid.

He had planned to take her on a late afternoon picnic. He had the whole scene planned out in his mind. The perfect spot in Hyde Park. Public. The spread of food. A bit of wine. Footman to keep guard. He wanted every last man to understand—*back off*. Whether his plan would work remained to be seen, but it would be worth it to try. In truth, as he had admitted the night before, he just couldn't stay away.

Then her note had arrived.

Deerhurst,

Thank you for always protecting me and ensuring that I arrive safely home. I shall take the day, maybe two, to rest.

Yours faithfully,
Phaedra

Nothing untoward or out of place with the note, nothing to suggest that Phaedra was anything but fine, and yet Deerhurst's gut had told him otherwise.

He was not fooled by her words.

Phaedra Sharp planned to avoid him. Cast him aside. Hide in her home.

After all that happened in the span of the night before, he couldn't blame her. And a part of him urged him to leave her be, respect her wishes—the wise part. He'd gotten too close. Too involved. Best to take a step away to catch his footing once more. But confound it. Would his heart listen to that sage voice?

No.

Deerhurst didn't want to catch his footing.

Which was why he found himself in the very drawing room that would probably put a blush on her face when entered—if she received him at all.

Then she appeared. A vision of swirling blue and, as predicted, soft strokes of pink glazing her cheeks. "Deerhurst?"

He released the breath he hadn't realized he'd been holding. He took in all of her. She appeared a bit tired, but she was still the most captivating woman in all of London.

"I received your note. I thought I would not be seeing you today."

Yes, he had sent her a reply. But that was before he'd gone into a spiral of resistance. "I wanted to make sure you've recovered from last night." He sounded like a madman.

A short silence followed.

"My mother found one of my slippers on the stairwell."

Deerhurst inwardly swore. "Did she suspect anything?"

"No," her lips twitched. "Puck got all the blame."

"I didn't even realize." Deerhurst inwardly cursed his negligence. She'd kicked off her slippers—or slipper—when she'd dropped onto her bed. He hadn't noticed there was only one. His eyes had been on her face, not her feet.

"It's my fault," he said softly, almost apologetically, because it felt like something he could have prevented. "I should have taken better care."

She waived his comment aside with a small smile. "You are not to blame, Deerhurst. At any part of the night, I could have said no. There is no need for you to take responsibility for my actions."

His gut resisted, but he said, "No one suspects you snuck out?"

"No, they believe Puck has an undergarment obsession, though I do not know how well they believe it."

"Undergarments?"

Her eyes suddenly lit up with a sparkle, and Deerhurst watched in fascination as every little aspect of her expression lifted in glee.

"Multiple items revealed themselves this morning."

He instantly understood. His gaze darted to the sofa. "That cat *is* always stirring up trouble."

She snorted. "It's not him doing the stirring."

Deerhurst chuckled but still couldn't help but muse that that wasn't entirely true. The cat had been the reason they ran into each other in his garden.

She cleared her throat. "About last night . . ."

He held up his hand to stop her. "You have nothing to feel alarmed about if that's what you wish to say."

"I behaved abominably."

So, he'd been right. She planned to avoid him. "You were drugged."

She looked away. "Not when I accepted your invitation. Not when I kissed you."

"Phaedra," he said and waited for her to meet his gaze. "I am the one who started this. I'm the one who kissed you first. I'm the one who took you to that ball. From the very first moment, if anyone's behavior has been abominable, it's mine."

"That may be true, but that doesn't excuse my actions in all of this. You've only ever protected me, even from myself. And I have caused you nothing but trouble."

If only she knew.

"I don't agree."

The corners of her mouth lifted, but the momentary sparkle had already dimmed, and her eyes didn't quite meet his.

Deerhurst felt panic rise.

"Be that as it may, let us end this courtship."

He almost doubled over as the punch of her request hit him square in the gut. He'd once ended a courtship. An ugly business that later evolved into an affair that ended in pain and anguish. Some for him.

146

Some for her. Back then he hadn't been worthy of her. Not to marry, at least. But she couldn't let go either. Not entirely. And he'd sought validation in all the wrong ways.

He had never found it.

So, he had stopped looking for it. Period.

But this . . .

The mess of his past could not compare to these simple words spoken from Phaedra's lips. They struck him in a place he had thought long dead.

"You truly want that?" he whispered when he recovered from the blow. "You want me to never bother you again?"

Doubt flicked in her gaze, so brief, but he caught it, and with it, hope.

"I want to end whatever this is between us before it goes horribly wrong," she said. "We could have gotten caught last night. What then? Have your views on marriage changed? Mine haven't."

Deerhurst paused. His views on marriage? That had never mattered. He had a secret. One that not only drove him but would influence the woman who joined his house too.

He would never marry.

Not unless he could trust the woman with the happiness of his daughter. Could he trust Phaedra? A moot point. It didn't matter if he trusted her or not. As she said, her views had not changed. Which, incidentally, also revolved around trust.

They were both people in this world who did not trust others with their most precious possessions. He, with his daughter, and she with her heart.

Sweat broke out on his palms. Phaedra was giving him an out.

He didn't want it. Neither could he refuse it.

Christ. Deerhurst couldn't breathe.

"You understand why this is for the best." She gave him a regretful smile. "I've had more fun with you in the past week than I've had the entire season. I hope you've had some fun too."

He ought to be relieved. He was not the knight she thought him to be. If she ever learned the truth about the list, his daughter, the messy details of his past, the danger therein . . . she would never again look at him the same way she had when she'd called him a knight.

He should leave before that happened. "It's done, then."

"Thank you for all you've done, Deerhurst. I truly appreciate your help."

"I have one request, my lady if you would grant it."

She looked startled. "What is it?"

"One last kiss."

She blinked. "Deerhurst . . ."

"To lay our deal to rest," Deerhurst said. He couldn't walk away without one last kiss. Refused to walk away without one last kiss.

"We might be caught."

Deerhurst reached for her hand and dragged her behind the door, pressing her up against the wall. He slammed his hands on either side of her face, locking her in with no chance of escape. If this was to be the end, let it end on the same explosive fireworks with which it had begun.

"Deerhurst, you—"

He cut her off with a kiss, then breathed against her lips. "Say my name."

"What?"

"One time, just one time, Phaedra, say my name."

A moment of pause, then a breathless whisper, one he'd only heard in his dreams. "Marcus."

He claimed her mouth. This time, there was nothing gentle about the kiss. His tongue swept into her warmth with one smooth stroke. All his frustration, his disappointment, and his regret poured into their last kiss.

She didn't hold back either.

She kissed him back with all the passion he'd come to expect from her. Her hands shoved into his hair like they had done their first night, and she pressed her breasts up against him.

Saints, he was going to miss her touch.

"What if I'm not ready to end it?" he breathed. How was he supposed to walk away from the first woman who made him feel like he was worth a damn? "What if I can't?"

"We have to."

We.

As though she couldn't do it if he didn't walk away too. She thought him a knight. She thought him strong. He didn't feel bloody strong at the moment. He felt weak in the knees.

But this wasn't just about him.

Deerhurst reluctantly broke away from her, his gaze traveling over her face, committing every line, every nuance, every dazed spark to memory.

Nothing had ever felt this hard.

"Goodbye, Phaedra."

"Goodbye, Marcus."

It was done. They were done.

He walked away without a backward glance.

Chapter Fourteen

PHAEDRA WAS STILL plastered in the same spot ten minutes after Deerhurst left, heart pounding wildly. There was no doubt Deerhurst excelled at sweeping her off her feet, and it was for the best that they had ended whatever had developed between them since the moment they met.

Deerhurst didn't want a wife.

She wanted cats.

Cats were safe. Cats didn't sweep a woman into a magical fairytale dream. Cats can't walk away after a woman entrusts her heart to them. Cats could be trusted.

Phaedra wasn't certain her heart would survive it if he were to walk away after she had completely fallen for him. Luckily, that hadn't happened.

She cared for him—Deerhurst—greatly. But that wasn't love.

Fortunately, not.

She placed a hand over her heart, pressed into the uncomfortable spot there. Not being able to stand the pressure, Phaedra flung herself from the wall and rushed through the halls until she burst through the doors that led to the garden.

She inhaled a deep breath and looked toward his estate, her heart in a frenzy.

They weren't allowing any callers at present. And Phaedra would avoid balls for the time being. Perhaps they could even retire to the country a bit earlier this year. Whatever these wagers were, they couldn't stand forever.

Soft, girlish laughter drew her entire focus to Deerhurst's house. Her brows drew together as she padded over to the gate that connected the properties.

Should she?

Dare she?

Better not, she told herself and started to turn away when the laughter rang through the air again. Soft. Melodious. Impossible to ignore. Before she could give it any thought, she was through the gate and following the sound as though it had woven a spell on her limbs, powerless to stop the pull.

And then she saw her.

A little girl in a blue dress, much the same color she wore today, a doll in her hand, and dancing on the grass patch of the earl's garden.

The girl smiled when she spotted Phaedra.

She stopped twirling. "Are you the lady that lives next door?" the little girl asked.

"Ah, yes, I am. Who are you?"

"I'm Abigail."

"Hello, Abigail," Phaedra said uncertainly. She glanced around. "Are your parents here?"

"Papa is inside."

Deerhurst must have family visiting.

Phaedra shifted awkwardly on her feet. She didn't want the earl to catch her after she'd just ended their fake courtship. How embarrassing. However, in the end, curiosity won and propelled her to ask, "What are you doing?"

"I'm dancing with Miss Trumpet."

Phaedra pointed at the doll. "Is that Miss Trumpet?"

Abigail nodded. "She wanted to dance."

Phaedra smiled. "Well, I shall leave you to dance with your Miss Trumpet."

"Wait," Abigail said. "Are you looking for Papa?"

"Your papa?" Phaedra shook her head.

"Oh," Abigail said, then piped up again. "But you're the wench that lives next door? Papa talked about you."

"I beg your pardon?" Phaedra furrowed her brows. "Just who *is* your father?"

Surely, it's not one of those fortune-hunting baboons?

"You know, silly," the little girl said, followed by a giggle. "He lives here."

"The Earl of Deerhurst lives here."

"Yes! I just call him Papa."

The entire world dropped from beneath her slippers. This was Deerhurst's daughter? As in *daughter*?

No.

That couldn't be.

She would have known about it, right? At the very least, her mother would have known! She hadn't said anything the morning she enquired after their neighbor. Why would no one know that the Earl of Deerhurst had a daughter?

Because he has no wife.

Phaedra froze.

For a moment she thought she'd missed that tidbit too. If Deerhurst had a wife that meant . . .

"Where is your mama?"

Please tell me Deerhurst does not have a wife.

But then would mean his daughter . . .

"Papa said Mama is in heaven."

His wife *died*?

Phaedra shut her eyes to calm her beating heart. Logic told her Deerhurst had never been married. The countess would have known and told her as much. So that meant this little girl had to have been born out of wedlock and was perhaps the reason Deerhurst refused to take a wife. Why no one knew of his daughter. He had kept her a secret from their world.

Phaedra smiled and approached the little girl. She lowered onto her haunches. "I heard that heaven is a wonderful place."

"Papa says that too."

"Then you should believe him," Phaedra said. "Have you always lived in this house?"

The little girl shook her head. "I live in the hills."

Phaedra blinked. "The hills? Do you mean the country?"

Abigail nodded. "There are lots of hills. I heard Miss Green once say that Papa saved me and brought me there, which is why I like it so much."

Phaedra suddenly thought of the orphanage Deerhurst had taken her to. She scrutinized Abigail's face. No doubt. The girl had inherited many of her father's features. The most undeniable . . . her vivid green eyes.

"I once thought your papa a knight." *Before he called me a wench to his daughter.*

She wanted to strangle Deerhurst.

The girl giggled. "Is he not a knight?"

"No."

"What is he then?"

A scoundrel. An *irresistible* scoundrel.

"I'll tell you once I've figured it out," she told Abigail.

A strong, familiar baritone came from beyond the garden, "Abigail?"

Oh, no.

Phaedra glanced around for a spot to hide. Too late. A moment later Deerhurst stepped outside. His gaze fell on her, and she swore all the color leaked from his face.

"Phaedra?" Her name sounded as unsteady as her heart.

She slowly rose to her feet.

"Papa!"

The unease on her face must have been palpable because he practically shot forward and reached them in three long strides.

"Abigail, sweetheart, why don't you go inside?"

Ever the protector, Phaedra thought, amusement reclaiming space in her heart. Did he think she would shun his daughter? Though if Abigail was illegitimate, she would not blame him if he feared so.

She would have done the same in his place.

Abigail waved her goodbye and skipped to the house. They both watched her until she disappeared into the house before they turned to one another. This time, he bore an aloof air, no emotion on his face to indicate what he may be feeling.

But Phaedra knew.

The orphanage. His aversion to marriage. The man before her protected women. He would protect his daughter.

Phaedra tilted her head to consider him. "Abigail is the reason you've not taken a wife."

"Ladies do not tolerate the offspring of their husband's affairs."

So blunt.

Cold even.

And yet all Phaedra wanted to do was to pull him close and kiss warmth back into his eyes.

She wondered who the woman was that he had an affair with, but promptly shoved that thought from her mind. She didn't want to know.

"Ladies are like that," Phaedra agreed. Most. Not all.

"Are you like that?"

Phaedra's heart ached for him. How could anyone shun that little girl? It was inconceivable to her. Children were to be protected, not abused in any way. "I would never shun your daughter, Deerhurst. If you don't know anything else about me, you should at least know that."

His eyes widened fractionally before they reverted to their impassive stare. "You say that now, my lady, but then, we are not wed. If we were to wed, would you still feel the same way?"

My lady.

The distance in those two words made her want to punch him even more.

Phaedra snorted. Loudly. "Earlier you called me Phaedra. Last night you called me love. Now you call me my lady. Why not just call me *wench* and be done with it? It's what you do behind my back anyway."

His lips parted, but no sound emerged.

"Just as I thought. Let me tell you something, you scoundrel, if we were to wed right this moment, I wouldn't feel any different. Unlike other people, I don't lay the sins of the father at the feet of his children. Best remember that."

He advanced on her, a dangerous glint entering his gaze. "What about in a year, two, three, ten, when the *ton* learns of Abigail's existence? You would be ridiculed right alongside her."

"I would protect the child with my life," Phaedra said with a lift of her chin.

"Your friends would mock you."

She scoffed. "They'd be no friends of mine if they mocked my daughter."

He stopped before her. So close, if she reached out, she could trace a finger over his marble face. But she waited, wanting to see how he would test her next.

"*Your* daughter?"

"Of course," Phaedra said. "My husband's daughter would become my daughter."

His eyes searched hers.

Whatever he was looking for, apparently, he did not find, for he said, "Go home, Phaedra."

So this was the withdrawn, detached, private earl her mother and aunt had spoken of. Phaedra had witnessed the warm, passionate, mischievous side of him, and she wasn't about to let him sink into a bog of coldness. He had helped her. She would help him.

"No," Phaedra announced. "You've seen the inside of my drawing room, but I haven't seen the inside of yours. It would be rude not to return the favor."

Deerhurst blinked, and Phaedra seized his momentary distraction to march past him and into his house.

"Phaedra!" he growled. "Where the hell are you going?"

There now.

That was much better.

⇶⇷

DEERHURST STARED AT Phaedra as she and Abigail laid out the blanket and spread for their picnic. Once she'd inspected every inch of his drawing room and learned he'd prepared a picnic before they'd called off their fake engagement, there was no stopping her. So, he had agreed—against his better judgment—to host the picnic in the garden. No amount of persuasion worked on the woman once she set her mind on something.

But then again, she was a Sharp.

And he still hadn't recovered from earlier. Deerhurst had never felt panic rise as swift and sure as the moment he spotted her with his daughter. Everything around him had slowed to unbearably slow motion, as though he were but a spectator of his life and not actively participating in it.

Not a feeling he ever wanted to experience again.

He'd been certain he'd find a hint of revulsion in her demeanor, some little clue that gave away her distaste. He hadn't found it, and she claimed he would not. Try as he might, Deerhurst had detected no artifice or malice in her tone or posture.

Now they were on a picnic, and he found himself relaxing more each moment he heard Abigail's laughter weaving and intertwining with Phaedra's—one innocent giggle, the other true delight.

It could mess with a man's bloody mind.

He regarded the setup with a skeptical eye. "I should have arranged to have a table and chairs set up."

"Nonsense," Lady Phaedra said. "We are perfectly fine with a blanket and some pillows. Is this not the point of a picnic?"

Deerhurst couldn't say. He'd never been on one before. "The ground is hard."

She tossed a pillow at him. "Then sit on this."

"It's not me I'm worried about," he said with a grumbling tone.

"Are you going to join us?" She sounded amused.

Deerhurst lowered to sit on the blanket.

"I love picnics!" Abigail exclaimed. "I want to have picnics every day."

Phaedra smiled at her. "I'm sure that can be arranged." She looked at him. "You are very quiet."

That's because he had no idea what to say. They were here with his daughter—an event he'd never anticipated. He had entered unchartered territory. The entire moment felt so surreal. Deerhurst almost imagined he had entered an alternative world. One where all his troubles and fears disappeared. Where secrets didn't weigh him down to the bottom of the ocean with no way to breathe.

He reached for the wine. "Shall I pour us some?"

She smiled at him. "It's not laced with anything it shouldn't be, is it?"

He snorted and poured them a glass. "It's light."

"Can I have some too?" Abigail asked.

"No, pet, maybe when you're older. I had Cook add some freshly pressed juice for you."

"I don't want juice. I want to pick flowers. Can I?"

"Of course, pet." His words were scarcely cold before Abigail ran off to a small patch of flowers growing beneath a tree.

Deerhurst shook his head and handed Phaedra her glass. "Didn't she moments ago say she loved picnics?"

She took a sip as she regarded him. "Children are a fickle bunch."

He returned her stare. "Has Puck run off again?"

"I beg your pardon?"

"Was that why I found you on my property again?"

The corners of her lips lifted. "No, I heard your daughter's laughter and followed the merry tune."

Deerhurst nodded slowly. "You haven't asked about Abigail's circumstances." Her mother. Phaedra must be dying of curiosity, yet she didn't delve, as he'd thought she would.

"It's not any of my business," she said softly. "And I meant what I said earlier. I would never spurn a child over the circumstance of their birth."

He believed her. "I've been keeping her away from the probing eyes of society."

"You are doing what you feel is best for your daughter." She took another sip. "So, I was the first woman you ever courted? Fake aside."

Deerhurst paused, deciding whether he should reveal a snippet of truth. Why not? This part was no secret. "I courted a lady before you."

Her eyebrows shot up. "Truly? She must have been some woman. What happened?"

Ah, there it is.

Unbridled curiosity.

"She ended our courtship and married a duke."

She choked on a sip of wine. "That . . ." She cleared her throat. "That must have been rather disappointing."

Deerhurst shrugged. Thinking back, that part of his past hurt the least. "Perhaps for a moment, but afterward I counted myself as the lucky one."

"Oh? Why is that?"

Deerhurst almost laughed. He could clearly hear the questions she didn't ask. *Who is this woman? Who is the duke? Have I met them?*

Deerhurst shrugged. "The duke shipped her off to one of his estates in Wales. You have a vivid imagination, love. Why would a man ship his wife off to barren lands?"

"Either he did something, or she did something."

"Exactly."

She pouted. "Now I'm dying of curiosity, Deerhurst."

"Save your inquisitiveness for the next picnic. Otherwise, what will we have to talk about?"

She laughed. "There will be another?"

"That's up to you, love." *It's always been up to you.*

"Papa!" Abigail came running back, breaking the spell. "Look what I picked!" She offered him a small white flower. "Do you know what it is?"

"A flower?" Deerhurst asked, unsure.

"Let me see," Phaedra said, and Deerhurst was surprised when she set her wine glass on the ground and crawled forward on her hands and knees, inspecting the blossom. "I believe it's jasmine."

"It smells nice." Abigail sniffed the bud and stuck out the flower to Deerhurst. "For you."

"Thank you, pet, but I don't know what to do with flowers."

Abigail leaned in to say, "You give it to a wench, of course." She looked at him as though he ought to know this.

Saints preserve him.

Deerhurst took the flower from his daughter, and when her stare became expectant, he said, "Oh, you want me to do it now?"

She nodded eagerly.

He smiled and offered the flower to Phaedra.

"Oh, right. *I'm* the wench."

"Do you accept the flower or not?"

"Accept."

Just as she reached for the flower, and before Deerhurst could think better of it, he leaned over and secured it in her hair.

"There," he murmured.

Abigail clapped her hands, and they both watched as she dashed off again.

"She is lovely," Phaedra said.

"She will have a harder life than most." Deerhurst paused. "You are right, she is the reason I gave up on taking a wife."

"Not all women would snub you daughter."

"Perhaps, but if she were your daughter, would you trust the man you married to love her as much as you do?"

"If the man were worthy, then yes."

"Interesting." He leaned closer. "How do you know when a person is worthy?"

"You feel it," she whispered. "Everything about him, or her, calls to you."

A hell of an admission coming from a woman who didn't trust men. "And yet you have decided to become a spinster and spend your life alone."

"Not *alone* alone. I'd have my cats."

"Of course."

"Cats are dependable."

"Naturally."

"But when I made that declaration, I hadn't met a man who could change my mind."

Deerhurst froze. His eyes searched hers. "Then have you met him now?"

"I might have."

The temptation to rise onto one knee and ask for her hand hit him hard. He didn't dare believe that he was that man, but he couldn't help but hope that he was.

If he was . . .

A woman such as Phaedra deserved to be wooed. She deserved poetry and candy. Sweet words of endearment and nights dancing away until her feet hurt.

She tilted her head. "You said before that you fell into the category of men that would marry when you find the right woman. Is that true?"

He glanced at his daughter. "As you can see, it would have to be the right woman or no woman at all."

She chuckled. "Everything you've said in the past takes on a new meaning now that I've met her." Her eyes met his. "Then have you met the right woman now?"

"I might have."

"Is she a wench?"

He leaned in until his lips hovered just over hers. "She might be."

"I think I've found someone, too."

"Are you going to kiss?" a small voice interrupted the moment. Deerhurst jerked away from Phaedra as the question pierced him like the cold water of an icy lake.

"I don't mind if you kiss, Papa," Abigail said. "So long as you kiss me too."

Deerhurst groaned.

Phaedra laughed.

He shifted uncomfortably as a certain body part strained against the fabric of his breeches. He'd been deuced uncomfortable since he met Phaedra—one would think he'd be used to it by now. With his daughter present, that discomfort grew tenfold.

Bloody hell.

He must have completely lost his mind.

"No kissing, pet." He picked up the bottle of red to distract himself. "More wine?"

She stuck out her glass. "Please."

"Why won't you kiss?" Abigail asked.

"A man doesn't go around kissing ladies." *Follow your own direction, man.*

"Why not?"

"It's against the rules."

We're breaking all the rules, aren't we?

He inwardly cursed.

"But I like kissing," Abigail said.

That sobered him instantly. "Who are you kissing?"

Abigail pursed her lips. "You, Papa. Miss Green, Miss Lockhart, and Miss Trumpet."

Deerhurst calmed. "That's fine. So long as you don't kiss any males other than me."

"Forever?"

Deerhurst shot a look at Phaedra. *A little help?*

Phaedra laughed but said nothing.

He had no choice but to say, "One day when you marry, you can kiss your husband. *Only* then."

"Your father is right," Phaedra said. "You should *never* kiss a man until you are married."

Why did it feel that was directed at him?

"Do you want to know why?" Phaedra asked Abigail, who nodded eagerly. "Well, that's because any man who wants to kiss you before marriage is a scoundrel, little one. Every last one of them."

He was doomed.

Doomed.

Chapter Fifteen

PHAEDRA PACED THE length of the room, unable to sleep. She wasn't usually prone to pacing, but in this instance, it was necessary since she had to hold back from racing over to his house and finding the man responsible for her restlessness and throwing herself into his arms and absorbing every bit of warmth and care he had to offer.

Pacing or racing.

Those were her options.

"Do not look at me like that," Phaedra said to Puck, who lay curled up at the foot of the bed, staring at her as though he knew her strength was waning. "This is all your fault, you know."

She liked Deerhurst.

And was it any wonder?

They were much alike, the two of them. They both had reservations about the opposite sex. Both had good reasons. Yet today, a major obstacle had shifted for them. He'd practically told her he found her worthy of his daughter. And she . . . well she had fought to prove herself worthy.

Yet a sliver of doubt remained.

Because they had spoken in might haves. Both wanting yet neither entirely willing to give in first. Which was why she was all but bouncing up and down in her chamber—she wanted to stomp on that sliver of doubt. Stomp the agitating feeling to dust. She wanted to discover what could be possible for her and Deerhurst.

And she had ample time to lay her doubts to rest. But patience had never been her strong point.

The biggest challenge for her had been to admit that she would change her mind for the *right* man. That she would forgo her vision of spinsterhood and place her trust in a man.

Was Deerhurst this man?

Absolutely, irrevocably, *yes.*

It didn't matter to her that he had a daughter. She adored Abigail. How could she not? And Deerhurst loved that little girl. It was hard to not admire a man who would sacrifice his life for his daughter.

Phaedra's resolve firmed.

To hell with patience!

She darted to the door, careful to make as little sound as possible as she slipped from her room. She quietly and quickly made her way through the hall, down the stairs, and to the French doors that led to the garden. Cold nipped her skin, but Phaedra ignored the chill as she dashed off to the iron gate she had grown familiar with the past week.

She hadn't given any thought to what she would say to him once she found him, nor that to find him, she'd have to sneak into his house. If that were even possible.

I'll find a way.

She was, after all, a resourceful woman. What she wanted she would find a way to get.

The gate swung open as she reached it, and Phaedra jumped back. Her jaw nearly dropped as Deerhurst appeared before her, dressed in nothing but a shirt and breeches, just like the first night they had kissed.

"What are you doing here?" Phaedra asked, shocked. Then she recalled, well, she was also there, so he could ask her the same.

"I . . ." He frowned, and narrowed his eyes on her, his gaze traveling over from tip to toe. "What are *you* doing here?"

"I came to find you."

"Wearing just that?"

Phaedra blushed as she fought the urge to cover herself. She wore the same chemise she'd worn the first night. She hadn't even thought to grab a cloak.

Confidence, Phaedra. You must show confidence.

She squared her shoulders. "What else should I be wearing?" He arched a brow, and she cleared her throat. "Well, you still haven't answered my question."

Amusement lit his face. "I came to find you too."

"Well, it seems we have found one another."

"It seems that we have." He snatched her wrist and pulled her through the gate. "Why did you come to find me?"

"I imagine the same reason you came in search of me."

He chuckled, forever patient. "How about you say it? Or better yet, whisper it in my ear."

"You need to hear it that much?" Phaedra teased.

He touched her cheek with the back of his hand. "I need to know I'm not dreaming."

"You're not dreaming." She stepped up to him and lifted on her toes to whisper in his ear, "I came to find you because . . . I wanted to kiss you."

His lips were on hers a moment later.

Phaedra circled her arms around his neck. There was no mistaking the raw urgency of his claim. He wanted her as much as she wanted him.

"I have this fantasy about you on a couch," he breathed against her skin.

"There's no couch here."

"Let's go inside."

He pulled back slightly and searched her face. Phaedra knew if she agreed, she'd be agreeing to a lot more than merely entering his home. But this was what she wanted. To explore Deerhurst. Explore the connection she could not shake.

She said yes.

Phaedra laughed when he seized her wrist and dragged her to the house. Her heart pounded so hard she was afraid she might run out of breath.

The warmth of the house sent a delicious ripple down her spine. Dark and quiet, the only sound seemed to come from their hurried footsteps, impatient to find each other's embrace again. He pulled her into his study and shut the door. A moment later she found herself pressed up against the door with his mouth claiming hers once more.

Phaedra almost sighed in relief.

"No other man will do for you," he paused to breathe with utter confidence.

"Such arrogance."

"You are here with *me*." His heated gaze found hers. "There is no gentleman that can quench your thirst."

Tiny prickles coated her skin as she held his gaze. She caught the thread of thought in the depth of his eyes. He was saying to her no other woman would do for him. *He was here with her.* No other woman could quench his thirst.

He was right about her too, and she told him so by kissing him back, her fingers finding their favorite spot in his hair, and she felt unspeakable satisfaction when he shuddered at her touch. If she could, she would crawl inside of him, his heart, his, mind, his soul, for he had surely crawled into hers.

His hands swept over her buttocks, and he pressed her up against the swell of his arousal. She gasped, her thoughts returning to that one little word—*carnal*. A moment later, she felt the sleeves of her chemise pull over her shoulders.

Oh, Lord.

Phaedra had expected desire to burn slowly and ignite into a burning passion. Not so. Desire came hard and swift. It stole the breath from her lungs, had her heart pounding in her ears, and sent all sorts of tingles down to the core of her womanhood.

He lifted her off the ground and carried her to the sofa, following her down as he gently, yet provocatively, lowered her to the couch without breaking their kiss.

She pushed at his white linen shirt, desperate to feel his flesh beneath her fingers. He drew back just enough to draw the shirt over his head, his gaze glowing with fire right before it dropped to her breasts.

Too much.

His gaze. His body. Phaedra didn't know where to lock her attention. In the end, his body won. Hard muscles bunched as he moved to draw down the rest of her nightgown, practically yanked, her breasts spilling for him as he drew the dress off her shoulders even more.

Heaven save her.

Was he replicating the scene they'd witnessed in the drawing room? Phaedra found the very idea beyond erotic.

He lowered his head to stroke his tongue over her nipple. She had thought his stare heated, but that was nothing compared to the fire that seared through her blood at his touch.

She reached out to touch his shoulder, or to hold on, she wasn't sure, and his flesh burned hot under her hands. The entire encounter reminded Phaedra of a turbulent volcano, ready to erupt any second, destroying everything in its vicinity.

He gathered the hem of her chemise and drew it past her knees, then farther up to expose her thighs.

"I need to touch you."

She couldn't get a word out but managed to nod. She needed him to touch her too. He tugged at the drawers she wore, and before she could blink, maneuvered them off her and tossed them aside. She gasped when his hand brushed her most private place.

"Tell me this is good," he said hoarsely as his finger pressed inside of her.

"Yes. Oh, Lord, Marcus, yes."

He kissed her jaw. "Touch me."

Her fingers instantly skimmed the hard edges of his chest. He shuddered against her. As though her touch was the only thing keeping him together. She trailed her fingers to the waist of his breeches, scraping the line where they connected with his skin.

"Christ woman, don't tease me, unbutton me," he growled while his finger moved and explored inside her in slow, almost infuriating caresses.

Phaedra had never felt this hot, this powerful before. She made do with the buttons of his breeches and practically purred at the moan that tore through his throat when she pushed the material over his buttocks.

His breathing had become harsher. Beads of perspiration gathered across his skin beneath her palms as he seemingly fought an inner battle. "Phaedra, love, what happens next . . ."

She understood. "Cannot be undone, I know."

"You also know what comes next?"

She thought back to what she witnessed in the drawing room and arched her back against him. "You thrust."

He choked. "Christ love, you cannot say things like that." He bit down tenderly on her shoulder. "It drives me mad."

"Good mad or bad mad?"

"Lust mad."

Phaedra grinned. She supposed that's a good sort of mad. Very dangerous. Very delightful. "I don't oppose."

He nibbled his way across her collarbone. "I'm going to thrust, yes, but first I'm going to bury myself inside of you. Do you understand what that means?"

Oh, Lord. *Yes.* Carnal.

"It may be . . . uncomfortable at first."

"*Marcus.*" Phaedra didn't want to listen to this anymore. She wanted him. Uncomfortable or not. This caution was much more painful.

He chuckled. "Very well love, hold on."

Phaedra would give him just about anything at that moment, but she wasn't sure she could give him that. Hold on? She was about to come undone!

And she couldn't wait.

⇶⫘

POSSESSED.

Deerhurst was madly, badly, and dangerously possessed. He hadn't been able to hold back. Lord knew, he had tried. But knowing exactly where to enter her house, how to get to her chamber, and staying away from her had slowly driven him insane. All the walls he had erected—and for good bloody reason—crumbled, brick by brick, the moment she entered his mind. It didn't matter that he'd built those walls to protect his secrets. He never imagined they'd be defeated this easily by the woman in his arms.

He hadn't been able to hold back.

He wouldn't hold back now.

Deerhurst inhaled the sweet fragrance of her skin.

Yes, completely possessed.

What the future held for them, time would tell. He couldn't dwell on that now. He had spent so much of his energy fighting against the pull that drew him closer to Phaedra. He had no more fight left in him. No more strength to resist. He didn't have that much to begin with anyway.

Let fate cast its die.

Let his past come back to haunt him.

He would face everything then.

Right now, the woman beneath him grew ever more impatient with his patience. Deerhurst rubbed the tip of his nose against her temple.

"What am I holding on for?" she asked, her voice soft and full of sin.

Deerhurst inserted another finger into her, chuckling when she gasped. "This."

"Scoundrel."

"Just for you."

She writhed against him when he ran his fingers along the silky folds of her core, his gaze drinking up every one of her nuances as he prepared her for what came next.

She sucked in a breath, the grip on his back digging into his skin. He loved that little sound. Loved her hands on him.

"So beautiful."

He brushed his mouth up the column of her neck to nip at her earlobe as he focused his attention on enticing more whimpers from her with his strokes. He wanted her ready. Wanted her to shout out his name in ecstasy. Wanted to claim every beat of her heart tonight.

She arched into the palm of his hand, urging with her body, demanding more.

Deerhurst would give her more.

He'd give her everything.

"Phaedra . . ."

Her lashes fluttered and she gazed at him with such acceptance, such wonder, it was all he could do not to plunge into her like the wild creature she made him feel like.

No regrets.

No regrets.

Deerhurst had done many things in his life that he regretted. Handled many situations not as well as he could have. But not her. Not this moment. This he would never regret. And for a thousand reasons, he didn't want her to regret this either.

"No regrets," he whispered, almost pleading as he placed soft kisses over her cheeks.

She grabbed his face between her hands and narrowed her eyes. "Marcus... the only regret will be you not taking me this very second."

He laughed, then gave her a scorching kiss. "Then I shall take you this very second."

"Are you going to do it with your breeches on your knees?"

"No love, this was just the warm-up." He grinned and quickly made short work of any remaining cloth still separating their skin from each other.

Christ, she was soft.

"What if someone comes in," she whispered.

Not this time of night. "No one would dare," Deerhurst reassured as he settled between her legs, spreading them wide, his erection nudging at her entrance.

"Love . . ."

She wrapped her legs around his waist in answer to his unspoken question. Deerhurst nearly came undone then and there.

"I've never wanted a woman as much as I want you."

"Then don't let me wait any longer."

Ever impatient.

He didn't mind at all.

"Christ," Deerhurst all but growled as he pushed inside of her. It took all his strength to be gentle, to go slow and not turn into a ravening beast. He had never unraveled in such a profound way as he did with Phaedra. Not in his four-and-thirty years had he trembled at a woman's touch.

Tremble, for heaven's sake.

Never.

Not until her.

"Oh, my." She threaded one hand in his hair while the other

gripped his back. "That feels . . ."

Bloody amazing.

Absolutely torturous.

Deerhurst softly sucked on her lower lip, taking care to be as gentle as possible. He was never going to be the same after tonight. Every last one of the defenses he had painstakingly built over the years after the nightmare with that woman, ever since he found his daughter, the secrets he held so close to his heart came crashing down with each inch he entered her.

Deerhurst inhaled a shaky breath, in awe that he had found a woman like her. A woman who had lived next door to him for years. And yet, they had only encountered each other when, perhaps unbeknownst to them at the time, they had needed each other most. Whatever the case, whatever the reason, there would never be anyone like her in his life again. He understood that down to his bones. She was the one for him.

Forever and always.

It was her or nobody.

One last push brought him home, and he couldn't help the shudder that rushed down his spine when he felt her innocence give way.

Mine.

Her entire body tensed around him.

"Are you all right?" His voice came out husky, guttural, ravaged with desire.

"Yes," she said with a smile and wiggled. "I feel so full."

Deerhurst grinned and captured her lips for a quick kiss. "Full of me."

"You sound very pleased with yourself."

"That's because I am," he admitted and trailed his tongue along the arch of her neck. Instinct demanded he move, but Deerhurst had to give her a moment to adjust. "Are you comfortable?"

"No."

He stilled, his heart dropping. Had he hurt her? "Should we stop?"

"No! Why would you want to stop?" She arched beneath him. "Stopping is the problem."

He let out the breath he'd been holding. "Thank the Saints. I might just go up in flames if you told me to stop."

She kissed his chin. "I need you to . . ." She hesitated.

"I know exactly what you need, love. Hold me tight."

She did as she was told.

His hands slid beneath her buttocks to keep her in place as he slowly began to thrust. She whimpered beneath him, a sound Deerhurst would cherish all his life. He worshipped her until her skin flushed a splendid shade of pink, until he could barely breathe with how tight she held onto him. A vision so damn beautiful, he nearly came like a boy who just discovered his first taste of pleasure.

"Is this what you need?" he asked, fire licking up his spine as he withdrew slowly and pushed in deep.

"*Yes.*"

His mouth closed over her breasts, hot and demanding, groaning at the sweetness of their taste. He teased the peaks of her nipples until she arched beneath him with pleasure.

"I feel on fire," she said with a slight moan.

The delight he received from each little sound that parted her lips was unrivaled. Like sparks of lightning shooting down his spine. She made him feel like a hero. A saint. *A knight.*

Her response to his touch inflamed him, spurred him on to thrust harder, deeper into her.

"Marcus," she cried. "I . . ."

"It's all right love, let it go. Surrender to the flames."

He sensed her near her climax and found the little nub of her sex, stroking it with his thumb. Teasing. Enticing. Urging her to let go of the reigns, to trust in something so much more magical, and bigger than whatever obstacles they feared to face.

She bucked wildly beneath him.

He quickened his pace while holding a steady rhythm with his fingers.

"Come for me, Phaedra."

Deerhurst couldn't take his eyes away from her as he watched her lips part and her face flush with pleasure. He'd never seen anything so beautiful in his life. He had done that. He had put that look on her face.

And then her entire body contracted around him. She called out his name, the sound so lush and sinful, Deerhurst's pace took on a wild pounding. He grunted, his control snapping as he drove into her until her voice turned to a rasp and he too called her name upon finding spell-weaving pleasure in her arms.

He brought his mouth down on hers, his tongue demanding entrance as he filled her with a shudder. Her hands circled his neck as she kissed him back. His whole body trembled.

He couldn't stop kissing her. Couldn't stop his hands from touring her body. His entire life he had waited for her. He knew that now. Understood it deep within his heart.

Deerhurst held her tight, vowing he would never let her go.

Chapter Sixteen

PHAEDRA WOKE TO the most delicious sensation between her legs. A unique, almost wonderful prickle with a slight touch of soreness. Evidence of a woman well loved. She loved this feeling. She could very well become addicted to this sensation.

To this man.

Oh, who was she fooling? She had long since become hooked on him. He was her drug. But not like the horrid wine she had consumed at the masked ball. No, this was very different. Surreal, almost. When with him, she experienced a euphoric alignment in every one of her senses. When she was not with him, everything inside her twisted out of order down to the marrow of her bones.

It still amazed her how sometimes the smallest step in the wrong direction could turn out to be the greatest step of your life. And one had to give credit where credit was due.

Thank you, Puck.

Phaedra grinned and stretched out her limbs before snuggling up against Deerhurst's bare chest.

He was warm, like a furnace.

Flushing for no other reason than recalling those wonderful memories, she hadn't thought she'd be able to move after the scene with Deerhurst in his study. Luckily, she didn't have to, for he had lifted her into his arms and carried her to his bed. Where, she was almost ashamed to admit, she hadn't gotten that much rest. The man had been insatiable. So had she.

She was a woman ruined.

How utterly delightful!

Phaedra had fallen hopelessly in love with the man beside her. She couldn't deny it even if she wanted to. Her body gave her away. The beat of her heart. Her thoughts. Everything pointed at Deerhurst.

She also couldn't be entirely sure, but she was fairly certain he felt the same way about her. And to think, she'd have been perfectly happy to venture into spinsterhood while raising her future cat family with Puck.

She inwardly snorted.

Spinsterhood with cats? She must have lost her mind. She'd have missed out on Deerhurst. *This.* Having tasted passion she never imagined even existed, she could no longer be content without it. Or, more aptly, the *man* behind the passion.

Cats couldn't give her this. They'd still have cats, but cats with Deerhurst were so much better than cats without him.

How had she gotten so lucky?

For one, Deerhurst was rich all on his own, so he could have no designs on her dowry. She'd never have to worry whether he'd used her or not. Not about that. Secondly, he protected her from awful men. And he helped orphans. Despite his past, he was an honorable and trustworthy man. A great father.

Even Puck approved of him.

The man beside her stirred and pulled her still closer against him, draping one heavy leg over her. A thrill shot through her.

"Hello, love." Sleepy eyes roamed over her face. His voice sounded hoarse. Phaedra loved it. "Did you sleep well?"

"Marvelously."

"Me too."

Phaedra traced little circles on his chest with a finger. "I love how warm you are, like a volcano."

"A volcano?" He chuckled. "You ignite the fire in me."

She laughed and pinched him. "Such a smooth tongue in the mornings."

He rubbed his face against hers. "Must be a scoundrel, don't you know."

"Oh, I know." She continued dragging her fingers over his body. "I've never woken beside a man before. It's quite nice."

"A man?" His gaze narrowed. "You mean me."

She laughed. "Oh, very well. I have never woken beside you before. It's quite nice."

"Better."

She gave a light snort. "As if I can imagine waking up with anyone but you."

"*Much* better." He traced his fingers up along her spine. "I refuse to share you with others." A pause. "Imaginary or not."

"What about Puck?"

"Animals not included. Just humans."

Phaedra laughed. "I may have a wild imagination, Deerhurst, but not that wild."

He kissed her hair. "I know this is stating the obvious, but just so that there is no misunderstanding between us," he lifted her chin to stare into her eyes, "our fake courtship has turned very real."

She nipped the stubble on his neck. "And for that matter, so that there is no misunderstanding between us, I'm quite happy that it has."

"You're going to make an outstanding countess."

"Like my mother." Phaedra found that endlessly amusing. "Do you think Abigail will be excited?"

He nodded. "She will love you."

Such a wonderful man she found. "You're very brave, you know. I don't know how many men would have retrieved their child as you did. They would just have washed their hands of the infant."

"Can I tell you a secret?" He pulled her close. "It's not very nice."

She pulled away from him to catch his gaze. "Tell me anyway." When he hesitated, she went on, "I know it hurt all those years ago, but it all worked out for the better, didn't it? You have a daughter, no matter how she came to be here. In fact, I'm quite glad for her. If she hadn't been born, you might be married to someone else right now and I wouldn't have you."

He scrunched his brows.

"Does that make *me* a bad person?" Phaedra asked.

"No," he said gruffly. "It makes you lovely." He kissed her jaw. "Perhaps a bit possessive."

She smacked him and laughed. "It does not!"

"No?" He rolled her over and nudged her knees apart, settling between them. "That's a pity. I wouldn't mind being the object of your possessiveness. I think I might even kidnap you away."

"Do not think I'll stand for being locked away in a castle tower in the middle of nowhere."

"What if I'm locked away with you?"

Phaedra gasped when he pulled away the bedding and lowered his head to tease her nipples with the tip of his tongue.

"What are you doing?"

"Worshipping your body. Ruining you for all other men."

Phaedra pinched one of his nipples between her fingers. "I was ruined for all other men the moment you kissed me in your garden."

He flinched away and then nipped at her ear. "Let me ruin you some more."

Phaedra inhaled sharply as his teeth bit down. "We can't."

He licked her neck. "Why not?"

"It's almost dawn."

"And that's a problem?"

She gasped as one of his fingers slipped inside her. A slight sting of pain kindled an ache between the swelling of her flesh. Enough that the splendid sensation of his fingers made her yearn for all the exploding stars in the universe. But . . .

"You wanted to tell me something."

His voice grew hoarse. "I'll tell you later."

"Deerhurst . . ."

"Marcus," he countered. "Say my name." Another finger entered, filling her. Stimulating. "Say my name again and again."

"Marcus . . ."

"Again."

"Marcus . . ."

"Again."

Unreasonable scoundrel. She clamped her legs shut. "Say mine."

His gaze met hers, amusement laced with heat flashed in their depth. "Are you rebelling?"

She clamped down harder. "Say it."

"*Phaedra.*"

The fullness from inside her disappeared. Replaced by a bigger object. Harder.

Heaven Almighty.

"I have to leave before anyone awakes."

He pushed into her. "Leave," he whispered against her collarbone. "I won't stop you."

"Liar."

"Who is lying? I just need to be inside you. *Now.*"

She arched against him, and he cursed. "You're so tight. Tell me if I'm hurting you."

In answer, she gripped into the flesh of his buttocks and jerked him to her until he filled her completely. She made what she wanted clear.

He grunted and started to slowly thrust. Her body acted on instinct, bucking against his movement. Every nerve in her body came alight with his shallow rhythm. She entangled her fingers through his hair, unable to resist the silky strands. She loved his hair messy. She loved that she made it messy.

She sighed as his tongue marked the skin of her ear before trailing down her the side of her neck, her throat, tracing the bone along her collar, and finally closing over her nipple. Sucking. Her body thrummed with touches of pleasure. Desire clawed and gripped at the manhood entering her, each thrust an equal measure of magic and agony.

"Do you know what you do to me?" He said, his pace quickening as his fingers reached to play with the place that produced tons of magical things in her body.

"Yes," she said, barely a whisper, for he was doing the same to her.

Soft sounds of the sun and moon and exploding stars filled the chamber as they made love until they were both crying out each other names and the universe erupted all around them in fireworks.

A new dream was born.

>>><<<

DEERHURST LAY WITH Phaedra tucked into the crook of her arm, listening to the soft breathing patterns of her sleep. He wasn't sure how he was going to let her leave. He liked the feel of her in his bed. He liked it a bloody lot.

He glanced over to the window where light began to pierce the darkness. Some of the servants were already up, but he wasn't worried too much about that. They had an understanding. He would still have to let her go soon. This must have been the best night—morning—of his life, and he'd found something precious in Phaedra, undeniable.

Yet . . .

He still had a crushing secret. Two, in fact.

The identity of Abigail's mother, who he could not hide if he married Phaedra because that woman was mad as hell, and he never knew when she might reappear. He kept tabs on her for Abigail's sake, and he couldn't foresee how she could leave Wales without the duke's permission, which he had on very good authority she would never get. However, a chance always existed, as did the danger of the duke discovering the truth. Deerhurst would never let his wife be caught unprepared. What she would think about him after his past was laid bare . . . Deerhurst couldn't contemplate that now.

And then another, most recent secret. His involvement with the list that had caused a wildfire of wagers.

Confound it.

He hated that he kept secrets from her.

Just a little bit longer.

At least, that was what he told himself every day he did not tell her about the list and the betting book. Plus, another problem that he had to face had occurred recently.

The betting book had been stolen.

Deerhurst might just as well have been living under a rock because he'd only learned about it yesterday. None of his friends had thought to inform him. Though, in all fairness, Deerhurst had been occupied of late.

But the missing book . . .

This was a big bloody problem. The list had left White's. It wasn't as if their names had been signed on it, but Deerhurst couldn't help the unease building inside of him.

It *was* possible the book might have been stolen by a concerned father, a suitor, or even an enraged brother. Who else would benefit from taking the book? In that case, they shouldn't have anything to worry about. Much.

Of course, Saville had come to mind. Lady Selena was his sister, and he'd been a grump ever since Cromby had found the list and made it public to the members of White's. He'd almost pummeled the man into the ground. Avondale had stopped him, but then, the damage had already been done. Deerhurst inwardly rolled his eyes at his friend. If he wanted to be annoyed and throw a fit, he should have done so when he discovered his sister had made Avondale's list.

He dismissed the notion of Saville being the culprit. The man could not keep a secret. Not from his friends, at any rate.

Deerhurst brushed a gentle kiss on Phaedra's temple. It was only a matter of time before she learned of the list's existence. And when she did . . .

No one except Avondale, Warrick, and Saville knew they were responsible for what had transpired with the list. And Deerhurst had heard, quite to his surprise, that Avondale was actually interested in Lady Ophelia—one of the women on the list.

His friends were probably just as rattled at the book's disappearance.

Be that as it may, sooner or later, Deerhurst would have to own up to his part in the bloody chaos. Phaedra didn't trust men who could be linked to a lack of money, and she'd been swarmed by them lately. He may not be a pauper, but Deerhurst's paws were still all over the madness that now reigned because of that damn list.

Would she string him up by his balls if she learned the truth?

Yes. Yes, she would.

His woman was a Sharp. Their passions ran hot, as would their tempers, no doubt. He wanted to secure her to him before he told her the truth. Selfish? Absolutely. But he didn't care. He'd found the woman who was meant for him. She could slice him into pieces all she liked—and he would let her—so long as he didn't lose her. But he had to secure her first.

He nuzzled his face against the top of her head. She stretched out like a cat beside him. Languid. Sated.

Ah, damn it. His cock stirred right along with her. Would he never get enough of her?

"Is it time yet?" she murmured sleepily.

It was well past. "Yes." He placed a soft kiss on her lips. "I shall let you go only if you promise that I will see you tonight."

She sat up. "A thousand ships couldn't keep me away."

He enfolded her in a hug. "We can discuss the details of our courtship then."

She arched a brow. "What details?"

"Aren't you a woman with rules and conditions?"

"Aren't you a man who breaks them all?"

He smiled at her. "That's only because you're irresistible."

She leaned in to kiss his jaw. "I only have one condition."

"Let me hear it."

"You allow me to touch you the way you touch me."

Deerhurst nearly choked. Once again, the woman surprised the hell out of him. She gave as good as she got. It was damn attractive. "Christ Phaedra, don't say things like that unless you want to stay in my bed the whole day."

She grinned. "Do I take that as a yes?"

"You can take that as an absolute must."

She laughed. "Good then." She gave him a thoughtful look. "What about what you wanted to tell me earlier? The thing that isn't so nice. It's about Abigail's mother, isn't it?"

Deerhurst had almost forgotten about that. It had been a spur-of-the-moment urge. One he regretted immediately after.

"I'll tell you later, I'm in no hurry to scare you off." *The God's honest truth.*

She pushed playfully at his chest. "You know you can tell me anything. I'm not the sort to get all tangled about things in the past."

He slowly nodded. "Right. But I'd rather keep you unentangled as long as possible."

"Oh?" she teased. "Weren't you entangled with me most of last night and all of this morning?"

"Little vixen, your tongue is just as smooth as mine."

She laughed, then sobered, a thoughtful look crossing her face. "You can tell me when you're ready."

"I will hold you to these words." Down to the very last letter.

She smiled, her gaze flicking to the crack in the drapes before widening. "It's daylight! Why didn't you wake me sooner?"

He shrugged. "You needed rest. And aren't you good at sneaking in and out of your home?"

She glared at him. "In the darkness, yes." She covered herself with a sheet and darted from the bed. Her gaze tracked the floor. "Where is my chemise?"

"You slipped away during the morning once before if you recall."

She shot him a narrow look. "Do you expect me to climb through one of the windows? What if I'm caught? Besides, if *you* recall, Mary was there that morning to keep watch."

"We'll be careful."

"Oh no, you're not setting foot on our property until proper calling hours."

Deerhurst frowned. "Why not?"

"Do you even need to ask me that? While our courtship has turned real, I'd rather not have the end of my father's pistol rush us toward a wedding or, worse, lose you in a duel with my father."

"I'm an excellent shot."

"So am I."

Got it.

Let Huntly win.

Deerhurst suddenly smirked. Life with Phaedra Sharp would never be boring. He quite looked forward to their future. He trusted that she meant what she said—his past was in his past. And the list . . . well, after they wed, any wagers concerning her would be null and void, and he'd cross that bridge when they got there. In the meantime, he would seduce her over to his side.

"Where did you put my chemise?"

Deerhurst rubbed the back of his neck. "I didn't put it anywhere."

Her eyes widened. "Does this mean . . ."

He stilled.

The study.

There was a knock on the door.

Deerhurst almost laughed as Phaedra launched for the bed and dove beneath the blanket that still covered him.

"Sir?"

"What is it?" Deerhurst called, though he already had a hunch.

"Sorry to disturb your rest, my lord. I have some items that you might require," a clear of the throat, "later."

Of course.

He rose from the bed and strode naked to the door, opening the door just an inch. The footman handed him the discarded clothes before scurrying off with an expressionless face.

When the door shut, Phaedra ripped the covers off her head. "I am ruined!"

"Yes," he grinned, then outright laughed. "Yes, you are."

So am I.

Chapter Seventeen

PHAEDRA STARED AT the betting book of White's with a mixture of numbness and fury.

A few hours ago, still in the lovely aftermath of Deerhurst's lovemaking, she'd received an invitation to join Lady Ophelia Thornton for tea.

Phaedra had been surprised. After all, she couldn't claim any friendship with the woman. But she'd also been curious. Why would Lady Ophelia invite her for tea? A hunch suddenly formed. Lady Ophelia was also an heiress. Rumors. Wagers. Cromby. She hadn't forgotten that man and his greasy manners.

Her curiosity exploded and quickly transformed into full-blown impatience to get to that tea party.

If only she'd known . . .

The invitation really ought to have come with a warning.

Danger: Hearts may break.

For hers was breaking as sure as the sky was blue.

The reason for the tea? Lady Ophelia handed her guests the betting book, which she had stolen from the men's establishment. An impressive deed. But what Lady Ophelia had been after was not the wagers, but the content of the list, which she had heard was quite expressive.

No wonder Phaedra's father didn't want her to attend events. It had been much worse than they'd let on. The comments beside their names were not only unforgivable but downright humiliating.

"We need to show those bastards we are not to be ridiculed or taken for granted. We must stand together from this day," Lady Selena said.

Lady Selena was sister to the Earl of Saville, one of the men responsible for the wagers, along with the Earl of Warrick, the Earl of Avondale—whose mother apparently drew up the list—and lastly, the Earl of Deerhurst. Phaedra found it rather remarkable how connected Lady Ophelia was to have discovered all this information so neatly, but a part of her wished she hadn't. Phaedra didn't want to learn this about Deerhurst.

Her Deerhurst.

The very man in whose arms she had woken up to this very morning. Who kissed her, teased her, and lied to her face. She had asked him if he was aware of the wagers.

What had they—he—commented about her on that list?

Laughter to scare an alley cat to death.

A bunch of bastard earls, they were. Unoriginal rat bastards. Her years of reading came in handy for curse words for the rage and betrayal she felt but didn't know what to do with yet.

For now she could only curse.

Curse Deerhurst to hell.

How many times had she laughed in Deerhurst's presence? Did Deerhurst truly believe her laughter was that terrible? She thought of all the times they laughed together, and she winced. He probably did.

She'd believed him a knight, a protector of women. He certainly hadn't protected them from this list. Deerhurst was a protector, but not of women. Children, yes, but not women. Which begged the question, how could he think this was all right to do?

He had a daughter.

He ought to have known better. Or was this his way to get back at the opposite sex for disappointing him?

And Saville? That bastard helped save her and Deerhurst in the park. Lady Selena was his *sister*.

How utterly wicked.

What exactly did they—Deerhurst—gain from this? She thought of when he had appeared in her life. The night he'd kissed her. Had he known about all this then? The list? The wagers? Had that been the start?

Their drawing room was filled with rogues the very next day. And, of course, hadn't he shown up at her window to rescue her? No matter how she mulled it in her mind, she couldn't find any good excuse for the earl.

Phaedra wanted to puke.

Had he *protected* her so that she could let her guard down and then swoop in to steal her hand in marriage and claim her dowry along with the prize money for every wager about her in this book?

Had she been such a fool?

No.

No. No. No.

She refused to believe that.

She *couldn't* believe that. However, the evidence pointed to the opposite. Luckily, they weren't married. Now they never would be. Deerhurst was dead to her. Or he would be after she found him to demand answers. She would have an explanation from him, or she would have his head.

His choice.

She just hadn't figured out how to confront him yet. The very thought caused her belly to clench painfully.

Cats. Cats were much more reliable than men.

"You are right. Something more must be done," Lady Louisa said.

Phaedra furrowed her brows. The question was what? They were women *and* unmarried. They held no clout in society. Who would take them seriously? All they had going for them, according to the list, was their dowries.

Not to mention she was having trouble keeping her emotions at bay. One moment she wanted to burst into tears, the next she wanted to punch the wall. But she did not want to lose face before these women. All so strong. All so determined. She certainly hadn't told them she had spent the night before in the bed of one of the bastard earls . . . that she had fallen hopelessly in love with him.

Lord, it hurt.

"So what are we to do?" Lady Harriet asked.

Phaedra shot to her feet as fury renewed in her breast. By Jove, they were *not* helpless. She refused to accept they were. "We rise up," Phaedra said. Lord knew how. They just couldn't sit back and do nothing.

Lady Ophelia grinned, then moved to fill their glasses with wine. Before she could respond, a footman cleared his throat. "My lady, your mother wishes a quick word."

Ophelia nodded. "If you ladies will excuse me, I shall be right back."

Everyone nodded.

When their hostess had disappeared through the door, Lady Theodosia spoke up. "Well, I think Phaedra has a good idea. So how do we rise up?"

Lady Phaedra drew in a deep breath as she stared at the ladies in the room. She'd met each one of them, but they hadn't conversed much before today. And the matter of the betting book was still a topic that stung. She stared at Theodosia, unable to answer. She knew what she wanted to do with the betting book—stomp it into dust. But that was out of the question. They needed to act strategically, not emotionally.

Easier said than done.

Louisa puckered her brows. "It could be a while before Ophelia returns, let's form a plan in the meantime. Since the book has been stolen, we must decide carefully how to proceed."

"We ought to make copies of it and rub it in their noses," Selena muttered.

"What good would that do?" Harriet murmured. "Except announce that we are in possession of the book."

"We should not announce it to *them*," Selena said, "We should announce it to the women on the list."

Phaedra's heartbeat slowly calmed, and a touch of amusement broke past the haze. "That's an excellent idea."

All eyes whipped to her.

"I'm teasing," Lady Selena said uncertainly. "That would be a terrible idea. Not to mention that it would humiliate the men who have reduced us to breeding stock. Humiliated men lash out."

Phaedra shook her head. "More reason to do it." More reason to teach these bastard earls a lesson.

"I agree," Theodosia King said with a nod. "And men have been reducing us to breeding stock for hundreds of years. I daresay that will never change. But with this mockery they have gone too far."

Way too far.

"We shouldn't be humiliated," Louisa said. "We have done nothing wrong. No, we should court outrage with the rest of the female populace. Selena, your insight might just be a stroke of brilliance."

"And it's not just us," Phaedra said. Their attention once again fixed on her. "Men have been reducing *all* women to breeding stock for centuries. This isn't just about our outrage. We're just the heiresses someone chose as potential brides. What about the heiresses who weren't chosen? What about the other women in this book who remain blissfully unaware of this knavish practice of betting books? Like horses with blinders, the men keep us on track by keeping our focus onward."

"What are you saying, Phaedra?" Theodosia asked slowly.

"I'm saying we should lift the blinders."

"Splendid idea," Selena said. "How do we do that?"

"We make copies of the book," Louisa said. "Distribute it amongst the *ton*."

"Where's the drama?" Theodosia teased.

"Well, I might have a plan about that," Harriet said. "But I cannot be part of it. Leeds keeps watch over me like a hawk. I wouldn't be able to escape him." And then Harriet proceeded to inform them of her idea.

"Excellent!"

"I love it."

"It will cause quite a stir."

"Which is exactly what we want," Phaedra said. "Let's do it. But let us keep the plan between us."

"What about Ophelia?" Harriet asked.

"She did steal the book," Louisa said.

"She also handed it over to us," Phaedra reminded. "She did that for a reason. I suspect she wants nothing more to do with it."

"Then it's settled," Theodosia declared. "At the Stewart Ball, three days from now."

Phaedra nodded and stood. They had much to plan and think about, but she had one last thing she had to do that had nothing to do with these women.

She had to find Deerhurst.

She wanted to look him in the eyes when she confronted him, and she was pretty sure she was about to become one of the criminals in the books she loved to read—she was about to lay waste to a handsome, mischievous, scoundrel.

⤜⟫⟩⟨⟨⤛

DEERHURST STARED AT Warrick in horror. "*Lady Ophelia* stole the betting book?"

Warrick sat back and crossed his legs. "Afraid so."

"How the devil did she manage that?"

"Snuck into White's dressed as a man and walked the book right out."

Bloody hell. This was a disaster.

And it changed everything.

He could no longer keep the truth from Phaedra. She was bound to find out now that the book was in the hands of one of the heiresses. Lord, he could imagine it now. The group of females gathering with pitchforks and fires out for their blood.

Panic rose, and Deerhurst fought—and lost—the battle to calm his heart.

Everything will be fine.

Will it? Deerhurst had his doubts, but he couldn't waver in his confidence now, so he dug his boots into the ground. He still had time. No good would come by rushing to the Sharp residence with a half-cocked explanation.

"How does Avondale feel about all this?"

Warrick shrugged. "Since he is the one who helped her walk out with the book, I'd wager he's chosen his heiress."

"Avondale helped? Is he bloody crazy?" For the first time in his life, he had no words for his friend. Did Avondale understand the consequences of what they'd done?

Of course, he did.

The man wasn't a fool. No wait, he bloody well was a fool. Men turned into fools for the women they wanted. Just look at *him*. He'd turned into a fool the moment he'd set eyes on Phaedra, so he couldn't completely blame Avondale. However, he only hoped his friend had considered the impact because he'd just made things a whole lot more difficult for Deerhurst.

Warrick dragged a hand through his hair. "I'm telling you because it's only a matter of time before she tells the other women on the list."

He'd gathered as much.

"How is Lady Selena fairing?" Deerhurst asked to change the topic. He needed to think about how to redeem himself to Phaedra but not with Warrick present. "You've been keeping an eye on her?"

Warrick sighed. "Only because the chit does everything Saville tells her not to do. She doesn't suspect me of keeping account of her whereabouts. She's going to kill Saville when she finds out. Why did he have to appoint me to be her bloody babysitter?"

Because you lost the damn list. "How is Avondale's search for his family treasure coming?"

"Dunno, haven't heard anything yet. Where is that little puppet of mine?"

"Stop calling my daughter a puppet. It's poppet. And she is shopping for ribbons."

"You haven't sent her back?"

Deerhurst shook his head. Abigail didn't want to go back yet, and he didn't have the heart to send her. He would in the next few days. Perhaps tomorrow. Soon, all eyes would turn to him and Phaedra, and it would be wise to keep his daughter out of the spotlight until she was older, and he could introduce her to society as his distant niece.

"I heard Saville say you and Lady Phaedra have formed an attachment. Good match. Does she know about our little puppet?"

"Poppet, and yes, Phaedra knows."

"The woman is a saint."

A beautiful, delicious one. He couldn't wait to see her again. He'd make love to her until she was breathless with pleasure, and then he'd tell her about the list. And then he'd make love to her again.

Yes, yes. The perfect plan.

The only one he had.

"I'm happy for you."

Don't be happy yet.

A racket outside Deerhurst's study drew both the men's gazes to the door, which slammed open.

"My lady, you can't—"

"Deerhurst, you bastard!" Lady Phaedra exclaimed, cutting off the butler's protest. The blood in his veins froze. So did Phaedra when she spotted Warrick.

"Well, well, if it isn't a gathering with *two* of the bastard earls. Where are Saville and Avondale? They should be here for the whipping you're about to receive."

Warrick's horror-filled gaze shot to Deerhurst. He ignored his friend, eyes only on Phaedra as he slowly rose from his chair.

"I can explain."

"So it's true then. The list. The book. You."

Deerhurst clenched his fists. "It's not what you think."

"Not what I think? You can't begin to fathom what's running through my mind. Laughter to scare an alley cat to death? I suppose I should be grateful that is the only flaw you could come up with. But you know what? When you think about it, *that* was the flaw you could come up with? My laughter? How simpleminded, *narrow*, and silly are four grown men. Truly, it boggles my mind."

Deerhurst winced.

"We only meant to cheer Avondale up," Warrick defended. Of course, it was the wrong thing to say. "His mother drafted the list."

Deerhurst cursed.

Her gaze settled on Warrick. "Oh? Then you find it entertaining to list out our incredible flaws? Did you have a good laugh at them?"

"I—"

"A woman has been married off because of your entertainment! Did you know that?"

"I heard Lady Harriet married Leeds," Deerhurst said.

"Yes." Her eyes met his. "All for a little jest. Were you just going to keep me in the dark forever?"

"No," Deerhurst said firmly. "I always meant to tell you."

"When?" she pressed. "After we married?"

Deerhurst grimaced as a vein nearly exploded in the delicate arch of her neck.

"You'd have been freed from the wagers then."

"Bloody hell, man," Warrick muttered under his breath, loud enough for Deerhurst to hear.

"But not from the comment you made. Not from everyone forever listening to and weighing my laughter against an alley cat. Do you even know how an alley cat sounds?"

Deerhurst thought it best not to answer that.

"I thought not." She laughed then, not a sound he'd ever heard before. Not the carefree melody he'd become so familiar with—that he adored. This laugh was a mirthless thing that chilled his heart. "Well, congratulations, Deerhurst, you succeeded where every man before you failed. You tricked me into believing you were someone you're not."

"I'm not like those men, Phaedra."

She nodded. "You're right. You are much worse."

Panic rose. He couldn't lose her. Not like this. "I didn't make the comment about you. I enjoy your laughter."

"Did you speak up against what was said?"

No, he hadn't.

Warrick rose to his feet. "I'll leave you two to work through your, er, discussion. I have business I must see to myself."

Neither spoke as Warrick all but fled the room. Deerhurst came around the desk to stand before Phaedra. She had every right to be angry. He was in the wrong. He'd been selfish since the night they'd met. He'd only wanted to keep her close, no matter what.

"Phaedra, that list was a damn mistake. I didn't laugh, I didn't find it tasteful either."

She gave him an astonished look. "And yet you did nothing to stop it."

"Because *you* were on the list."

"Why thank you," she snapped. "I feel so honored."

Deerhurst inhaled deeply. He couldn't afford to lose his cool. "It was after our first kiss," he explained. "When Avondale showed us the list, I was aghast to find you were on it. I couldn't explain the why of it then, but I was afraid Avondale would choose you. So, I stayed quiet and let the shenanigans play out. I don't even know what was said about the other women on the list. I was too concerned with thoughts of you."

"That doesn't make what you did after right. You lied to me."

"I know now," Deerhurst said softly. "I didn't think the list would ever get out. Warrick misplaced it by accident."

She was silent for a moment. "Do you agree with my supposed flaw?"

"No! Dammit, I love your laughter. I've never thought your laughter to be anything but musical."

"And yet you allowed them to write those things because you what? Kissed me and didn't want your friend to *court* me? Do you know how absurd that sounds?"

Maybe. Yes. No. He didn't know. All he knew was that he loved this woman to distraction.

"We're done, Deerhurst. Done. Do not court me. Do not call on me. Just stay on your side of the fence, and I shall stay on mine."

That snapped him out of his thoughts.

"No." He dragged both hands through his hair. "We're not done, Phaedra. I made a mistake. We move past it. That's how relationships work."

"I cannot move past this."

Deerhurst clenched his jaw. "Because I sat by while they made a list?"

"Because you betrayed me. I asked you about the wagers and you acted like you weren't aware of anything. You pretended to be a hero when you were the villain all along."

He couldn't deny that. Deerhurst had always known he was a beast. Selfish in ways he couldn't explain. And when he first glimpsed himself as a knight in her eyes, that selfishness hadn't gone away. It had only expanded, demanding to occupy all of her, keep her by his side.

"I didn't want you to believe me to be a scoundrel, Phaedra. The moment I found out the list had been lost and then resurfaced in the book, I decided to protect you."

She nodded. "Protect me from the very wolves you set on my trail, right?"

"Yes."

She retreated two steps.

He stiffened. "Phaedra . . ."

"Did you ever, at any time, have any other motive to approach me other than being my so-called protector."

He shook his head. "No."

"All this time, all the moments we spent together—it was all just because of that list."

"At first—"

"Stop," she interrupted him. "I don't want to hear it."

"Love—"

"No! You made a fool of me, Deerhurst. Nothing you say can convince me that you meant a word you said in our time together. I don't trust you."

"You can still trust me."

She shook her head furiously. "Don't ever approach me again."

Panic had him launching forward. With a yelp, she pulled a pistol from her skirts and pointed it straight at him.

Deerhurst's blood ran cold.

He held his palms out in surrender. "What are you doing, love?"

"Consider this a warning, Deerhurst. Stay away from me or I will shoot you."

She backed out of his study, and Deerhurst let her. In her frame of mind, she might just put a hole through him.

Confess.

Tell her you love her.

But it was too late. The moment he opened his mouth to say the words, she was gone. He let them brush the air, a soft whisper in an empty void, and inside, Deerhurst's world crumbled.

Chapter Eighteen

The Stewart Ball

LADY PHAEDRA WAS about to cross a line she could never step back from. And she was not the only one. Theodosia, Selena, and Louisa stood beside her at the top of the stars that looked down at the ballroom, their backs straight and chins lifted high. They'd timed their arrival perfectly.

The ball was in full swing.

No regrets.

At least, that was what Phaedra repeated to her herself over and over again. It occurred to her that in every woman's life, at some point in time, there came a moment of truth. The moment a woman must decide what sort of woman she wanted to be—in her case, either a woman who played by society's rules or a woman who flaunted them. A woman who would sit back when wronged or one who would rise and meet the challenge head-on. This moment was rarely ever a grand event and often entirely missed. It was also a moment often decided for them by society's rules or their guardian's judgments.

But for a rare few, depending on their path, a third branch at the crossroads sometimes presented itself. For Phaedra that turning point came the second she stepped into Lady Ophelia Thornton's drawing room and received news that pulled her world right from beneath her feet.

These men had made a mockery of her. Of all of them.

So fine, Phaedra might have a boisterous laugh. Was that so bad? She had half a mind to go in search of an alley cat and compare their vocal cords. Which only infuriated her more. Because why should she compare herself to an alley cat? Why should she even *care* what a few dastardly lords thought of her?

Her opinion of them wasn't so favorable either.

But Phaedra understood why she cared.

Him.

Deerhurst.

The scoundrel earl next door. She hadn't seen him since that day when she'd confronted him. He hadn't made any attempt to call on her either.

And she missed him.

She hadn't had a good night's rest since then. Thoughts of Marcus consumed her. And when she did fall asleep, dreams of them together tortured her.

She even debated whether she had overreacted or not. Had she been too harsh cutting him off over this? But she hadn't wanted to sink into that line of reasoning. *Couldn't.* Resistance would instantly rise at the mere thought.

So, Phaedra directed all her focus on getting through tonight.

A hush fell over the room as the crowd started to notice them and, in its wake, the hushed titters of guests who instinctively knew a scandal was on the rise.

Why?

Because all four women were dressed in the crisp clothes of a gentleman about town—boots, breeches, white shirt, waistcoat, cravat, top hat, and even a cane. They were aiming for full impact, to cause such a scene the like of which London had never witnessed.

Her heart pounded in her ears as Phaedra's gaze fell on the very men who had made a mockery of them as she pulled a stack of papers from the pocket in her jacket. She clamped down the anger that threatened to swell in her chest.

Tonight, they would have their revenge.

She flicked her wrist.

Satisfaction made its way down her spine as hundreds of copies of pages from the betting book of White's danced above the sea of astonished faces gazing up at them. Their intentions, however, were as clear as the crystal glasses the partygoers sipped champagne from.

They were done.

Done being made fools of. Done acting the biddable and dutiful creatures to the very men who made a mockery of them. Done allowing men to get away with their actions.

The time for accountability had arrived.

Phaedra gripped the cane in her hand when she spotted her parents in the crowd. Her father's face was devoid of any expression, but her mother wore a look of shock. Of all the things Phaedra had done in her life, this was the most extreme. Because it was public. She could not escape the consequences. Consequences Phaedra, and the other heiresses, were fully prepared to face.

This was the only uncomfortable part of their entire plan. They not only went up against the men of society and their flaws, but they revolted against their parents as well. But Phaedra hoped that the women at the ball would join their outrage and rebel against the atrocious behavior of the men behind the wagers.

It was their hope to start a movement.

The ton, however, had always been terribly fickle. One never knew if the wind would blow east or west and whether it would be warm or freezing. They figured they had about a fifty percent chance of the ladies joining their cause for accountability.

The men of White's wanted to arrogantly note down horrid wagers; well, let the rest of the world see, then. They imagined themselves entertaining and clever; let others be the judge of that.

They thought to mock the women; well, let them be the subject of ridicule for once.

Yet no amount of imagination could have prepared them for the riot that would soon follow.

Phaedra's gaze was pulled in by a dark set of eyes.

Deerhurst.

Her heart sped up, but she averted her gaze. That one look had been all it took for her to glimpse the lines of horror wrinkled at the corners of his eyes. She'd also caught a glimpse of Saville, Avondale, and Warrick, who appeared just as appalled.

Good.

Let them be shocked right out of their polished black boots. They hadn't foreseen this, perhaps not even in their wildest dreams. Well, Phaedra thought with a satisfied smirk, it was about to get wilder. Their copies weren't just being distributed here but to every home in London, the theatres, Almack's, and even Vauxhall gardens. By tomorrow, the streets of London would be littered with them.

By the end of the week, Phaedra had no doubt word would have spread throughout Britain, making every member of White's either a laughingstock or the subject of some womanly ire.

Below them, curious people snatched up copies of the paper and were studying them with interest. Nash was the first to pull her aside. Phaedra wouldn't have much time before her parents dragged her from the ball.

"This was your grand plan?" Nash asked with a frown. "When Ophelia stole the betting book from White's, we never expected this would be the outcome."

"What did you expect?" Phaedra countered.

"Well for one, not for you to publicly announce that you all are in possession of stolen property."

Oh, that.

"No one can prove anything."

"You also didn't have to show your faces. Lord, Phaedra, could you not have paid actors to do this?"

"No, because we aren't that cowardly, Nash. We don't hide in clubs with betting books. We are better than that." She poked his chest. "And you, did you know about the list? About Deerhurst?"

His face flushed, and no more needed to be said. "It wasn't for me to reveal this truth."

Phaedra averted her gaze.

He lowered his voice. "I didn't know about the list the last time we spoke. And I only recently discovered who was behind it. If I had known about Deerhurst, I would have told you, but Phaedra, Cromby is responsible for the list hitting the book."

She shuddered at that name. "I know."

"What about Deerhurst? He's been courting you."

"Not anymore."

He instantly seemed to understand. "You're not willing to forgive him?"

She snorted, stomping her cane into the ground. "He lied to me." She suddenly had a need to confess, and softly admitted. "We've kissed."

She had kissed the biggest wolf in town. She had done much more but would never admit that. In fact, at this very moment, all she wanted to do was forget.

Nash's brows lifted, and Phaedra couldn't tell whether it was in shock or intrigue. Perhaps both.

"And?" Nash prompted. "Do the others know you have cavorted with the enemy?"

"Enemy is a bit strong is it not?" Deerhurst wasn't her enemy. Just a wolf. A scoundrel. The real enemy was that book full of wagers and the hands that wrote them.

"How about the kiss?" This time the delight was clear in his tone. "Did you enjoy it?"

She shrugged to hide the flush of emotion that rushed to her heart.

"The kiss was passable."

"Only passable?"

Phaedra froze. That hadn't been Nash's voice. She whirled to find Deerhurst behind her, peering at her with an unfathomable expression. "And here I thought you shifted the world beneath my feet."

Nash made a gurgling sound in the back of his throat. "Am I in the presence of true love happening right before my eyes?"

Phaedra imparted a glare to Nash. "This is not true love happening." To Deerhurst she directed, "The world did not shift for either of us."

He crossed his arms over his chest and looked down at her, his lips slightly pursed. "I've never known you to be a woman of denial or pretense."

Her heart seized.

She couldn't believe *he*, of all people, would accuse her of such things. What made it worse was that he wasn't wrong. But Phaedra didn't take issue with what he was accusing her of being but rather the gall he had to accuse her at all.

She wanted to whack him with her cane. He'd fooled her, seduced her, and broken her trust. Which was much worse than breaking her heart.

Even Nash shook his head in that way that said, *Man, you must have lost all your marbles.*

"If you'll excuse me." She couldn't stand to be in the traitor's presence. She turned to leave.

"Wait," Deerhurst said, moving to block her away. "A moment, please, Phaedra."

"No," she said. "You get nothing from me ever again."

He caught her wrist.

"Deerhurst," she hissed when he pulled her from the room. She glanced around frantically, but no one seemed to take any note of them, too immersed in the pages scattered all over the ballroom. All around her, she could hear the soft curses of men and the intake of breaths as ladies read the contents of the copies they made.

Phaedra twisted her hand to escape Deerhurst's grip, but he merely stooped to pick her up and set her over his shoulder.

The nerve!

"Let me go, you barbarian! Scoundrel! Oaf!"

Why did she not think to bring her pistol?

⟫⟫⟫⟪⟪⟪

DEERHURST HAD MADE many questionable choices in his life. But never had he regretted any of them the way he regretted not telling Phaedra the truth from the start. Her cold indifference chipped away at the calm he'd forcibly instilled in himself these past few days. He'd wanted to give her space, time to get over the worst of her outrage.

Perhaps that hadn't been such a good idea. Deerhurst couldn't help but wonder if he had pressed, if he had crawled on his knees before her, if she would have made a different decision. Because tonight, he had watched as the consequences of his mistake caused what could only be described as the biggest scandal the *ton* had ever seen.

He didn't know whether she could recover from this. No, there was no need to wonder. She couldn't. None of those women could. And perhaps that had been their point. They had already been laughed at and wagered upon. Why not expose the very men who had hurt them?

But then, they hadn't exposed him, Avondale, Warrick, or Saville. The true beasts behind it all.

Deerhurst entered the Stewart library, shut the door, and twisted the lock in place. He strode to the center of the room, a good few feet away from her only route of escape, and only then lowered her to her feet.

205

She whirled on him, her face flushed with anger. He wanted nothing more than to pull her into his arms and kiss away the harsh lines that creased her eyes as she glared at him. He refrained from the impulse, but only because he wasn't sure she wasn't carrying some sort of weaponry on her. God's breath, the way those breeches hugged her curves, Deerhurst was surprised he hadn't fallen to his knees when he first saw her on the stairwell dressed in such a provocative outfit.

Of all the outfits they could have chosen—what the devil were they thinking dressing like this? How many men must have ogled her? A spark of annoyance filled his heart. Not just because of jealousy, but because he had no right to be jealous.

"What's the meaning of this, Deerhurst? I told you I never wanted to speak to you again! The least you could do is respect my wishes as you certainly cannot respect anything else!"

"I'll respect any of your wishes after you hear what I have to say."

"And what is that?"

Deerhurst clenched his fists. He should have prepared a proper speech, but he had never been good with flowery words. He'd thought he was doing the right thing by giving her space, yet it turned out just to be yet another one of his many mistakes. He shouldn't have let her storm out of his study that day. He should have told her clearly . . . he should have told her sooner . . .

"I love you."

Her eyes widened. "I beg your pardon?"

"I love you."

"No, you don't."

"Yes, I do. I should have confessed to you the night we spent together." He dragged a hand through his hair. "I should never have let you leave my house without telling you that I love you."

"But not that you lied? What kind of love is that, Deerhurst? I fell for your lies once. I won't fall for them again."

"I never lied to you, Phaedra."

She snorted. "There are many forms of lies, Deerhurst. Skirting around the truth is one of them, keeping the truth from me is another."

Deerhurst bit back a curse. "After all we've been through, you find me to be that unforgivable?"

"You made a fool of me."

"Is this what it's about? Pride? Then you don't feel any affection for me at all?"

"What I feel for you is irrelevant."

"How the bloody hell is it irrelevant?" Deerhurst wanted to punch his fist into a wall. How could one woman be so stubborn? He rubbed his temples. "Distributing copies of the book doesn't just get back at the men who issued those wagers. It will also rile up the women."

She pursed her lips. "That is the point."

"But what about after the point? What happens when the men tire of the women's rebuke? Or haven't you thought that far?"

"It doesn't matter what happens in the future. What matters is that women are made *aware* and that the men in all the clubs understand there are consequences for their behavior as well."

"And what about the consequences of tonight?"

"I am prepared to accept them." Her gaze met his. "Why are men the only ones who can play dirty? Why should we simply accept injustice just because we are told we are the lesser sex?"

"I don't believe you are the lesser sex, love," Deerhurst said in a low voice. If he could go back in time and rip up that list, he would. "I believe you are the strongest."

She shook her head furiously. "You are merely saying that out of guilt."

He took a step closer to her. "Guilt? Yes, I feel guilt, love. I also feel regret. And pain. I broke something beautiful. Still, I'm a beast enough to ask for forgiveness. A second chance."

She retreated a step, pointing her cane at him to keep the distance.

"Stop."

He didn't. Couldn't. "You're the bravest person I know, Phaedra, and at times I can't keep my footing for what I feel for you. I can't quite catch my breath—it belongs to you."

He grabbed the cane and pulled her toward him. She gasped as he held her in his arms. He needed to get through to her. Needed her to believe him. "I love you. There will never be another woman for me but you. You must know that."

She shook her head, wiggling out of his arms. He let her go. "I know you lied to me. I know you betrayed me. I know I shall never forgive you for that."

"What about the night we spent together? Do you believe I faked that? Did you think it a lie every time I kissed you? Every time I was inside you?"

She looked away, her face losing some of its color. "Don't say such things."

Deerhurst tried again. "Can you honestly say you have no feelings for me whatsoever?"

The look of hurt she shot him iced the blood in his veins. She truly wouldn't forgive him. Her next words confirmed it.

"I would rather live the rest of my life as a pariah than share even one more minute with a man as deceitful as you."

Christ, his chest hurt. Actually *hurt*. As if it was more than a mere organ beating in his body. Deerhurst backed away a step. If he didn't, he was afraid he'd kidnap her away in a desperate attempt to persuade her of his heart.

"You could be carrying my child."

Her gasp told him she hadn't thought about that. Hell, he hadn't thought about it until this very moment. He decided to be as blunt as possible, "I will not allow another child of mine to be born out of wedlock," Deerhurst warned, deadly serious. He'd rather slit his wrists.

"*If* I am with child, I shall consider marriage. If I am not, I will not suffer your presence again," she returned just as bluntly. Hell hath no fury as a Sharp woman scorned.

Deerhurst wanted to shake some sense into her.

So, he was present when his friends discussed the list. So, he had made a comment or two. So, he hadn't stopped them. But what about what he *had* done, how he had tried to protect her? Did that count for nothing?

"You would condemn us both to misery because of pride and stubbornness."

She pointed that damn cane at him again. "If you are miserable, it's because of your own doing, Deerhurst. I told you my dreams, my fears. You understood how I felt about deception. How do I know this wasn't an elaborate plan on your part all along?"

And there it was—the crux.

She didn't trust him.

"Shall I send my man of affairs over with my account books? You already have the betting book. I made no wagers," Deerhurst bit out. He didn't mean to be rude, but the growing distress swirled in his gut.

"It won't change anything."

Deerhurst grabbed the palm of her hand and covered it over his heart. "Do you feel that? That's my heartbeat. It belongs to you. Every single beat. Do you get it now? The very heart of me, the essence of my soul, it's yours."

She hesitated, then said, "I never asked for this."

He dragged a hand over his face before his gaze met hers. "You are not your aunt, Phaedra. And until you realize this, you will never be free of your fears."

Her gaze narrowed, in their depth a thousand daggers. "My aunt has nothing to do with this!"

"She has everything to do with this," he countered, feeling as though he had nothing left to lose. Why not just get everything off his chest? "And despite what may have happened in her marriage, she seems as though she is enjoying her life still, as we have both witnessed." Her intake of breath riled him even more. "Are you shocked I brought it up, or that I am right?" Deerhurst asked.

She gave him nothing.

That list would forever be the bane of his existence. "Casting me aside is one thing, love, but do not lie to yourself that you're doing it over that damn list. You've got something real in front of you, yet you refuse to reach out and seize it because you're scared."

She shook her head.

Deerhurst had had enough. He grabbed the cane and tossed it aside before sealing her lips in a demanding, torturous kiss. She didn't push him away. Perhaps she was too shocked. He wanted this woman to distraction, but he wanted everything else too. Her heart. Her trust. Her forgiveness.

He tore away from her in bitterness. Bitterness at himself. At her. His friends. The entire bloody situation.

"I love you Phaedra, but I'm not going to beg you to be with me."

With that, he turned on his heel and strode from the room.

Chapter Nineteen

"**Y**OU ARE RUINED!"

Phaedra flinched as her father's voice echoed off the walls of the parlor and carried through the halls of their home. She had never heard him raise his voice to this degree. Not surprising, considering that she *was* ruined, yes. In more ways than her father could ever imagine.

But not because of tonight. One might say she'd been ruined the first night Deerhurst kissed her in the garden, or certainly by the night they'd spent together. But since no one knew about any of those things, they did not count. At least, not where society was concerned.

She was ruined in other ways too. Her heart for one. Her heart was utterly and unequivocally ruined.

I love you, Phaedra.

She had wanted to believe him so badly, but how could she ever trust him after he'd kept the truth from her? He had betrayed her, lied to her, and kept secrets from her. He'd been one of the reasons men wanted to trap her into marriage. No rational woman could forgive such betrayal, right?

Which was another thing that was ruined: her trust.

"You are ruined," her father exploded again.

Phaedra grimaced. She was starting to hate that word. Ruined, yes, and with her actions, she had placed them all in a terrible position as well. Scandals were like that. They never just touched the person embroiled in it, but the entire family crest as well. It was almost as if it were a living, breathing creature. One that had tentacles that reached far and wide.

Phaedra sighed. This was as angry as she'd ever witnessed her father. They'd caused a scandal, yes, but she doubted after the ladies of society read some of those wagers, they would condemn Phaedra for what she and her friends had done. Those women ought to be outraged, as they had been. But Phaedra could not forget this world belonged to men, and men had a long history of keeping women in their place.

One of those men was her father.

Phaedra lifted her chin. "I merely took a stand."

"A stand!" A vein popped in her father's neck, and he just about turned purple in the face. "This is what you call a stand?" He motioned at her clothing. "You started a mutiny!"

Phaedra's temper flared. "Well, good! If that is what it takes to teach those rogues a lesson, I am glad!"

"Who do you think will be taught a lesson when all is said and done?" Her father bellowed.

"Robert, that's enough," Phaedra's mother attempted to intervene in the face-off between father and daughter. "We are all civilized beings, let's talk about this calmly."

"Calmly?" the earl asked incredulously. "Your daughter is wearing breeches and you want to talk calmly? Do you have any idea the consequences of what she has done?"

Her mother nodded. "More women will be wearing breeches from this night on, dear husband."

"This is no laughing matter, Eleanor. This is serious."

"I daresay that no one is laughing at what transpired this evening," her mother, answered. "At least not at her."

"Not now," her father said. "But when the dust settles, where do you think society will cast their eyes? If all this goes wrong, Phaedra and her friends will be blamed."

Of course, her father was worried about that, and not how she felt about being the object of countless wagers. She didn't blame him. This was the way of the world, which was why they had sought to push against it in the corridors of power. Winning or losing didn't matter. Awareness had been their goal.

But she had thought it would feel more satisfying.

Phaedra rubbed the bridge of her nose.

She was tired, both from this evening's excitement and the emotional turmoil she faced in the library with Deerhurst. Before that train of thought could run out of control, her father's next question made her back snap up straight.

"How the hell did you get your hands on those pages?"

He meant the copies of the book they'd gleefully fed to the unsuspecting crowd at the ball that night. That it did not occur to her father that they had copies made from the book itself spoke volumes of the deep arrogance that made up the character of men.

Phaedra lifted her chin. "They fell into my lap."

"Don't be tart," her father said. "Besides the scandal of your unruly behavior tonight, the betting book was stolen from White's—a criminal offense. Then copies of the pages are found in you and your friends' hands. I am surprised Bow Street has not knocked on our door yet."

Bow Street? Phaedra almost snorted.

"I didn't steal the book."

"But someone did. Who gave you those copies?"

Phaedra held her own. "As I said, we happened upon them."

"Phaedra," her father said, his face red with fury and frustration. "This is bloody serious."

"Phaedra, dear, your father is right."

Phaedra furrowed her brows. This was not the time for her mother to side with her father. "I am aware of that, but as I have said, the pages happened upon us."

"How did they happen upon you?" her father asked. "In *Bond Street*? By pigeon carrier?"

"Should we not leave the cross examination for Bow Street?"

Her father gave her an exasperated look. If Phaedra hadn't been so exhausted, she'd have laughed.

"Shall I call Bow Street over myself to get to the bottom of this?"

"That's enough, Robert." Her mother's voice turned whip sharp. "Leave our daughter be. You men have done enough."

Finally.

Phaedra watched her father sputter for an answer, then settle for, "*You men?*"

"Our daughter has been the subject of ill-conceived wagers and I'm horrified you allowed that to happen. When you told me about the wagers you said nothing about a list of heiresses being the subject of mockery."

"I had nothing to do with the list or wagers," her father protested.

"Neither did you do anything about them," her mother countered and lifted a copy of a page in the air. "Neither did you inform me Phaedra's name had been part of this horrid list. Why, I'm shocked *you* didn't steal that book and burn it to ash."

Phaedra rather agreed.

"And before you say it's club affairs," her mother went on. "Let me remind you that there is nothing I won't do for my daughter, and if you continue to badger her, I will walk out of this house with her if that is what it takes to make you see reason."

The earl paled. "You will do no such thing!"

Phaedra paled too. The last thing she wanted was for her parents to separate because of her.

"Then do not test me, Robert."

"What did you want me to do, Eleanor?" Her father said. "Rip the book to shreds? They would have produced another. By the time I learned our daughter's name was plastered over the betting book, it was too late. The damage had been done."

The countess squared her shoulders.

"Your daughter is standing right here." Phaedra decided to intervene. She hated to admit it, but her father had a point as well. Those rogues would just have opened another book. They probably already had. While she was glad her mother stood by her, witnessing her mother and father argue did not bring Phaedra any satisfaction.

"While I would have handled matters differently, I do not fault Phaedra's actions tonight," the countess said.

The earl's face turned solemn.

"You have raked our daughter over the coals long enough, Robert." She turned to Phaedra. "Why don't you go rest, dear? We shall speak in the morning."

Phaedra didn't want to leave, but neither did she want to fight anymore, so she reluctantly nodded, and with one last parting look at her family, she hurried off, but came to an abrupt halt when her aunt stepped out from the receiving room.

That wasn't what caught Phaedra's attention. Her aunt was not alone. Following in her wake was the man Phaedra had seen once before—quite naked. And there was no mistaking this was the man she had seen that night, nor what these two had been doing before they arrived.

What on earth was her aunt thinking?

"Robert?" Portia asked. "Why are you hollering your ire in the middle of the night?"

Her father glanced at Portia, then beyond her to the man at her back. "Brayton? What are you doing here."

Brayton?

As in *the* Jack Brayton? The infamous hotelier?

Phaedra's exhaustion suddenly disappeared.

According to the gossip, if this was him, he was no gentleman. Not by birth. Not by character. And apparently, not in bed.

"Do not try to shift the attention to Portia and her guest, Robert," the countess hastily put in. "You have some explaining to do!"

"*I* have explaining to do?" A short pause. "Her *guest*? What sort of guest is he?" her father demanded.

Phaedra glanced at her aunt, who winked at her and mouthed for her to go. She instantly understood. Her aunt was diverting her father's attention away from her, and quite possibly to a bigger scandal looming on the horizon.

Phaedra fled the room.

She didn't want to admit it, but Deerhurst's confession kept playing in her head, making her dizzy. The moment she shut the door to her chamber, tears spilled down her cheeks, and she finally let out the emotion she'd been holding at bay.

⋙✦⋘

DEERHURST TOSSED BACK a tumbler of brandy, welcoming the burn of the liquid spreading down his throat. He did his best to ignore the pain that pounded in his chest as though it had a life of its own. His heart was shattering from the loss of her.

After the mess of his youth, he never thought love would be in his future. He certainly had never imagined it could be this painful. After all, his responsibilities required him to be practical, and caution had become the grounds on which he rebuilt his life after he'd discovered his daughter.

Now he had lost the woman he loved. And for what? He couldn't even say. Yes, he had made mistakes. But were they unforgiveable? No.

Maybe.

Perhaps her rejection was punishment for his past. After all, he'd had a torrid affair with a married woman and a secret child out of wedlock. And what had he done now? Had an affair with an unmarried woman.

It was Olivia all over again.

Only this time *he* was the one obsessed. It was only now that he could somewhat understand Olivia's actions. The letters. The tears. The relentless pursuit.

Warrick and Saville plopped down at his table.

"Go away." He was in no mood for his friends tonight. He wasn't even in the mood for White's, but he didn't dare go back to his house. The temptation to go to her was too great.

"Why so sour?" Warrick asked.

Deerhurst shot his friend a glare. "You lost the damn list."

"Bloody hell," Warrick growled. "How many times do I have to be raked over the coals for that?"

"My apologies," Deerhurst said deadpan. "You wrote down every damn word on the list."

"Cannot argue with that," Saville said. To Deerhurst, he murmured, "You've got Sharp troubles, I gather."

"Phaedra will have nothing to do with me."

"She will come around," Saville said, accepting the drink the waiter brought over. "Lady Ophelia did, and it was Avondale's list."

Deerhurst tossed down another brandy. They wouldn't understand. Lady Ophelia did not share the same fears Phaedra did. Besides, Lady Ophelia loved Avondale. Phaedra didn't love him. She would have forgiven him if she had. She cared for him, yes, but he'd seen nothing but distrust in her eyes in the Stewart's study.

She's hurt.

So was he. He'd confessed his love, bared his soul. And she had spurned him. There was only so much rejection a man could take. So much punishment.

"I was there when she confronted Deerhurst," Warrick told

Saville. "I've never been so scared of a woman in my life."

Saville nodded. "I've heard the Sharp women are not women to be trifled with."

"And yet who is the one that compared Phaedra's laughter to an alley cat?"

Saville cursed. "I haven't had it easy either, old chap. Selena hasn't spoken to me for days. She won't even look at me."

Deerhurst sighed. "Can't say I blame her."

They all drank their brandy in silence.

"I saw how she looked at you the day in the park," Saville said. "Trust me, your lady will come around."

Deerhurst couldn't be so sure. "Her anger is born of fears that run much deeper than the wagers."

"Show her she has nothing to fear from you," Saville said.

Warrick nodded. "Fight for her."

"I told her I loved her."

Saville whistled. "Perhaps she won't come around."

Warrick kicked him beneath the table. "Don't listen to his foul mouth. "When have words ever repaired a woman's trust? That's why Selena hasn't forgiven this rogue, her own brother."

Deerhurst took another swill of brandy. "I can't fight her fears for her."

"You don't have to fight her fears," Warrick said. "All you have to do is show her they are meaningless with you."

Deerhurst pursed his lips in thought.

Show her they are meaningless with him. He turned the idea over in his mind. It wasn't the worst advice. In fact, for Warrick, it was perhaps a stroke of genius. Only, Deerhurst had no idea how to go about showing her what *more* he could do. Confessing his love hadn't even been enough.

Because she didn't believe you.

"More brandy," Saville called to the waiter. "A bottle."

Warrick leaned back in his chair. "Agreed, let's get foxed tonight."

Deerhurst nodded. Anything to forget tonight. Brandy eased the discomfort that stabbed with each intake of breath.

Deerhurst suddenly recalled that Lady Selena, Saville's sister, and been part of the scandal on this eve. "Where is your sister?"

Saville winced. "Locked herself in her room. I've put four footmen on her watch tonight. This is a disaster."

"Well," Deerhurst said. "If there is one woman who would have taken badly to your connection to the list, it's your sister."

"She cut up all of my clothes." Saville pulled at his coat. "All I have to wear are the clothes on my damn back. She even destroyed my boots. Luckily, I still have some shirts and trousers at my bachelor's apartment."

Warrick snorted. "I wouldn't put it past her to find out about your apartment and torch it. Always thought of her as a sweet girl. But now I don't know who scares me more, Selena or Lady Phaedra."

Deerhurst arched a brow. "You were there when his sister confronted him?"

Warrick nodded. "I believe all the porcelain in the house had to be replaced."

"Centuries old porcelain," Saville griped. "And she's not done. I had to forcibly remove her from my study after she got into my liquor cabinet and threw a two-hundred-year-old cognac against my wall. My office still reeks of spirits."

"I take it that was before she stopped speaking to you?" Deerhurst asked.

"Don't know what's more unnerving, her shouting or her silence."

So Deerhurst wasn't the only one with problems. But then, Lady Selena would eventually forgive Saville. They were family, after all. This was why he had wanted to secure Phaedra's hand before he told her the truth. They would have been family then. Family forgave family. Simple as that.

"What do you suppose will happen after tonight?" Deerhurst asked. It had been a question that plagued him ever since Phaedra appeared on the top of the Stewart stairwell with a top hat and cane. He couldn't think about the rest of her outfit. It made him hard, which given the circumstances, was quite beastly.

"Depends on how deep the women's outrage goes," Warrick said with a shrug.

"I was thinking more in the lines with the betting book. One of the women has it. White's will want it back."

"That is correct." A new voice joined their conversation.

Deerhurst lifted his gaze to find the Duke of Mortimer stepping up to their table, face devoid of any clues as to what he might be thinking.

"As a patron of this establishment, I'd like to see the book returned."

Saville scowled. "We don't know who has it."

"However, the suspects have been reduced to four."

Deerhurst cursed. Mortimer must have been charged with investigating the theft and finding the book so that the club's reputation didn't suffer a greater blow.

He was not a man to be trifled with.

"Good luck with that, old chap," Saville drawled, a careless grin hanging on his lips. "You come near my sister, you and I will be facing off."

"Your sister started a revolt."

"Revolt?" Warrick said. "I haven't heard anything about a revolt."

"I agree with Warrick," Saville drawled. "How can one slip of a woman start a revolt?"

Deerhurst inwardly snorted.

"One woman, no. Four? Perhaps," Mortimer said.

Saville merely laughed. "You suspect them just because they reacted to a disservice that occurred in this club."

"You know all about that, don't you?" Mortimer said.

Deerhurst cursed when Saville's smile froze. He recognized the look that entered his gaze—trouble. Mortimer's words were a kick in the teeth.

"The real disservice done here," Deerhurst spoke up, "was by the man that found a list and showcased it like a peacock in heat."

Warrick nodded. "Cromby, if you haven't heard."

"I heard," Mortimer said. "He, however, did not remove the book from White's. I suspect one of the names on that list did."

Deerhurst regarded Mortimer with a dark look. "And any male associated with the name on the list, I hope."

Mortimer smiled. "Why do you think I'm here discussing the matter with you?"

Saville cursed. They were Deerhurst's sentiments exactly. He hoped by the Saints that the book was not in Phaedra's possession.

"What punishment will be doled out to whoever stole the book?" Warrick asked.

Mortimer's hawk eyes shifted over them. "No punishment. If the book is returned to the club."

The table reeked of skepticism.

"You think there would be punishment for a lady of breeding?" Mortimer snorted. "Will never happen. The club just wants the book returned."

Naturally, so long as the book is returned to its rightful place, they could all pretend that nothing had ever happened, that none of them had behaved badly, that no ladies had been treated shamefully. Deerhurst understood. He also felt disgusted.

Mortimer's gaze missed nothing. "Of course, I am merely acting as a representative of the club."

Saville sneered. "You still had to agree."

"How could I not? There are ladies involved. Would you rather I had given way for Cromby to hunt down the book?"

Deerhurst stilled.

"In any event," Mortimer went on. "I've heard rumors that there are many gentlemen who are as outraged by tonight's events as the women are about the wagers on those pages. Already, talk had begun of wives bolting their chamber doors shut. Some men will want retribution for that. I'd keep an eye out for your ladies if I were you."

It was a warning.

One Deerhurst felt it best to heed.

Chapter Twenty

PHAEDRA REFUSED TO leave her chamber for five full days. On the sixth day, the soft blue wallpaper covered with colorful sparrows finally chafed her nerves, so she ventured to the library, one of her favorite rooms in the house.

Drawing rooms were off limits. They reminded her of Deerhurst.

The one used to receive callers had been used in the most carnal ways by her aunt, and Phaedra herself had shared a passionate kiss in the same one. The other one, well that drawing room held memories of a different sort. Deerhurst's appearance. Climbing through the window. His arms wrapped around her.

Phaedra pushed the memories from her mind. The library wasn't much better. While she hadn't shared a moment here with Deerhurst, she had been introduced to the word *carnal*.

However, the smell of hundreds of books gave her more comfort than the discomfort of that one memory could dispel.

These past several days, Mary had kept her abreast of household activities. They hadn't received any callers since the Stewart ball. Apparently, Mary had overheard rumors that many wives were revolting against their husbands, including Phaedra's mother, who hadn't spoken to Phaedra's father since that night. And Aunt Portia had also been ordered to break off any connection with that man, Brayton.

She sighed.

She hated that her parents were at odds because of her. Which was one of the reasons—besides her bedchamber wallpaper—she had ventured from her room. If her mother saw she was out and about, she might forgive her father.

"My lady." Phaedra looked up to find a footman at the door. "You have callers, a Lady Selena and Lady Harriet."

"Please direct them here."

The footman inclined his head and left to return a few moments later with two of Phaedra's newfound friends.

"We heard about Deerhurst," Selena wasted no time in saying as they each took a seat on the chaise longue.

"You have?" Panic erupted in her heart. What exactly had they heard? An alarming thought, since Phaedra and Deerhurst were the only two who were supposed to know about *them*.

"You ended your courtship," Harriet said. "I didn't even know the earl was courting you."

Selena nodded. "We were quite surprised. You never said anything at Ophelia's."

Right.

Their fake courtship that had become real. And then fake again.

Her heartbeat settled. "It wasn't that serious."

"It's serious enough that he's been drowning himself in spirits ever since the Stewart ball," Selena said.

Deerhurst had been drinking?

It's none of your business, Phaedra. And it wasn't. He'd been the one to betray her, not the other way around. Still, curiosity blossomed in her breast.

"How do you know this?" Phaedra asked.

"Warrick told Avondale, who told Ophelia, who told me," Harriet said.

"My brother has been drowning himself with Deerhurst, that's how I know," Selena said.

Phaedra blinked.

"It seems like it was serious for him," Harriet said softly.

Phaedra furrowed her brows. "Is that why you are here, to plead his case?"

"We are here to see how you are holding up, nothing more," Selena said. "Apparently, Warrick told Avondale who told Ophelia who told Harriet that Deerhurst is in love with you. We naturally assumed you felt the same way and might be feeling a bit glum, so we decided to come cheer you up."

"It's more complicated than that," Phaedra said slowly, her mind still working through that mouthful of words.

"Seems quite simple to me," Lady Harriet chirped.

"*You* are in love with your husband," Selena said with a scowl. "Your opinion doesn't count."

"People in love cannot have an opinion?" Harriet asked incredulously.

"People in love want the entire world to be in love as well. *And* because your husband had no part in the list or the wagers."

Harriet snorted. "My husband isn't entirely blameless. He took gross advantage of those wagers. And trust me, I am not in love with him." Her gaze narrowed. "Have you not forgiven your brother?"

"Forgiven? Hah! We called a truce after he told me the Duke of Mortimer suspects the betting book is in our hands and plans to find out whose."

"The Duke of Mortimer?" Phaedra asked.

"He called on me yesterday," Harriet said, shivering. "The man has the awful ability to intimidate with one look. I began to ramble about drapes and carpets almost immediately. Had it not been for Leeds, I'm sure I might have blurted something incriminating."

"Mortimer called on Ophelia a few days ago as well. Set Avondale off in a fit. We came to warn you, he might be knocking on your door next."

Dear Lord.

Because Phaedra had the book. Selena had given the book to her after she had made copies of the pages because she didn't trust her brother not to snoop through her things. "What happens if he discovers I have it?"

"He might ask for it back nicely?" Harriet said. "He said there will be no consequences if the book is returned to the club."

That made Phaedra want to hide the book all the more.

"And you believe that?" Selena said. "Since our theatrics at the Stewart ball, as my brother so prettily put it, he'll probably threaten to involve Bow Street if we continue to go against him."

"Perhaps that is why he is approaching the ladies who are attached to it first," Phaedra murmured in thought. "Besides, he can't know for sure we have the book."

"If that's the case then we can probably assume he'd approach Louisa next," Selena said.

"Why is that?" Phaedra asked, a dreadful suspicion forming.

"Her father is arranging a husband for her as we speak," Selena confirmed. "She's fighting him every step of the way, but in the end, she might not have a choice."

"Knowing Louisa, she'll come out at the top," Harriet said.

But she shouldn't have to, Phaedra thought darkly. That list had caused too much trouble already. She hoped those bastard earls were suffering too, even if just a little.

"We can't hand the book over to Mortimer. If we do, they win," Selena said.

"Agreed," Phaedra said. "Let the duke come. He'll learn soon enough that Sharp women don't crack."

Harriet grinned.

"What will you do about Deerhurst?" Selena asked.

"There is nothing to do," Phaedra stubbornly held her position, and that was all she had to say on the matter. She'd been alone these past five days, but she refused to dwell on Deerhurst. She'd read books, too many to count, to divert her attention.

"Well, they are loathsome beasts to be sure."

"It does seem that they are trying to protect all of the women on the list," Harriet said.

Selena snorted. "Saville has been avoiding me."

Harriet arched a brow. "But Warrick has not."

Selene snorted.

Phaedra's lips quirked for the first time in five days. Their banter was like the crispness of a fresh breeze.

Harriet's gaze flashed to Phaedra. "I suspect Deerhurst has been keeping close to you as well."

"I cannot say," she murmured. "I haven't been out and about."

"Before that," Harriet pressed.

Phaedra couldn't deny that. He had, to some extent. But she still questioned his intentions.

"Who has been protecting Louisa?"

"I believe her younger brother has been quite the bodyguard," Harriet remarked.

"What about Theodosia?" Selena asked.

They all stilled.

Saville.

"Surely not." Phaedra found the idea laughable.

"If this is true, Theodosia is going to maim my brother when she learns of it," Selena said gleefully.

Phaedra agreed, though inside she felt anything but happy. She couldn't help but wonder if she was the only one who couldn't find amusement in all this for more than a few seconds at a time.

She missed Deerhurst terribly.

What if you are carrying my child?

Ah yes. The thing she had most tried to suppress these past five days. The reason she had secluded herself. She might be carrying

Deerhurst's child.

And she didn't know what to do about it. Didn't have anyone she could talk to, anyone she could ask how she would know if she was or if she wasn't. No book had been able to enlighten her either.

She felt numb inside.

A footman announced, "The Marquess of Leeds."

Three pairs of surprised eyes jumped to the library entrance, then beyond, as Leeds appeared behind the servant. Phaedra's immediate thought jumped to *something must be wrong*.

"My Lord," Phaedra greeted as she slowly rose to her feet, sending a curious glance to the girls.

"Lady Phaedra, my apologies for interrupting your visit," his eyes darted to Harriet, who pursed her lips. "May I join you?"

"By all means."

Harriet gave them a sheepish glance before shooting a much more heated one at her husband. "Did I mention my husband keeps showing up during all of my excursions?"

"Since your excursions always take you away from me, can you blame me?" he countered.

Selena rolled her eyes.

Harriet harrumphed. "I have a life, you know."

"I have one too—you."

Phaedra blinked. And this was *not* a love match?

Selena groaned. "Can the two of you please stop? I do not know how much more of this I can take. Does Eton not teach that it's unfashionable to show affection to your wife?"

Leeds settled comfortably next to Harriet. "Since you've decided to cause a scandal and my wife is friends with you, I'll do what's necessary to keep her safe."

"Of course, we all need protecting from the fire and pitchforks marching upon us."

"That your brother has not locked you in your chamber and tossed away the key astounds me."

"He can't." She pulled a key from her sleeve. "When he is locked away himself."

Phaedra laughed. By Selena's grin, she couldn't tell if the woman was serious or not, but for some reason, she believed something—or someone—had been locked in a chamber or basement somewhere.

Something else filled her heart.

Envy.

The way Leeds looked at Harriet—Phaedra wanted a man to look at her with that much care and devotion. She had a man who looked at her like that.

Too bad he was a scoundrel.

⫸⫷

"YOU LOOK LIKE hell."

"Thank you," Deerhurst said as Avondale joined him. He felt like hell too. He hadn't slept a night through in almost a week, longer perhaps. But recently, it was Mortimer's warning that had been keeping him up at night, so he spent his evenings at the club, which, apparently, hadn't gone unnoticed.

"You've been spending a lot of time in White's."

"It's where all the gossip lives." This was about all he could do. Keep an eye out for news and ulterior motives.

"Ah, this is about Mortimer."

Deerhurst glanced at his friend. "He paid you a visit, did he?"

"Ophelia," Avondale said, lips turning down. "Then he got a visit from me."

So, Mortimer was making the rounds. Deerhurst suddenly felt uneasy. Had the duke called on Phaedra? He did not like the idea one bit. Not that he didn't think she could hold her own, but Deerhurst became restless over any man who was not him who could spend time with Phaedra. However, his footmen hadn't reported anything back to him, so he didn't think Mortimer had paid Phaedra a visit yet.

"Does he suspect who is in possession of the book?" Deerhurst asked.

"Not that he voiced."

Deerhurst studied his friend's face. "Do you know?"

Avondale shook his head. "Not even Ophelia knows which one of the ladies has the book, and since she indicated she was done with it, they are keeping her out of their plans in consideration."

"Understandable."

Avondale swirled his brandy in his palm. "They might also be keeping her out of their plans for fear word would get back to the other men. You."

"Probably the truth."

They sat in silence for a moment, each deep in thought as they sipped their golden liquid. Mortimer hadn't been the only reason he'd not slept. His night of loving Phaedra haunted him day in and day out. Whenever he closed his eyes, she was there.

On his bed. In his arms. The touch of her hands. The stroke of her tongue. The cry of his name on her lips. It drove him mad thinking about how one mistake had doused all the passion inside her. Did she not miss him? Crave his touch? It drove him even crazier knowing she lived in the house next door to his. So close and yet so bloody far. He couldn't even bring himself to walk past her residence anymore.

So, he just stayed here.

Abigail had finally stopped kicking up a fuss and had gone back to their country estate with a promise that he would visit soon. She'd even asked if Phaedra would come as well, and they could have a picnic in the field. He did not have the heart to tell her that she wouldn't be joining them on picnics anymore.

He'd grown angry then.

Phaedra refused to forgive him because of a sense of betrayal, spurned him because of her fears. While he respected her fears as genuine, he could not help but resent them. They were the only obstacle between them.

How could he ever hope to overcome them?

No. He couldn't. And it bloody ate at him.

You still haven't told her the full truth about Abigail. Yes, there was still that. Christ, it was all one big mess.

"Ellington is going to ask Lady Phaedra to marry him."

Deerhurst lifted a brow at that, but inside his blood iced. "And you know this how?"

"He told me so himself."

"Ellington is a puppy. Phaedra will chew him up and spit what's left of him to the wolves."

"Are you sure about that?"

I'm sure.

"Things seem to have changed recently," Avondale continued with a thoughtful look. "Perhaps she changed her mind about certain things as well."

Deerhurst full out scowled. "What things?"

Avondale smirked. "You should know better than I do."

Phaedra change her mind? Never.

But what if she did?

What if she married Ellington out of spite? She would never do that, Deerhurst was sure.

But what if she did?

Deerhurst tossed back another brandy. "It's got nothing to do with me."

"So you're *not* going to chase after your woman?"

"What do you mean what am I going to do about it? She rejected me. Twice."

"You are in love with her, are you not?"

"Are you deaf?"

Avondale waved a dismissive hand. "You love her. That ought to be enough encouragement to motivate you into action."

"Who says I love her?" How bloody lame. It was written all over his misery.

"I've never seen you in such a wretched state, old friend. Only a woman can do this to a man. Go home. Go take a bath. Shave. And go get your woman."

Avondale didn't understand. If it were that easy, he would have done it already. But the way they had ended things was decisive, as was the threat he had tossed at her feet. How close had he been afterward to paying a visit to Huntly to confess his deeds and ensure her hand? But he hadn't. Not because he was righteous and would never do that to Phaedra, but because he wasn't sure Huntly would give him his daughter's hand.

"You didn't see the loathing in her eyes."

"Are you sure it was loathing?" Avondale asked.

"There was also hurt, distrust, perhaps a touch of distaste."

Avondale choked. "Christ man, what did you do to the woman?" His eyes suddenly widened. "Tell me you didn't seduce the chit."

"Would you shut your damn mouth?"

Avondale held up his hands in surrender. "Well, did you?"

"It's complicated."

"So you did." Avondale gave him a once over. "There must be something else going on here. Why else would she reject you?"

"She doesn't trust easily. I betrayed her trust." Deerhurst sighed. "Whatever she's grappling with, I can't fight it for her no matter how much I want to."

"Perhaps, but it's your life, and if you want her in it, you'll find a way to stay in it. You get my meaning?"

"We can't all be as lucky as you."

But already Deerhurst's mind spun in all directions with all the ways he could stay in Phaedra's life. If she was carrying his child, of course, it would be a done deal. But he didn't want her to come to him out of responsibility. He wanted her heart. He wanted her to choose him. He wanted what he had lost.

Her trust.

Else it would be like him and Olivia, only he would be Olivia in this scenario. Refusing to let go. Always showing up in her presence. Allowing obsession to become an ugly, tangible thing. That had been a nightmare. He refused to be a nightmare in Phaedra's life.

His attention caught on Cromby and one of his cronies sauntering into the club and plopping down at a table behind them. He tried to pay them no mind, but their voices cut through.

It's done," Deerhurst heard the man at the table behind them say. Cromby's friend.

"Good," Cromby replied. "My pockets will be filled when morning comes."

Deerhurst met Avondale's gaze. Cromby was an arse, and he had also caught Deerhurst's attention. The man had scared and tried to compromise Phaedra, Deerhurst was sure, and Deerhurst would never forgive Cromby for that. While he would like nothing more than to roll his eyes, this topic of pockets being filled was a sensitive one. He listened harder.

"You will have more blunt if you do it yourself."

Deerhurst stilled, his head tilting to the side as he listened to their conversation.

Cromby grunted. "I have a reputation to uphold. Don't like my hands to get dirty. Besides, that bitch spurned me at Morewood's ball. She's going to get what she deserves tonight."

Deerhurst's heart dropped to his shoes, his eyes lifting to meet Avondale's, who sat up in his chair.

"And you're sure you gave the right address?"

Deerhurst frowned as the man repeated Huntly's address. Then his blood turned to ice shards in his veins, their painful flow stabbing throughout his body.

Phaedra.

Deerhurst leaped up, the chair scraping back in an eerie sound before he directed a murderous glare at Cromby. The man paled. Good, he still had some instinct for self-preservation. Too bad for Cromby—and good for him—he was dumb as horse shit, openly discussing such a matter in public without a damn care in the world.

Deerhurst grabbed him by the collar and hauled him to his feet.

"What have you done?"

"Nothing," Cromby croaked out, grabbing at his wrists to relieve the pressure. Deerhurst didn't allow it.

"Don't lie to me," Deerhurst warned, though he almost sounded like a threatened animal with such a low growl. "I heard you. What are you planning to do to Lady Phaedra?"

A wicked glint entered Cromby's eyes, a look that turned Deerhurst's heart to stone. "It's too late. Your pretty lady will be damaged goods after tonight."

Behind him, Avondale cursed.

"What's going to happen to her?"

"Don't worry, nothing too bad. She's just going to find herself in need of a husband soon."

"Kill the plan."

Cromby laughed. "It's already in motion. There is no stopping it. It's as good as done."

Deerhurst threw the man against the table, the loud clatter alerting fellow patrons. Fury clawed at his throat. "If anything happens to Lady Phaedra tonight, if even one hair on her head is harmed, I will kill you."

Deerhurst didn't waste any more time, he ran from the club and got his horse, setting off at a dead run to Mayfair. In anything happened to her he would never forgive himself.

Please God, don't let me be too late.

Chapter Twenty-One

PHAEDRA SHOT UP in bed, pulled out of sleep by a mysterious force, heart beating wildly in her chest. Her eyes darted over the shadows of the room, stopping at one particular spot that appeared somehow strange. She couldn't exactly explain what had prompted her sixth sense to flare up. Perhaps it was because she hadn't been sleeping well lately or perhaps because she hadn't let her guard down since she cut Deerhurst from her life.

But she just *knew*.

She was not alone in her chamber.

Lord, help me.

She wanted to scream. She even opened her mouth to cry out in alarm. It didn't matter if she woke her family and she'd be compromised when they'd find her with whoever was in her chamber. All that mattered was getting help.

But no sound emerged.

It was as though the distress had cut off her vocal cords. Phaedra measured the distance between the door and her bed. If she were quick and nimble on her feet, she would make it. But she had to be fast. Her gaze flicked to the shadow again.

Yes. She'd have to be very fast.

Phaedra ripped the covers off her and leaped from the bed. A curse ripped from her throat as bed linen entwined with her feet and she landed in a tangled heap on the ground.

Now her voice reappeared.

She kicked out her legs to untangle herself and tried to scramble to her feet.

"Phaedra?" a low whisper came.

She stilled. She knew that voice. Would never forget that low timbre in all her life.

"Deerhurst?" She squinted in the darkness. "What are you doing here? You scared me near to death!"

Phaedra's heart settled somewhat. Only a bit, for it had turned frantic for another reason—the man she loved and loathed at the same time was in her chambers.

No one would ever know that it had taken all of Phaedra's strength to reject Deerhurst at the Stewart ball. She wanted to trust that his words were true, that he loved her and hadn't used her in any sort of way. But she couldn't.

She felt his presence draw close, and from the shadows, an outline of a man appeared.

"Why didn't you scream?" he asked as he knelt before her.

"If I could have, I would have."

A beat of silence.

"What are you doing here?" she asked, finally drawing her legs from the sheets, and rising to her feet. He rose with her.

"I had to make sure that you are all right."

I'm not. "Why wouldn't I be?" A sudden thought occurred to her. "Has something happened?"

Another beat of silence.

"Something has happened, hasn't it? Do not think about keeping anything from me." She pointed a finger at him. "Why are you hiding in the corner of my chamber like some scoundrelly thief?"

He said nothing.

"Why aren't you speaking?"

A soft sigh echoed through the chamber. "I'm here to stand guard and to make sure you don't encounter any unwelcome surprises."

"You're the only surprise here."

He nodded, then dragged a hand over his face. "Cromby is out for blood."

Phaedra's heart stuttered to a stop. "What?"

"It seems that he has targeted you, which is why I'm here."

"For what exactly? I've done nothing to that man." Her eyes suddenly widened. "Is this about what happened at the Morewood ball?"

"Yes, he feels spurned, and from what I can tell, he wants to ruin you."

"That's ridiculous. The man's an oafish goat. I'd be surprised if he's not spurned daily."

"Normally, I'd agree, but this is about more than just spurning him. Apparently, there is a lot of money on the line."

Of course.

As Phaedra understood it, Cromby was the one who found the list Warrick had lost and entered it into the book. He was one of the worst sorts of devils born into a title. Sadistic down to his rotten heart.

"Well, thank you for warning me," Phaedra said and had to firm her wavering heart. "Now please leave."

He didn't budge. "Phaedra . . ."

"I can handle Cromby and his cronies."

"Like you handled him the last time? This is not a game, Phaedra. He has a plan in motion as we speak." He removed his jacket and tossed it over the chair of her writing desk.

"What do you think you're doing?" she demanded, but she needn't have asked. He had made his position perfectly clear.

Still, he said, "I'm staying the night."

"No, you're not. I told you—"

"Yes, I know," he cut her off. "You don't want anything to do with me. I'll leave you in peace once the threat has passed."

"You truly believe that? It seems the threat will pass only when I have a husband."

"I can be that too."

"You are surely full of bright ideas tonight, aren't you?"

"My only crime is not speaking up. You're allowing your fears to rule your life."

"Do not speak to me of fears when you have a daughter you lock away from the world because of yours."

A short silence ensued, then, "I want her safe, you know that."

Yes, she knew. The moment those words had left Phaedra's lips, she'd regretted them. But it was still the truth. "And I want a future that's not built on tricks and schemes, you know that."

"Yes, I feel the sting of it in your words every time you speak," he muttered in a low voice.

"Good," Phaedra snapped. "Then I am getting my message across."

He sighed but still bent to remove his boots.

"Deerhurst, I'm warning you . . . get in this bed and I will club you over the head with a . . ." she paused to look around for a weapon to wield. "A book."

He paused. "You're right. This is a bad idea."

"Finally, you see the light."

"You need to come with me. You're not safe here."

Her jaw went slack. "You are mad if you think I'm going anywhere with you."

"Scared you won't be able to resist me?" he challenged.

"On the contrary, I don't trust your motivations."

"My motivation has always been to protect you."

"Well, what if I believe you would do anything to win my hand in marriage?"

"That's absurd and you bloody well know it." He moved to loom over her. "If I was prepared to do anything, Phaedra, you'd be wedded to me already. If you don't trust in anything else, trust in that."

Phaedra glared at the man, wanting to refute him. But she believed if he had wanted to force the issue, he could have done so after their first kiss. She missed him terribly. She hadn't wanted to admit it, had fought for a week to ignore it, only for her heart to crack open the moment he appeared.

"I trust that you are a man."

He chuckled. "Naturally."

Phaedra gasped. "Are you mocking me?"

"No," Deerhurst said. "I am challenging you to trust what you feel in your gut and not only what you can see, hear, and touch."

She changed the subject. "What exactly is Cromby's plan?"

"He wouldn't say."

Her eyes widened. "You confronted him?"

"A small altercation," he admitted. "Are we staying here or moving to my house?"

A thrill shot through her. She didn't just trust that he was a man. She also trusted that he wanted to protect her. But what to do with that trust? She still felt betrayed and confused. So many conflicting emotions rampaged through her heart, Phaedra didn't know how to make sense of it all.

All she wanted to do was pull him into her bed and snuggle tightly, and she nearly did just that, but a small noise, almost too faint to hear, caught her attention.

Almost as if . . .

A shadow moved on the balcony of her bedchamber. Her eyes flicked to Deerhurst, who had also gone utterly still.

"Who is that?" she asked softly. Cromby? Could he even climb up to her window?

A soft finger grazed her lips indicating complete silence. Fear spiked in Phaedra's belly. This was no ploy or trick. Deerhurst had been serious.

She watched wide-eyed as Deerhurst crept to the balcony door, careful to keep to the shadows of the room and not alert the intruder. There was a faint scratching sound, as though the burglar was now picking the lock, before the balcony door slowly opened.

Saints help her. Surely it wasn't that easy to break into her chamber? With Deerhurst she didn't even dwell over the matter. She just assumed he'd slipped through the same back door to her house he'd used the last time, the one Phaedra also suspected her aunt used for her lover.

But this . . .

She'd never feel safe in her chamber again!

The moment the man stepped into her chamber, Deerhurst grabbed him by the shoulders and threw him into the wall with a loud crash.

"Deerhurst!" Phaedra cried out when the man tackled him to the ground.

The pistol! She had a pistol.

She scrambled from the bed and darted to the drawer of her writing desk as the men pummeled each other on the floor, each blow and crunch of bone sickening to Phaedra. The cold steel grip of her pistol was the only comfort as she swung around and pointed it at the men.

Her door burst open.

"What the devil is going on here?"

◦◦◦❯❯❯❮❮❮◦◦◦

DEERHURST WIPED THE blood from his nose as he straightened to his full height, yanking the intruding bastard to his feet as well. His eyes instantly gravitated toward Phaedra, who stood, pale as snow, with a pistol pointed at the intruder.

She hadn't been harmed. A relief.

However, Huntly stood in the doorframe, behind him was the

countess as well as a woman he recognized as Phaedra's aunt and another man. Jack Brayton? What was he doing here? He had a sudden epiphany.

Bloody hell. So many witnesses . . .

At least Phaedra was pointing a pistol at them. He had expected when he entered her chamber he might be staring at the end of a barrel once again tonight. Luckily, it had happened. Not quite as he thought, but this would do. No one would suspect anything less or anything more than what they were privy to at the moment.

"Huntly," Deerhurst spoke up when no one said a word after Huntly's roar. Shock, he presumed. "I overheard Cromby say he'd sent a man to Lady Phaedra's chamber. I arrived just in time to intercept him."

Huntly's frosty eyes moved to the intruder, who they now recognized as Lord Neville Howard, third son of Viscount Purbeck.

"Is that true?" Huntly demanded.

Howard clenched his jaw, refusing to say a word.

"Speak or I'll dust the floor with your face," Deerhurst growled. His grip on the man's shoulder tightened. He was not in a charitable mood. If he hadn't been on his guard, hadn't overheard Cromby—if anything had gone differently tonight, Phaedra would be hurt right now.

"I wouldn't have harmed her."

"No?" Huntly said. "You being here right now harms my daughter."

Lord Neville lifted his chin in deviance. "I only meant for you to find me in her chambers."

"And how would I have found you?"

The man shrugged. "Cromby said all I had to do was sneak into Lady Phaedra's bed. Her commotion would wake the household and she'd be ruined when they found me. I never intended to force myself on her."

"Only into her bedchamber," Huntly growled, clenching his fists. "Scaring my daughter to death. What does Cromby get out of this little deal?"

"A portion of her dowry."

Deerhurst cursed.

The bastard had lied to him. He'd made it sound as though the only winnings he'd received were from the wagers. He should have known that jackanapes wouldn't tell him the whole truth.

"I should shoot you where you stand," Phaedra bit off in anger. "You vile goat."

The countess slipped past Huntly to shield Phaedra. "What are we going to do with this ruffian, Robert? I vote to shoot him."

Lady Portia followed, taking the pistol from Phaedra. "Give me that dear, I am more than happy to take the fall if a hole appears in the man's heart."

"I, however, won't be happy about that," Brayton said as he strode over to the women and snatched the pistol from Lady Portia. "I'll hold onto this, angel. Don't want you to accidently harm yourself or end up in prison."

Huntly cursed. "Brayton? What the devil are you doing here again? Didn't I tell you to stay away from my sister?"

Lady Portia snorted. "He's with me."

"With you?" Huntly's face flamed when the implication of that statement penetrated. Even Deerhurst held back a whistle at the woman's spunk.

"I'll deal with the two of you later. One damn scandal at a time." His gaze settled back on Lord Neville. "Howard, you have two choices. Either you leave London tonight and what happened here stays between us, or your body is removed from my home in a casket. Choose."

Lord Neville paled. "You wouldn't dare. I'm an aristocrat."

"You're a man who broke into my home and stole into my daughter's chamber. She screamed. What else can I believe but your intention was to harm her? It's dark. A pistol fired. An unfortunate death. Am I painting this vision vivid enough for you?"

Lord Neville lifted his chin. "She will still be ruined."

Deerhurst wanted to pummel the man.

"My daughter is stronger than the gossip columns. She will prevail. So, what's it to be, Howard? You have thirty seconds to choose."

Howard shrugged out of Deerhurst's hold, and this time, Deerhurst let him go. The man was done for no matter what the outcome of his choice now. He knew that. Besides, Huntly was being courteous. Deerhurst still wanted Howard to limp from the house.

"I'll leave London tonight."

"Within the hour."

Howard gave a curt nod.

"And I'll have your word that you do not speak of tonight with anyone. Unfortunate accidents happen all year round," Huntly pressed.

Howard gave another nod.

Brayton strode to Howard and yanked him by the lapels of his jacket. "I'll make sure he leaves the city without any more incidents."

Huntly inclined his head. "I expect you back, Brayton."

"Couldn't keep me away, Huntly."

Huntly narrowed his eyes on Brayton. Deerhurst had to hand it to the man—he had balls as big as the ones rolling on bowling greens. Truly impressive. Truly inspiring.

"Deerhurst," Huntly said when Brayton dragged Howard away. "You are courting my daughter?"

Deerhurst winced. "We had an understanding."

"Had?" Huntly queried. "Ah, Avondale's list."

"You know?" Phaedra asked.

"Since you and your friends exposed the wagers in such a flamboyant way, the dowager countess has admitted to drafting the list for her son."

This surprised the hell out of Deerhurst. Huntly had known but hadn't confronted him. But then, why would he? The Sharp family were peculiar to be sure. All Deerhurst had to do was look at Brayton's presence. But he didn't expect Huntly's next question. That knocked the air from his lungs.

"Are you prepared to marry my daughter?"

God, yes.

"Papa!"

"You are ruined, Phaedra. Howard might say nothing tonight, but we cannot guarantee he won't say something tomorrow."

"Robert," Portia began but was cut off with a hot stare.

"Not a word from you, Portia. Consorting with Brayton? Have you learned nothing of your past marriage?"

"That is not the same," Lady Portia defended. "Neither will any good come from forcing Phaedra to wed."

Christ, Deerhurst didn't want to go through this again. How many times would he have to be rejected in one night? But considering what had happened with Howard, he had no choice. He'd wanted to keep this between him and Phaedra, but that no longer seemed possible.

"I have no problem wedding your daughter, Huntly, if she will have me, but she has made her position clear."

"I won't marry," Phaedra said. "Not because of that lout, Lord Neville."

Deerhurst's breathing stopped.

"I beg your pardon?" Huntly thundered. "Are you in any position to argue?"

"You said it yourself, Papa. I am stronger than gossip columns. If Lord Neville breaks his word, I will face whatever comes."

"With Howard yes," Huntly said. "But what about Deerhurst? Or should I ask how he knew where to find your bedchamber? How did he enter the house? When did he enter the house? How perfectly timely that he intercepted Howard in your bedchamber."

Confound it.

Deerhurst had hoped Huntly wouldn't notice or question any of that.

"Papa, I—"

Deerhurst couldn't listen to this anymore. "Her decision has been made, Huntly."

Huntly's lived gaze whipped to him. "Have both you and my daughter lost your minds? This is not up for debate."

"In that, you are correct. It's not up for debate," Deerhurst held his stance. Phaedra didn't want to marry him, and he wasn't going to force her. He might be a bastard, a beast, selfish to the bone. But he wouldn't stoop so low as that.

There had to be a line. A line he couldn't cross.

Unless she carried his child, in which case, she'd have no choice but to seek the shelter of his title. None of them would have a choice then. On one hand, he hoped she was with child. A part of him wanted her any way he could get her. On the other hand, he wanted her to marry him of her own choosing—because she loved him too.

He felt her gaze burn into him, but he refused to look at her. He would stumble, then, and agree to Huntly's every demand. He'd bared his heart to her, and she'd spurned him. He'd protected her and she'd spurned him. He'd offered her his future and she'd spurned him.

There was only so much a man's heart could take.

Deerhurst strode from the chamber.

Chapter Twenty-Two

P HAEDRA STARED AT Deerhurst's back until he disappeared from her chamber. She wanted to run after him, but her feet wouldn't move. They seemed stuck on the fact that Deerhurst had just told her father they would not wed.

"This is a deuced dream I'm never going to wake up from," her father said. "This is your fault, Portia. Having a man over at night? Brayton of all men? No wonder the child refuses to wed."

"Do not put the blame on me, Robert. Jack and I both value privacy and discretion."

Laughable, Phaedra thought.

"Shall we expand on the topic of values? Do you know what they are?" Huntly countered.

"Do not take that tone with me, brother. I'm not a child."

"You may not be a child but what of your faculties? You've lost them all!"

Phaedra sighed. Her mind's eye was still staring at the door Deerhurst had disappeared through.

"That's enough," her mother ordered. "We have plenty to worry about without you two at each other's throats. We are a family, and we must remain united no matter what happens."

"Our daughter refuses to marry, Eleanor, despite what's happened. What do you suppose we do?"

Her mother took her hand, both cold and soft to the touch. "Dear, are you sure you don't want to marry? The earl seems to care for you a great deal."

"Deerhurst only cares for—" She stopped.

He only cares for . . .

Me.

He did care for her; she couldn't deny that. They'd spent too much time together for her to dismiss his feelings completely. The problem was her sense of betrayal. It was difficult to see past that. But that wasn't his shortcoming. It was hers.

He had been right.

Oh Lord.

She couldn't let him leave like this—angry, hurt, disappointed. She'd used her anger to lash out at him and all he'd done was protect her. She shuddered to think what would have happened if he hadn't come tonight—if he'd done as she'd demanded and stayed away from her.

They'd shared so much together. Kisses. A mad dash. A passionate night.

And she'd turned on him the moment she'd discovered he'd made a mistake. Hadn't she made plenty over the years? Hadn't she had enough of mistrust in her life?

Phaedra started for the door and then set off at a dead run after Deerhurst. Behind her, she could hear the calls of her father, her mother's admonishment, and her aunt's approval. She dashed down the stairs, through the hall, and out into the garden, where she finally caught up to him.

"Marcus, wait," she called, stopping to catch her breath. He had stopped as well but didn't turn around to look at her. Suddenly, she didn't know what to say. She had pushed him away, now she wanted to pull him a bit closer again. Even she had to admit that a person didn't do that, not without confusing them both even more.

"Thank you for saving me," Phaedra said slowly. "I should not have doubted you."

"Doubted me tonight or for everything else?"

Phaedra hesitated.

"Why did you follow me?" He turned and she almost gasped at the unrestrained torment in his eyes. "I am not fit to breathe in your presence."

Phaedra shook her head, her heart stumbling over every beat. "I never said that."

"Not with words, no." *With everything else*, his eyes seemed to say.

"I don't know what I believe," she confessed softly.

"Do you truly believe that I don't love you? That I have no care for you in my heart at all?"

"I know you care for me."

"But not that I love you."

At her silence, he clenched his fists, and Phaedra felt that motion right to her bones.

"It's not that I don't *believe* you. I just don't . . ." How to say it? "I just don't . . ."

"You don't trust me," he finished for her. "Let me ask you this, love. Do you care for me?"

Phaedra nodded. *Of course I do.*

"Do you love me?"

I do. But again, as when she'd woken with a feeling of being watched, her voice failed her. She couldn't form the words on her tongue. She couldn't even part her lips. She wanted to, but the words wouldn't seem to form outside her mind.

Deerhurst dragged a hand through his hair. "I thought as much."

No!

"The worst part of this is that I know you love me, which makes me want to shake some bloody sense into you."

Phaedra inhaled sharply.

"I have done nothing but try to atone for my sins. From the night that list came into being straight to tonight."

I know.

"I have opened my heart, my very soul to you. I trusted you with my daughter. With parts of me that I've shown no other person in this world. Still, you would only see what I didn't do."

Phaedra's breath hitched.

He advanced on her. "And what exactly is it that I haven't done? Not stopping my friends. Not informing you about the list and wagers. Those are my only crimes. And yes, I am aware of the severity of all this, all the things I didn't do, but I have done nothing but try to make up for it since then."

"I have a right to be angry."

"But you're not angry, love, are you? You're punishing me. You are punishing us both."

"No," she said shaking her head. "I'm not."

He just stared at her.

Was she punishing them both? He for his betrayal and her for almost allowing the same thing to happen to her that happened to her aunt.

But it's not the same.

And Deerhurst wasn't the same either. Yet she couldn't bring herself to take that one step toward him. If she was with child, then she wouldn't have to make the choice. It would be made for her. Wouldn't that simplify things? Then she wouldn't be responsible for deciding her fate.

How utterly cowardly of her.

"I can't meet you halfway this time," Deerhurst said. "If you want to be with me, love, you're going to have to come to me."

Tell him, Phaedra.

Be with him.

Just take that one step.

"I . . ." Words failed her.

He took a step back, his lips pressing together before he said, "You can either choose love or choose misery for us both, but regardless of your choice tonight, if you are with child, we will marry. If I must drag you to the bishop kicking and screeching, I will."

For the last time that night, Deerhurst turned on his heel and walked away.

Numbness settled over her limbs.

"He is right, you know."

Phaedra whirled to find her aunt hovering in the doorway.

"Aunt, I . . ."

"No need to explain. I understand more than you know, but that doesn't change the fact that he is right—your fears are keeping you paralyzed, and you both are paying the price for that."

"I know our situations are different."

"Yes," her aunt said thoughtfully. "You love him, don't you?"

Phaedra looked away.

"I've experienced something quite similar to you recently, I believe. I might love someone, but I don't want to admit it out loud for then it becomes real, and when that happens . . . the possibility of being hurt also becomes real."

"Deciding to trust someone with your future is a fearful thing, aunt."

"I know," she said. "So is not trusting someone, especially if that someone is yourself."

Phaedra felt as though a cold bucket of water had been splashed over her head.

"I was the same with Rowley. For years I denied the truth about him and our marriage because voicing it meant I had to admit a painful truth—I hadn't walked away from him because I hadn't trusted myself to be strong. Be brave, Phaedra. You are a Sharp, after all."

Phaedra was a Sharp, yes.

But brave?

She had thought so once. She had thought it brave to walk away from society's expectations and live life single and on her own terms.

But no.

That hadn't been bravery. It has just been another form of coward-ice. An escape.

Her aunt was right, Phaedra was paralyzed. She couldn't move toward the man she loved, and neither could she speak the words she longed to speak. She could only stand frozen as he walked away from her each time.

A voice that could scare an alley cat? She hung her head. No. She *was* the alley cat. And she was scared. Beaten and bruised. Stuck in a dark passage with nary a spark of light in sight.

⟫⟨⟨

DEERHURST FELT SICK to his stomach as he entered White's two hours later. He'd caught up with Brayton and Howard after leaving the Sharp residence, wanting one last thing from that bastard before Brayton sent him off.

Phaedra had pulled a pistol on Howard. How deuced ironic that he was the one with holes through his heart.

How foolish of him to imagine she'd chase him down to declare her affection and allow them to be together. She should have accepted Huntly's direction. But if he was unhappy now, he didn't want to imagine how miserable he'd be if he forced her into a union she didn't want.

Yet he could not convince himself that he meant nothing to her. He just couldn't.

He was such a bloody hopeless fool. He couldn't even convince the woman he loved to be with him. The only thing that would help swallow down the bitterness of that taste was brandy. And a fight. Which he was ready to pick.

Hence, White's.

He had come to realize that he was no good at letting the things he treasured most in life go.

Not his daughter.

Not Phaedra.

Not a chance at happiness.

So much regret clawed and fought for domination. He ruthlessly pushed it down. Regret served no one.

Which was how he'd come to a decision—to give Phaedra what she wanted. Space. It would be deuced hard, but he had meant what he had said. She would have to come to him. Although, honestly, he might have meant what he said at the time, but he regretted it thirty seconds later. If she didn't come to him . . .

Well, Deerhurst had never been a man to give up easily.

He almost felt sorry for her. He almost felt sorry for himself.

He would woo the stockings right off her perfect legs. But first he had to wait a bit. If she wasn't with child, then they could put that chapter behind them and start anew. Then again if she was . . . it still didn't matter. Whether she was with child or not, he would still use every weapon in his arsenal, every resource at his disposal to win her over.

He would not stop. Ever.

And since he told her she would have to come to him, he had to figure out how to woo Phaedra from a distance. Luckily, he didn't live that far away from her. He also had the upper hand with her cat.

There was no letting Phaedra go. Not while there was still breath left in his body.

However, there was still the matter of Cromby. He spotted him almost instantly on the first floor of White's. Wasn't that hard. He still sat—smug smile plastered on his face—in the same spot Deerhurst had left him.

Fool.

Deerhurst clenched his jaw and strode over to Cromby's table, plopping down lazily in a seat across from him. "I just thought I'd inform you that your plan has failed. Lady Phaedra is well, and Howard is leaving London as we speak."

Cromby's eyes hardened, the muscles in his own jaw clenching. "I have no idea of which you speak."

Deerhurst ignored him. "There is, however, still a matter we need to settle."

"Not that I can see," Cromby bit out.

Deerhurst quirked up his lips in one of those smiles that mocked. "Tell me, why *did* you put that list in the book? You could have tossed it away."

Cromby sneered. "Where would be the fun in that?"

Deerhurst bit down on his jaw. Fun? He wanted to punch the man in the face, but he all too well remembered what he and his friends had thought as fun when the list had been in their own hands.

"And tonight? You never thought twice about ruining an innocent woman's reputation? About what she might go through?" Of course, he hadn't, but Deerhurst wanted to hear Cromby say it.

"She is to marry one way or another. What does it matter how it comes to pass? What do you want, Deerhurst? By your own account my supposed plan failed. I've done nothing wrong."

From the corner of his eye, Deerhurst saw Mortimer and Leeds glance their way.

"Retribution."

Cromby scoffed. "For what exactly?"

The man couldn't be this daft. He truly thought he could get away with what had happened tonight. "You sent a man to compromise a woman's virtue as part of a plot to get your hands on a portion of her fortune," Deerhurst said loud and clear.

"A plot you cannot possibly prove."

Deerhurst felt the presence of two men flank him. He didn't need to look to know they were Leeds and Mortimer, and both wore grim expressions. He smirked at the man opposite him.

"Cromby," Leeds spoke first, his voice cold as ice. "Tell me you haven't done what Deerhurst is accusing you of."

"His claims are nothing but hearsay," Cromby said with an arrogant lift of his chin. "He can't prove anything."

Deerhurst removed an envelope from his jacket and slammed it onto the table. "As a matter of fact, I can."

Cromby scowled at the document. "What is this supposed to be?"

"A signed confession from Neville Howard that you concocted a plot for him to ruin Lady Phaedra and that you'd receive a substantial amount of the dowry as commission if it succeeded."

"That's horseshit!" Cromby spat. "If Neville did do this then he acted on his own."

Mortimer pointed to the envelope. "May I?"

Deerhurst nodded.

Mortimer's lips thinned as he read the content of Howard's confession. "This is damning indeed."

Cromby paled. "He is lying. They all are."

"What do you think we should do about him, Deerhurst?" Leeds asked as he too read the confession.

Cromby leaped to his feet. "There is nothing to be done."

"I don't know about that," Mortimer drawled.

"Revoke his membership," Deerhurst said. And that was just the beginning of what he had planned for Cromby. The man would be lucky to be accepted into polite society anywhere after Deerhurst was done with him.

"That's madness!" Cromby exclaimed.

"It's done," Mortimer growled. "And let me impart another warning, Cromby, in case this one doesn't penetrate your skull. If I find out you're behind any more such schemes, I will personally reduce you to nothing."

Deerhurst watched Cromby stalk off with a stiff back. Impressed, he inclined his head toward Mortimer. He hadn't known what to expect of the man, but it appeared that he needn't have been worried. Mortimer once again proved he was on their side.

"Well, that was interesting," Leeds murmured. "I'll make sure he is blacklisted from every other club in the city."

"Many thanks," Deerhurst said. "The man is an ass."

"Agreed," Mortimer said. "I take it the woman you referred to was Lady Phaedra?"

Deerhurst gave a curt nod.

Leeds patted his back. "You saved her from a lifetime of misery."

Yes, but Deerhurst might also have caused her a lifetime of misery as well. He didn't know how they had all gotten to this point.

No, that wasn't true. Secrets. That was what got him here, at least. All secrets, no matter the intention behind keeping them, became a deep well of obscurity. Became dark.

"I was lucky enough to overhear Cromby boast," Deerhurst admitted. "The man is a fool. Fortunately."

"Howard?" Mortimer asked. "I overheard you say he left London."

"He knows what will happen if I see him back here this season." Not to mention anything about Huntly.

"Good, we need to settle this before the season ends," Mortimer said. "There is no telling if there'll be a next if this madness continues."

"As long as the book is in rotation and copies are being circulated there's not much we can do," Leeds pointed out.

"Once we get the book," Mortimer said. "We can address the matter of the copies."

Good luck with that, duke.

"You're hoping tempers will die down once the book is back at White's?" Deerhurst guessed.

Mortimer ached a brow. "You don't think it will work?"

"I think as long as coin is being collected at the expense of these women, tempers will remain high and foolish action will take precedence over common sense," Deerhurst said.

"What do you suggest?" Leeds asked.

"Clean slate," Deerhurst said. "If the book is to be returned to White's, let it return without the wagers in it." It wasn't much but it was something.

"Declare them null and void," Mortimer said thoughtfully. "You believe that will work?"

"I believe it's a start," Deerhurst said.

Leeds nodded. "A compromise."

"These women are smart," Deerhurst said with a smile. "They know they can't control whether we open another book or not. They just want to be acknowledged. Then again with both sides of the coin offended, it will be a herculean task."

"At this point all we can do is try," Mortimer said. "Does Lady Phaedra have the betting book? Do you know? I need to find it first before we can begin a compromise."

Deerhurst didn't envy Mortimer's task. These heiresses weren't easy to deal with. Just look at his sorry state. "Unfortunately, that, I do not know. If she does, she hasn't said anything to me."

And she wouldn't be saying anything to him for a while.

Chapter Twenty-Three

PHAEDRA STILL FELT queasy and dazed the following evening when she entered the drawing room—the first time in a week. It was three o'clock in the morning. Sleep proved impossible.

There was no escaping Deerhurst.

His words played in her mind like a carriage wheel rolling down a hill. And every time it came to a crashing halt, another wheel would start rolling down the hill. An endless loop of accusations and hurt.

But what stuck with her most . . . *You can either choose love or choose misery for us both.*

And no doubt, she was choosing misery for them both. Why else would she be wandering around the house restless and miserable when all she wanted to do was dash the distance between here and the house next door and fling herself in a certain earl's arms?

Yet she didn't.

One way or another, Phaedra had to face her cowardice, the reason her feet held her in place. With a sigh, she plonked into a chair and lowered her face into her hands.

"Can't sleep?"

Phaedra nearly leaped from the chair in fright. She glanced around the shadows of the room. A silhouette stood in the doorway.

"Mr. Brayton?" She looked past him. "Where is my aunt?"

"Kitchen."

Oh. She didn't ask any more. Who knew what answer she might get, given what she knew of the two.

"May I?" He motioned to one of the chairs and she nodded. May as well. Mr. Brayton seemed to have become part of the household as her aunt's companion. She wondered if her father was aware of this. Probably not, Phaedra thought with a touch of amusement. The Sharp residence was run by women. Of that there was no doubt.

"You're not surprised to find me here this late?" Mr. Brayton asked.

"You'd be surprised how little shocks me these days."

Mr. Brayton lit a candle and sat down. "Not sure if that's a good thing."

"I daresay neither is it a bad thing." She shot him a look. "Since I've been witnessing all sorts of displays of affection."

He arched a thick, bushy brow. "You've witnessed such displays recently?"

"In this very drawing room."

"I see."

"What exactly are your intentions with my aunt, Mr. Brayton?" Phaedra asked. "You must know she has been through a lot."

"I'm aware," he said slowly. "My intentions are to provide your aunt with whatever she desires."

"Whatever she desires? What if she desires marriage?"

"Then she will have it."

"What if she doesn't?"

A pause. "Then she won't have it."

Phaedra smiled then. She liked this Mr. Brayton. "That is good, then. My aunt seems to trust you. If I may ask . . . when . . . at what point . . ."

"Did she trust me?" He smiled. "Always."

"I find that hard to believe."

"Let me rephrase," he said. "Portia trusts me to be exactly who I am, and she accepts that."

Trust him to be exactly who he is . . . and accept that.

"A rogue?"

He chuckled. "A rogue. Ruthless. Always getting what I want. I do not deny who I am, and neither does your aunt."

"Interesting." Her aunt sure knew how to pick a man. A true wolf.

"My point is that Portia is aware of who I am, and rather than condemn me, which she has every right to do, she embraces me, faults and all."

She pursed her lips in thought. "No one is without faults." She wasn't without faults, neither was Deerhurst. The trick was acceptance.

That was what it all came down to then. She had to accept Deerhurst with his faults, just like he seemed to embrace hers—and she did have them.

The only reason Phaedra had claimed Deerhurst's actions unforgivable was because her betrayal stemmed from being deceived from the start—the very essence of all the fortune hunting scoundrels that courted her. They were decked out in the very essence of deception.

But had Deerhurst deceived her?

No.

He had merely kept a secret. And the secrets Deerhurst kept were to protect the people he cared for, and it appeared he kept his secrets at great cost.

And here, right across from her, sat the very man who proved that despite her aunt being fearful and mistrusting because of what happened in her marriage, even she could take a leap of faith.

Deerhurst had been right. Her fears might not be unfounded, but they were holding her back from happiness. From love.

From *him.*

In the end, for all he'd done and not done, Deerhurst had always protected her in his way. It was time someone protected him. His heart. His daughter. And his love. And Phaedra was the woman to do it. It was time for *her* to take a leap.

She surged to her feet. "I must go."

Mr. Brayton frowned, seemingly understanding it was not her bedchamber she was returning to. "It's three in the morning."

"The perfect time."

Brayton rose to his feet. "I cannot in good conscience allow you to dart off into the night to God knows where. At least wait for Portia and we will accompany you."

"I'm not going far. Just next door."

"Forgive me, Lady Phaedra, but the household will be sleeping. It's best to wait for a few hours."

Somehow, Phaedra knew Deerhurst wouldn't be sleeping at all. Plus, Mr. Brayton's attempt to have her do the right thing was truly amusing. "Mr. Brayton, I have seen you with your breeches around your ankles." Both his thick brows rose. "Please do not preach to me on propriety."

And with those parting words, leaving a slack-jawed Mr. Brayton in the drawing room, Phaedra dashed through the quiet house and out to the gate that led to Deerhurst's garden. It was dark, and there were some close calls with furniture on the way, but Phaedra knew the layout of her house well enough to avoid a broken neck.

If Aunt Portia, who had lived through the atrocities Phaedra had merely witnessed, could take a leap for love, so could she. She only hoped Deerhurst would forgive all the hurt she had caused him with her coldness.

Now that she had decided, she realized just how much her lack of trust had hurt him. Hurt her. Because when she thought about it, deep down, she *did* trust him. She trusted him to be exactly who he was—a protector. Even when he made missteps, he always gravitated back toward who he was in his heart.

Phaedra only hoped she hadn't completely ruined things. She

yanked open the gate and rushed through only to come to an abrupt halt.

Deerhurst stood in the garden. And not just in any spot, but the exact place where they'd shared their first kiss. He seemed to have lost a bit of weight, and a few days of stubble coated his jaw. An air of gloom surrounded him, so palpable it made her heart ache. At his feet, a ball of fluff curled.

Puck?

They seemed like the best of friends.

Deerhurst looked up then, straight at her. Their gazes locked. Her breath stuck in her throat.

"Phaedra? Is something amiss?"

Yes.

Everything.

She hurried to him, and after the third step broke into a run and threw her arms around his neck as she planted her lips on his.

Let that be her answer.

I'm sorry.

Forgive me.

His arms shackled her waist instantly before his tongue swept home and he retuned her kiss like a man who'd been starved for weeks. The night charged with emotion, and within this hot, demanding exchange, they both vented all their grievances and fears.

And hope.

"Christ, Phaedra."

She pulled her head back just enough to catch his gaze. "I love you, too. I love you too. Do you believe me?"

He sealed his mouth over hers again. *I believe you,* his kiss seemed to say. Phaedra relaxed in his arms. Unfortunately, he ended the sweet kiss too soon.

His questioning eyes searched hers. "What changed?" he asked softly.

"Brayton put some things into perspective for me."

Deerhurst frowned. "Brayton?"

"We ran into each other in the drawing room. I couldn't sleep."

He touched her cheek with his fingertips. "You're really here."

"I'm really here," she said softly. "You were right. I couldn't look past my fears. It's a terrifying thought to entrust my heart to another person's hands."

"I'm also entrusting mine to you."

She nodded. "I know. I've been so blind."

"You pushed past your fears now, that's all that matters."

"Then you're not angry with me?"

He shook his head. "How could I be angry with you? I'm the one at fault here."

Phaedra gasped when he lifted her up into his arms and strode back to his house. "Where are we going?"

"Bedchamber."

"You're incorrigible."

He kissed the arch of her neck. "Always," he breathed against her skin. "Do you know how happy I am at this moment? All that matters is that you're here with me, love. Nothing else. Which leaves us with bit of a problem."

"Oh?"

"I refuse to spend another moment without you."

Phaedra tightened her hold. "What shall we do?"

"Marry me. Tomorrow."

"We can marry that fast?"

"I'll make it happen." He paused. "Three days at most."

"So long as I can spend my nights with you."

"There is no other way, love."

And then Deerhurst proceeded to show her just how motivated he was for their wedding to be arranged posthaste.

HAPPINESS.

Deerhurst had never given much thought to the concept in his youth and as years went on it had almost become an abstract concept to him. A dream. A myth. Always just beyond his reach.

When he learned of his daughter and brought her into his life, his focus touched on this concept of happiness once more—in all the ways he could make his daughter happy.

It wasn't until this very moment, with Phaedra in his arms, having confessed her love and intention of marriage, that Deerhurst felt the full scale of happiness. The world no longer seemed so empty. His secrets no longer appeared so big and ugly.

He realized: happiness wasn't a state to be achieved but a decision to be made.

"Why aren't you sleeping?"

He smiled and placed a kiss on her temple. "I can ask the same of you." For two people who hadn't been able to sleep well the past week they ought to be out cold.

"Too excited." She lifted her chin. "What are you thinking about?

Deerhurst pulled her closer. "There is something I still haven't told you."

She nodded. "About Abigail's mother."

"How did you know?"

She pinched his skin. "Of course, I know. What else is there to tell me? In any event, it doesn't matter to me."

"It matters to me . . ." he said slowly. "Because once we marry, if the truth ever comes to light, you will be affected as well."

She lifted onto her elbows, eyes searching his. "How?"

Deerhurst sighed. He had to get it out. "I told you I courted a woman before."

"Yes, she married someone else."

"Even though she married someone else, she came back to me. She might have cared for me, I don't know. Perhaps she just didn't want me to marry someone else, too. But an affair began."

"And Abigail is the result of that affair."

He nodded. "She went into hiding from her husband during that time, and once she gave birth, she sent the baby away. The maid in charge of this came to me and let me know she left my daughter at an orphanage."

"That's horrible. Where is this witch now?"

"Exiled to Wales by her husband. It seems I was not the only affair after I ended our relationship." He dragged a hand through his hair. "Her husband is the Duke of Ruthbridge."

Her eyes widened. "Ruthbridge? Isn't he . . ."

Deerhurst nodded. "Ruthless. Prone to violence. Powerful friends."

"If he ever learns of Abigail, that she is the product of you and his wife . . ."

"There is no telling what he might do."

A short silence followed, and Deerhurst held his breath. This had been the deepest secret he had carried for seven years. Phaedra had accepted Abigail, so logically, there was no reason for her not to accept the past behind his daughter. Behind him. But still, he couldn't help the small bit of hesitation to linger. Would she condemn him? Loathe him? Suspect him of more beastly acts?

"Well then," she began. "We shall just have to make sure that the duke never learns the truth."

Deerhurst blinked.

"What?" she teased. "You thought I would judge you for your past?"

"You don't think I'm a beast?" he asked.

"A beast?" She grinned. "A scoundrel, maybe, but not a beast. Not even a full scoundrel. Perhaps half of one."

"Phaedra . . ." He loved this woman beyond measure.

"We all make mistakes, Marcus. I've realized a lot of things this past week, but the most important thing I've realized is that it's less about the mistake, and more about how we move on from it."

He buried his head in her shoulder. "Christ, I love you."

"I love you too," she said softly. "And I'm glad for this wicked woman, for Abigail. Else you would probably be married to another right now. Everything happens for a reason, don't you agree? I am exceedingly grateful not to have missed out on you."

Deerhurst nodded. Everything did happen for a reason. How comforting to know. "The reason is you," Deerhurst said.

She laughed. "The reason is *us*." She combed back his hair with her fingers. "You must send for Abigail at once. We aren't complete as a family without her."

Deerhurst nodded, and his heart swelled. "I shall send for her at daybreak."

"Good. We will introduce her to the world as your distant niece. We shall raise her well and find the perfect husband for her in the future."

Deerhurst chuckled. "Husband? What if she doesn't want a husband, or have you forgotten your little discussion with Evie, Maddy, and Macy?"

"Well, I have changed my mind since then."

"Oh? How have you changed your mind?"

"One needs a partner to share adventures with. Cats make good partners, they are also good to snuggle with, but they lack one thing."

Deerhurst smiled. "And what is that?"

"Loyalty."

He laughed, remembering she'd caught him and Puck red-handed earlier.

Ah, yes. *Happiness.*

All his moments with Phaedra were happy, even when they were at odds. A moment shared with her brought him happiness even when it brought him pain.

Happiness only ever needs a moment.

And he prepared to share all his with the woman he loved.

Epilogue

Two days later

"YOU WANT ME to keep the book?"

Phaedra nodded, pushing the wrapped box across the tea table. "Yes, I believe you are the perfect person to keep it safe. You're also the only one I could get hold of."

Lady Harriet stared at the book wide-eyed. "What of Theodosia or Louisa?"

"I'm not that familiar with them. Selena hasn't replied to my missive, so I can only hand the book over to you. If you wish to pass it on to one of them, you may do so."

"What about you?"

Phaedra smiled. "I'm to wed tomorrow and will probably go traveling for a bit in a few days. I'm not confident in hiding things and I cannot travel with the book. It's also best for it to stay in London, should it be needed."

Lady Harriet nodded absent-mindedly. "You do realize my husband watches me like a hawk. That man is more protective than a bear over her cubs."

"I do." She glanced toward the door. "Which is why we probably don't have much time before he comes in search of you." Phaedra pointed at the box. "This a *gift* from me to thank you for cheering me up the other day."

266

"You want me to take it today? In broad daylight?"

"How else?" Phaedra laughed. "Is it not the best way?"

"It's the most terrifying way, to be honest."

"Who would suspect a ribboned box? Besides," Phaedra gave her friend a foxlike smile, "you haven't read through all the wagers. Aren't you curious about whether Leeds's won any?"

"Leeds has wagers in the book?"

She shrugged coyly. "That is for you to discover, no?"

Lady Harriet pursed her lips as she glanced at the book.

A footman interrupted to announce. "My lady, the Duke of Mortimer."

Both women's gazes whipped to the footman in equal parts shock and thrill. Mortimer? The duke who's on the hunt for the betting book.

Oh Lord. How positively eerie!

Phaedra refrained from shooting a glance at the box sitting neatly on the tea table before her and smiled at the footman. "Well, let's not have the duke wait. Send him in."

"Phaedra!" Lady Harriet hissed.

"Not to worry," Phaedra said, raising both her brows at her friends. "It's not like he will rummage through our belongings."

Lady Harriet groaned, just as the duke entered the drawing room, bowing in greeting. "Lady Phaedra." He looked over to her guest. "And Lady Harriet. What an unexpected surprise."

Truly? Phaedra thought not.

"May I?" He motioned to the sofa.

"Of course," Phaedra said. "Please, join us. We were just discussing ribbons and trinkets."

The duke took a seat. He didn't mince words. "You know why I am here?"

Phaedra titled her head to convey a thoughtful look. "I've heard rumors."

"Rumors?"

"That you are searching for White's book of curses."

His lips twitched. "That is no rumor but a fact."

"In which case I am confused as to your presence here, Your Grace."

"You distributed copies of it, did you not?"

"I shared what was shared with me," Phaedra countered. "Is there something wrong with that?"

He considered her for a moment. The man's eyes had an intensity that would probably have ninety percent of women cowering with just this look alone, but Phaedra was not part of that percentage.

"Wives have been running away from their husbands, stacking up debtors' notes, and some have even brought their lovers home to flaunt, my lady. This is all thanks to you sharing those copies."

"Well, imagine how we women felt when we read those wagers."

"It's atrocious, I agree, but something needs to be done to settle this matter."

"You mean the club wants its property back."

The duke inclined his head.

"And what exactly do you think that will accomplish? In fact, I'm surprised they haven't opened another book."

"As long as the missing book is in circulation, the club feels this matter will never be put to rest."

"And by club you mean the men of the *ton*, right?"

The duke stared at her a moment before switching his gaze to Lady Harriet. "My lady, what do you think?"

Lady Harriet blinked. "I . . ."

The footman appeared again. "The Marquess of Leeds."

"Oh, thank God," Harriet said and jumped up. "If you will excuse me, my husband and I have plans we cannot miss."

Leeds, who entered the room, lifted a brow. His gaze flicked over the duke and narrowed, but he said nothing. "Lady Phaedra."

"Leeds."

"Then we shall be off," Lady Harriet said.

"Do not forget your gift, Harriet," Phaedra said and picked up the box to hand it to the fleeing bird. "I truly do appreciate you being a friend."

Lady Harriet took the box hesitantly, shooting a quick glance at her husband. "You really did not have to get me a gift."

Phaedra waved her hand. "It's just a token of my gratitude."

Lady Harriet nodded and hurried to her husband, who merely inclined his head at them before taking his wife away. Phaedra sat back down and smiled at the duke, who had no idea the very object he sought had been under his nose the entire time.

So much fun.

➤➤➤❮❮❮

"Is THAT MY mother and my father?"

Deerhurst followed her gaze to the drawing room. It was past midnight, and they'd decided to walk back from the Carrington ball since it was only a few blocks, and they were passing Phaedra's old home.

He pinched his lips together to keep from laughing. "I'm afraid so."

"Are they . . . dear Lord! They are! I sat on that sofa only yesterday!"

"Are you shocked? Given the den of iniquity in which you lived, I'm surprised," he teased.

She glared at him. "We Sharp women are very passionate."

He couldn't argue with that.

"Then what's the matter?"

"It's my *mother* and *father*, Deerhurst! This is not a sight any daughter ever wants to witness."

"Then look away."

"I can't."

Deerhurst stepped into her view. "You watching them is more

disturbing than them doing the deed."

She snorted and peered around him. "Not when it's like two objects approaching a collision and you want to look away, but your gaze is melded to the impending crash."

"Well, there will certainly be a collision here."

"What position *is* that?"

"Not one we've tried before," he tugged on her arm. "Come, let's give them some privacy."

"Privacy? If they wanted privacy, they should have confined themselves to their quarters!" She turned a suspicious gaze at him. "How many times have you witnessed their, er, coupling?"

"Trust, me, you do not want to know."

"Well, now you have me curious beyond measure." She grinned. "Do you think we will be as bad as they are in our old age?"

"We might be worse."

"Well, it certainly seems like the Sharp women aren't partial to beds."

Deerhurst chuckled. "I'm not complaining."

"You wouldn't. You're insatiable."

"That's all your fault."

"Oh, no, husband, you cannot place the blame on my shoulders."

"How am I supposed to keep my hands off you when you look at me as though you wish to devour me?"

She grinned at him. "That look is never going to change."

"In which case I shall never be able to keep my hands off you."

She shot him a thoughtful look. "We've never done it in the drawing room."

"Once, almost."

"Almost doesn't count," Phaedra said. "What is it about that drawing room that draws the passion of my aunt and mother?"

"The exhilaration of being caught, perhaps?"

"We shall have to give it a try."

Deerhurst furrowed his brows. "You want to do it in your parents' drawing room?"

"Well, I certainly can't be the only Sharp woman left out of the tradition."

Deerhurst pulled her in for a kiss. "We could start a tradition in our drawing room."

She arched a brow. "You've not given that statement any thought, have you?"

Ah right, Abigail.

"Your father's drawing room it is," Deerhurst said.

"Good. Let's sneak into the house tomorrow night, and after that, Deerhurst, we are moving. You better find us another house to live in where our neighbors are not prone to drawing room shenanigans."

He did laugh then until something else occurred to him, and his laughter quieted into an uncomfortable chuckle.

"What's wrong?"

"I just realized, if you birth us a daughter, she will have Sharp blood."

Phaedra grinned. "And if she is anything like her mother, she will not wait to engage in shenanigans until she's—"

He kissed her.

She was teasing him, of course, or—hell, he couldn't be sure. But one thing he had absolute certainty over—he would cherish this woman forever. As for his daughters . . . well, he'd just have to practice his aim.

A cry came from the drawing room.

"Oh, Lord, let's go. I can't listen to that."

Deerhurst seconded that. He lifted her into his arms and strode to their home, fully intending to make it to their bed and strip his wife naked.

Wouldn't you know, they never made it that far.

The End

About the Author

Tanya Wilde is an Award-Winning author that developed a passion for reading when she had nothing better to do than lurk in the library during her lunch breaks. Her blazing love affair with pen and paper soon followed after she devoured all their historical romance books! In 2020, she won the Romance Writers Organization of South Africa (ROSA) Imbali Award for Excellence in Romance Writing for Not Quite a Rogue.

When she's not meddling in the lives of her characters or pondering names for her imaginary big, white greyhound, she's off on adventures with her partner in crime.

Wilde lives in a small town at the foot of the Outeniqua Mountains, South Africa.

Website – www.authortanyawilde.com
Instagram – instagram.com/tanyawilde
Facebook – facebook.com/groups/843373666456177
BookBub – bookbub.com/authors/tanya-wilde

Printed in Great Britain
by Amazon